A Bullet for the Utah Kid

OTHER FIVE STAR WESTERNS BY T. T. FLYNN:

Night of the Comanche Moon (1995)
Rawhide (1996)
Long Journey to Deep Cañon (1997)
Death Marks Time in Trampas (1998)
The Devil's Lode (1999)
Ride to Glory (2000)
Prodigal of Death (2001)
Hell's Cañon (2002)
Reunion at Cottonwood Station (2003)
Outlaws (2004)
Noose of Fate (2005)
Dead Man's Gold (2006)
Gunsmoke (2007)
Last Waltz on Wild Horse (2008)
Shafter Range (2009)

A Bullet for the Utah Kid

A Western Quartet

T. T. Flynn

FIVE STAR

A part of Gale, Cengage Learning

GALE
CENGAGE Learning™

Detroit • New York • San Francisco • New Haven, Conn • Waterville, Maine • London

GALE
CENGAGE Learning

LIBRARY OF CONGRESS CATALOGING-IN-PUBLICATION DATA

Flynn, T. T.
    A bullet for the Utah kid : a Western quartet / by T.T. Flynn.
    — 1st ed.
        p. cm.
    ISBN-13: 978-1-59414-910-8 (hardcover)
    ISBN-10: 1-59414-910-0 (hardcover)
    1. Western stories. I. Title.
    PS3556.L93B85 2010
    813'.54—dc22   2010024667

Published in 2010 in conjunction with Golden West Literary Agency.

Printed in Mexico
3 4 5 6 7 14 13 12 11

PERMISSIONS

TABLE OF CONTENTS

★ ★ ★ ★ ★

JOHNNY'S ONE MAN INVASION

★ ★ ★ ★ ★

Mike Tilden was the acquisition editor for Popular Publications' Western pulp magazines, including *Dime Western*. He preferred to title each story in every issue himself, so authors took to calling their stories for submission to him "Western". They would find out what the story had been titled upon publication. "Johnny's One Man Invasion", the title given this story, was submitted on January 10, 1942 and the author was paid $171.40. It appeared in *Dime Western* (7/42).

I

All the long afternoon Johnny Stevens sat moodily in the train smoker and watched the hills clad with cedar and pine drop behind. The wailing whistle blasts from the engine were like sad farewells. Farewell to the bright lights, the gaudy saloons, and cordial cattle offices of Kansas City, far back across the dry plains. Farewell to the busy towns and placid ranches along the railroad. Farewell to all that long panorama of peace and contentment for which Johnny hungered when the trail horses ranged the border country, and guns and the sharp hard core of a man were all that kept his neck safe.

Ahead in Thunderbird were Big Tim Mara, Denby Frisch, and Solano Romero. Somewhere back in the mountains beyond Thunderbird were Chihuahua Keene and an even dozen of Tim Mara's men. At the salt springs of the Yamma Matta *malpaís*, Denby Frisch had spoken his mind about those riders.

"Thirteen," Denby Frisch had counted off. "It's a bad luck number."

Tim Mara had hooted.

"Ain't any bad luck for us. We're set for big things. Johnny an' me have figured everything."

The trip to Kansas City had been part of the figuring. Buyers now were waiting for cattle shipments from Stevens and Mara, soon to be operating in the Thunderbird country. Johnny had done most of the figuring, and he'd figured well. But he had not figured on Linda Watersford and Tim Mara, whose hard-eyed laughing ways usually got what Tim wanted. Over Linda Watersford had come the first hard flare of temper between himself and Tim. And it was Tim who had slanted the moment off into boisterous good humor.

"Get on to Kansas City, feller." Tim had laughed. "It's her old man's ranch we want, ain't it? I've got to jolly Linda along."

"She's too damned good to be hurt," Johnny had warned. "Lay off her, Tim. You know why."

Tim's laugh had taken the edge from his reply. "Sounds like you've got an eye on her yourself. Make that Kansas City trip, Johnny, and I'll look after the Thunderbird end of it."

Sundown had brought dusk when the train stopped briefly at Thunderbird. Tim Mara, Frisch, or Solano Romero were not among the loiterers at the station. But they hadn't known he was coming.

Thunderbird was a few dusty streets, frame business buildings, and a red brick courthouse at the far end of the main street. Corrals along the railroad marked Thunderbird for what it was—a small cattle center and little else. But summer grazing was good on the high mountain slopes. The grassy valleys gave winter protection and graze. A man could ranch peacefully and prosperously on the Thunderbird range and be contented and happy.

Johnny put the thought out of his mind as he walked toward the hotel. He was a lean, leathery young man, carrying the heavy suitcase effortlessly. A dark suit and conservative Stetson gave him a steady, reliable look.

He turned his head as a team of fast-pacing horses whirled a polished buggy along the main street. Tim Mara was driving and speaking to Linda Watersford on the seat beside him.

From the corner of his eye Tim sighted the suitcase. By the way his head jerked around he was surprised and startled. Then with a wave of his hand Tim swept on, leaving a drift of yellow dust.

Johnny's face was set as he carried the suitcase into the hotel. The flushed, happy face of Linda Watersford was proof that Tim had played the *caballero* these last ten days.

In the hotel room Johnny stripped to the waist, shaved, washed, and was opening a clean shirt from the suitcase when Tim Mara walked in.

"Might have sent word you were heading back," Tim greeted breezily. He was an inch taller, with the wide ready smile that made most strangers instinctively like him.

Johnny answered briefly: "I got done and climbed on a train. . . . Linda Watersford looked mighty happy."

Steel-gray irritation entered Tim's look as he stopped smiling. "Why shouldn't she? Don't start preaching, Johnny. I know what I'm doing."

"So do I," Johnny said patiently. "We might as well settle it, Tim. You know we didn't come over the border to put that look on any girl's face."

"And I didn't come up here tonight to talk about it!" Tim snapped.

Johnny tossed the shirt on the bed. Hot temper was flaring in his own eyes. "We'll talk about it anyway."

For a moment something ugly and dangerous struck between them. Tim Mara was the first to put it away with a quick laugh and a shrug. "Get it off your chest tomorrow, Johnny. What we want is that Running R Ranch of the Watersfords, don't we?"

After a moment Johnny grinned wryly and reached for the shirt. "That's right. Has Frank Watersford made up his mind about selling?"

"Not yet. How'd you make out in Kansas City?"

"All we need is a shipping ranch along the railroad to make us respectable . . . and everything we load in a car is sold."

13

"We know how to load 'em in a car." Tim chuckled. "Look, I'm going to see Frank Watersford. He's in town, too. We'll talk everything over later."

Tim was grinning as he went out. Johnny smiled ruefully after him. Tim had his bad points, but they had pulled pretty well together since that day, several years back, when Tim and two of his riders had found Johnny Stevens unhorsed, wounded by a sheriff's posse, and helped him across the border to safety. Each had qualities the other needed. Only Tim shouldn't have tried to play the *caballero* to a girl like Linda Watersford. Even for idle amusement.

Johnny went downstairs for supper in the hotel dining room. Tim did not return. Solano Romero and Denby Frisch evidently were eating somewhere else.

During the meal Johnny thought back over the trip, conning the moves that remained to make the Thunderbird country a profitable outlet for the activities of Tim Mara and his riders below the border. It had been Johnny's idea—one of those neat plans Tim Mara never thought of, but could recklessly carry out. Denby Frisch, with his baldhead and square, solid look of honesty, would manage the Thunderbird end. Tim Mara and Johnny would stay across the border in the reckless life Tim liked and Johnny Stevens had to take.

Supper finished, Johnny sat smoking, enjoying the peace that came seldom enough in his dangerous life. He looked up, faintly smiling, when the buxom young waitress spoke as she cleared the table: "You don't seem in a hurry to get to the wedding."

"Wedding?" Johnny repeated, still smiling.

"Him, your pardner, and her the prettiest girl around Thunderbird. A body'd think you'd be right there in the front row to kiss the bride first," suggested the waitress archly.

A cloud shaded Johnny's smile as he ground the cigarette in his plate and stood up. "I guess I forgot. Where's the wedding?"

The waitress tossed her head, thinking he was joshing her. "You wouldn't think it'd be out to the ranch, would you? I could have told you before she got engaged, that Linda Watersford'd have a church wedding in town."

Johnny nodded, and walked out of the dining room and up to his room. He started to roll another cigarette after he closed the door. Half through, he dropped paper and tobacco on the floor.

It seemed now that from the first he had expected this to happen. Tim Mara never turned back when he set his mind on a thing. And for once Tim Mara could not have his way. This trip north into the Thunderbird country was business—all business. It had been Johnny Stevens's idea. There was no part in it for a girl like Linda Watersford. The future held no place for the heartbreak Tim Mara would give her.

Johnny left the hotel with the weight of gun belt and gun under his coat. He knew Tim Mara perhaps better than Tim knew himself. And he knew Linda Watersford better than she realized.

The white-painted frame church was near the courthouse, on the side street. The colored glass windows were lighted. Wagons, buggies, saddled horses were hitched in front. A group of men and boys crowded around the open doors and overflowed on the steps. As Johnny came up with long strides, he heard the organ playing inside, and he saw the lithe, narrow-hipped Solano Romero holding the matched horses hitched to the polished buggy. Solano was waiting for the married couple to come out of the church and leave in the buggy.

"Where's Tim?" Johnny asked.

Solano's white teeth showed in a doubtful smile as he jerked a thumb at the church.

"Where's he going in the buggy?"

"I t'ink eight o'clock train east," Solano said after a moment's hesitation.

He hadn't been surprised to see Johnny here. He had known Johnny was back. He and Denby Frisch had stayed away from the hotel to avoid talking about the wedding. They were Tim's men. Johnny had always known they'd stick with Tim Mara.

"There they are!" exclaimed a voice at the doorway. "Ain't she a pretty one, though."

A man would have a time trying to push quickly through that crowd at the doorway. Johnny thought of the side door near the back of the church and headed there.

The organ music had stopped as he ran lightly up creaking wooden steps and entered a little side room.

An inner door was open. He looked through into the front of the church, at filled seats, at the bridal couple, with the best man and the bride's father standing before the minister.

Denby Frisch had his broad, solid back to the doorway. The lamplight gleamed on Denby's baldhead. Thunderbird had never seen a more substantial-looking character than Denby Frisch, standing there beside the bridegroom. Those solemn, proper people in the church pews wouldn't have believed that the knife always snug up Denby's sleeve or the gold-mounted Derringer that was in the special pocket, low down on Denby's vest, out of sight. Denby could slash a man's throat or blast Derringer lead through his heart while still talking reasonably at arm's length away. And had. And would again.

Johnny was sorry for old Frank Watersford, a little stooped against his cane, looking proud and sad, too, on the other side of the bride. The old rancher, with his drooping mustache, must have once been a fine figure of a man until crippled by a rolling horse. Now Frank Watersford looked what he was, a four-square, successful old rancher, married late in life, failing fast now, and proud and lonely, too, as he watched his girl being taken by another man.

The girl looked up at the man who would be her husband in a few moments, at tall Tim Mara, handsome and assured. She was slim and lovely in her dark traveling dress, with excitement pink on the curve of her cheek, which was all Johnny could see. But he had seen her eyes before and faced her smile. Now, Johnny knew, she was giving her heart to Tim Mara for the years to come.

Tim glanced at Denby Frisch and sighted Johnny standing just inside the doorway. Tim's eyes narrowed. Johnny gestured to stop it. Tim scowled, and moved a shoulder in a shrug as he faced back to the minister, who was clearing his throat.

"If there be anyone among you who can show why these two should not be joined in holy matrimony, let him speak now or forever hold his peace," droned the minister, and paused perfunctorily.

Johnny took a long breath in the instant of quiet that followed. His low voice out of the open doorway barely reached the minister. "I'm speaking now, Preacher."

II

The minister was startled, uncertain as he looked around to see where the voice came from.

"Over here in the doorway," said Johnny in the same low voice. "Those two won't be hitched. Tim Mara's got a wife in Mexico."

"G-good heavens. . . ."

Denby Frisch whirled to the doorway while Johnny was speaking. The man's broad, placid face was smiling queerly.

"Come outside an' talk it over, Johnny," Denby said under his breath.

And then Denby Frisch stopped as Johnny's gun inside the doorway covered him. "Try one of your slick tricks and I'll blow

17

you back over the preacher."

"Now, Johnny," Denby pleaded.

"Shut up, you baldheaded snake," Johnny said softly. "You helped on this behind my back."

People in the church seats were stirring, murmuring. Tim Mara was talking rapidly, hotly to the minister and Linda. Johnny caught some of the words.

". . . his idea of a joke. Finish it up quick, Preacher."

But old Frank Watersford lifted his voice as he pushed past them. "Hold everything, Reverend, while I look into this."

Tim Mara got in front of him and caught Denby's arm. "Throw that fool outta here," Tim raged under his breath.

"You do the throwin'," Denby muttered. "I ain't arguin' with him now."

Graying mustache bristling, brass-ferruled cane thumping the floor, Frank Watersford thrust into the doorway. "Did I hear you right about Mara having a wife in Mexico?"

"One that I'm sure of, mister. She'll do, won't she?"

Frank Watersford looked older, haggard, almost pleading. "This ain't some kind of a hooraw on your pardner?"

"We're not pardners. This has busted us. Tim'll be after me with a gun soon as he gets the chance."

The old man's eyes blazed. He lifted the cane, and then lowered it. "Why didn't you say something? Why'd you wait until it went this far?"

"I warned Tim before I left town. Maybe I should have kept my mouth shut tonight."

Frank Watersford turned away without answering. He walked to the railing and lifted his cane to the seated people. The suppressed excitement quieted as Watersford's shaken voice addressed them.

"There won't be any wedding, friends. I . . . ah. . . ."

A woman cried out as Watersford took a stumbling step and

crumpled, still clutching his cane. Linda cried under her breath and dropped to her knees beside him.

Tim Mara's face was a furious red as he stood with shoulders hunched and head lowered, as if weighing the chances of seeing it through.

But men were on their feet and starting forward. One man in the front row turned to another behind him and spoke loudly: "Seems like he's already got one gal tied to him! Ain't this a hell of a trick to play on one of our girls?"

Tim gave it up and headed out of the church through the doorway where Johnny stood. Johnny stepped back watchfully, thumbing the gun hammer. Tim Mara's wild rages were deadly.

"Don't come back across the border," was all Tim snarled as he passed without stopping.

Denby Frisch silently followed him out. Their boot heels stamped down the wooden steps. They'd keep going, for anger was flaring among the Thunderbird men as they realized what Tim Mara had tried.

Johnny looked back through the doorway. Linda Watersford, still on her knees, looked up and met his gaze. She was so lovely that Johnny's heart turned over. But Linda looked pale, frozen, and her look said that she would hate Johnny Stevens as long as memory persisted. Johnny shook his head regretfully as he holstered the gun. He put his back to her and walked out of the church, heading for the hotel, knowing these were his last hours on the Thunderbird range.

From now on he was on his own. Tim Mara and all of Tim's men would shoot him on sight. The long, dry reaches of the border country and down across the line in Mexico were no longer safe for Johnny Stevens. But up north here, there was no safety, either. Tim Mara would see that the law again picked up the trail of the man who had been calling himself Johnny Stevens. Tim was that way, too, never resting until he had struck back at a man who had done him injury.

Tim Mara was not waiting at the hotel, which surprised Johnny. He was impassive in his room as he emptied the suitcase on the bed and made up the saddle roll he had brought into Thunderbird. His rifle was in the corner, his horse and saddle at the livery barn. Once more it was farewell—for good this time—to those faint hopes of peace and a placid life that had stayed in his mind like a mild, gnawing hunger.

He paid the room bill on his way out. The hotel clerk's tight, disapproving silence showed that the clerk had heard what had happened at the church.

Tim Mara was not waiting at the livery barn, either, which surprised Johnny still more. The hostler had heard, also, Johnny guessed as soon as he spoke to the man. But the hostler was a sly, talkative little man who could not keep quiet as he saddled the horse.

"Your friends left town fast," he said innocently. "You leavin' us, too?"

"Which way'd they go?" Johnny asked briefly.

"Headed north past the courthouse. Didn't say where they was going."

Johnny rode to the north, too, for the hostler's eyes, and at the edge of town swung west and south. Tim Mara, Frisch, and Romero would be heading back into the mountains after Chihuahua Keene and the other men. It would not be healthy to have the bunch cut his trail as they rode for the border with the long trip and all plans wasted and Tim Mara seething and raging.

Six days later, his third day in El Paso, Johnny was still undecided whether to head for California or down into the Texas brush country. He was turning the matter in his mind when he cashed in at a stud game and walked through the night to his hotel room.

He walked into the dark room, lit the oil lamp in an iron bracket by the washstand, and was whistling softly between his teeth and stripping off his coat as he turned. And then with an oath Johnny tried to snatch at his gun and failed with his arms tangled in sleeves of his half-removed coat. The gun would have helped little. They were five, spread out on both sides of the doorway. They could have jumped him when he entered the dark room, but they had waited, guns covering him until he lighted the lamp.

Three of the five Johnny recognized as Thunderbird men. Frank Watersford was one. He looked old now and shaky, his face haggard and drawn, pouches under his eyes. But the eyes were cold and dangerous and Watersford's voice rasped like a file on hard metal.

"Where is she?"

"I'm going to shuck back in this coat," Johnny warned. When the coat hung straight again, he answered Watersford's demand slowly: "So Linda went with him after all?"

But something was wrong with that guess. The five men had a hard tension, as if they had judged Johnny Stevens and had passed sentence on him before they entered the room. Frank Watersford stepped out from the wall. He was without his cane; he moved stiffly, like a man driven by inner fires that ignored bodily weakness.

"Don't trifle about it, Stevens. You know damn' well that wolf pack of yours took her. We cut their trail next morning, and, when they split up, these men sided me on the likeliest tracks that headed this way. Where is she?"

A hot helpless anger drove blood into Johnny's face while the old man was still talking. He understood everything before Watersford finished. Tim Mara hadn't given up. Linda Watersford had been in Tim's blood like fire. That was why Tim had left the church and had ridden out of Thunderbird without settling the tally with Johnny Stevens.

"Tim got her that same night?"

"You know damn' well he did."

The breaking edge was in old Watersford's voice. The gun muzzle wavered a little in his hand. It was easy to believe control might snap any moment and let his gun cut Johnny Stevens down.

The other four men had moved out from the wall and were covering Johnny from three sides. Their silence was more threat than words as Johnny said: "You followed my tracks to El Paso and laid for me?"

Watersford moved the gun impatiently. "We lost the tracks, but they was still headin' this way. Linda didn't have any more use for him. We'll get her if it means killing, starting with you."

"Couldn't blame you," Johnny said. "But it wouldn't help. If I wanted Mara to have her, I wouldn't have bothered about the wedding. Any of you stopped to think of that?"

A younger, square-jawed cowman, who Johnny had not noticed around Thunderbird, snapped the answer: "We've thought of everything. But the tracks headed this way. You're here in town. An' you were one of the bunch."

"Not now," Johnny told him. "And if Linda's in town here, it's because she wants to be. Tim Mara wouldn't bring her to El Paso any other way. They'd lynch him here as quick as in Thunderbird if a girl said he was holding her as prisoner."

"She's probably afraid to talk," said Frank Watersford huskily.

"You don't know your own girl," Johnny retorted almost angrily. "She wouldn't be that afraid of anyone. She's not here in El Paso. Neither is Tim Mara or any of his men. I've been here three days with my eyes peeled. Had two men I know watching for them."

"Been expecting them?" the square-jawed young cowman blurted.

"I've just been careful not to get caught with my back turned. You think Mara will leave me alone after I busted up his wedding?"

They were silent, not knowing what to believe. They had sighted him around town and made this move, and now reason was telling them he must be right.

Frank Watersford muttered: "I'd owe the devil thanks for stopping that wedding." He holstered the gun. The Thunderbird men took it as a silent order and did the same. They watched Watersford address Johnny almost pleadingly. "Where'd he go with her? You know him. I . . . we don't."

Johnny reached for tobacco and papers. The five men watched his set, weathered face as he rolled a smoke and lighted it and stared at the floor, thinking.

"The tracks split up?"

"Yes," said Watersford. "Wasn't more than two horses kept together after they split."

"How many made the trail you cut?"

"Six or seven was in the bunch that stopped our buggy on the way back to the ranch. We ain't figured yet where the others come from to help Mara."

Johnny did not explain Chihuahua Keene and the dozen other men. "Mara came from across the border, and he's gone back," he said. "He travels fast when he moves. If tracks headed this way, some of Mara's men made 'em for a blind. You can bet Tim took Linda across the line as fast as he could travel. He knows what he'd get if he was caught with her on this side."

"Where does he hang out across the border?" Frank Watersford burst out. The old man's gnarled fist balled up; pent-up grief and fury burst from him. "We'll follow him to hell!"

"Hell," said Johnny, "is about where you'll have to follow if you catch him. It's a long border . . . and a long way south across Mara's range. If you're lucky, you won't catch him."

"What do you mean by that?"

"Mara usually has fifteen or twenty good gun hands near," Johnny told them. "More than that when he's in the right spots across the border. They could outride you, outfight you, and deal your men more grief than the Yaquis. Think it over."

He broke Frank Watersford with those words, as he knew he would. But it was the truth they had to face. The bitter uncertainty of it crawled over the faces of Watersford's companions. They were ranchmen who could deal with rustlers on their home range, ride in a hard-shooting posse, face guns, and not back down. But following Tim Mara across the border was suddenly something else.

"What can I do?" Frank Watersford asked with husky weariness. And now he looked as if he needed the cane. Hopelessness was bearing hard on him.

"I don't know," Johnny admitted. Then he added: "You can talk to a sheriff, you can take a chance trying to trail him . . . but it will be a slim chance."

Frank Watersford swallowed. "We'll see you before we leave town," he muttered, and he seemed to be walking blindly as he made for the door and his men followed him.

Johnny tossed the cigarette into the waste pail beside the washstand. He had stayed calm before them; now, alone, he began to swear under his breath. He felt no better for the outburst. If he had bothered to think about it, Johnny would have guessed he was not feeling. It didn't help. The facts were like cold figures in a ledger. Two and two made four. It would always make four.

III

An hour later Johnny did not look back as he rode across the wooden bridge planks that spanned the Río Grande. A backward look would reach clear to Thunderbird and that nebulous hunger for peace and contentment that a man might find ranching on the placid Thunderbird range. And there was no peace ahead.

Tim Mara's tracks had been printed from Baja California to the steamy thickets of the Mexican Gulf. Tim might be anywhere in the mountains, plains, and deserts in a thousand southward miles. But he would not be far from his men. Not even for Linda Watersford. Knowing Tim Mara's habits made the hunt a little simpler.

In the days that followed, Johnny rode a great swing southeast, below the south-dropping Río Grande, and finally circled toward the west. He followed rutted pack trails and cut over dry desolate country to hidden water holes, studying the tracks of shod horses, sifting idle talk of the trails, lazy gossip of native huts and little *placitas. Gringo* strangers in the back country were not forgotten.

Nineteen mud-chinked polo huts and squalid adobe houses—and no church—were in the isolated *placita* called St. John of God. And a *gringo* without hair on the top of his head and a Mexican who traded *gringo* tobacco or corn-shuck cigarettes had passed days back. They had asked about water holes on the mountain trail to Cordova—as if any woman or man in St. John of God had ever ridden over the mountains.

"*Sí, señor,* there was a man in my father's time who went there, but he did not return. . . ."

Johnny rode his gaunted horse from the misting years that drowsed about St. John of God. And he was grinning coldly. He might have guessed that Tim Mara would head for the Cordova country, where Tim had often stopped before, and law and order was a matter for the indifferent military governor at Chihuahua City, far away. The shod horses of Denby Frisch and Solano Romero had puzzled out the faint trail across bleak dry mountains. One water hole in the rocky bottom of a deep, sheer-sided barranca was dry. The sun-dried goat's meat from St. John of God was like sawdust on Johnny's bloating tongue before he reached a meager water seep near sundown on the next afternoon.

He had to rest the horse there overnight. Blackened fire embers, scattered cigarette ends, and the buzzard-cleaned bones of a mountain sheep were proof that Denby Frisch and Solano Romero had been forced to do the same.

But west of the mountains the country opened up. Two days later through the driving blaze of the setting sun Johnny saw the far dust of a wagon train that was plodding into Cordova.

He was gaunt and dry and his eyes were watchful as he rode in among the adobe houses where dogs barked in the early night. If Tim Mara were around Cordova, so were some of Mara's men. Any one of them sighting Johnny Stevens would make the long hard trip useless. Pete Cruces was the answer, if that Apache half-breed still lived with his latest wife in the same adobe house west of the plaza.

Pete Cruces did. He opened the door himself, swearing in surprise as the lamplight streamed out over the visitor.

"*Aii, Dios* . . . ees the devil heemself w'en I t'ink of him!"

"Why think about me tonight?" Johnny demanded alertly as he stepped inside.

Pete Cruces was slender, wiry, dark-skinned, with agate eyes and a derby hat worn at a jaunty angle even in his own house. He closed and barred the door and uttered an order in Spanish that sent his good-looking young wife scurrying meekly from the room.

"Why I t'ink about you tonight?" said Pete Cruces. He

crossed the room lightly and took bottle and glasses from a shelf. White teeth showed in his dark face as he sat across the corner of a table from Johnny and passed the bottle. "I hear today thees Mara no like you now."

Johnny's eyes narrowed as he drained a stiff drink. "Who'd you hear it from?"

"Celestino Garcia, who ees ride weeth Mara."

"So," said Johnny. "Garcia's in town. Who else?"

"Many you know. *Señor* Mara, too, I t'ink."

"Got a woman with him?"

Pete Cruces's bright eyes shifted quickly in the only sign his interest had been caught. "How I know? What woman?"

Johnny shrugged, watching the man drink and put down his glass.

"You any more friendly with Mara now than you were the last time we were through here?"

This time Pete Cruces's smile had a snarling edge. His hand unconsciously touched a small scar on the side of his chin.

Johnny nodded. He'd gambled that Pete Cruces had not forgotten the night Tim Mara had knocked him across a *cantina* table laden with bottles and glasses. The blow hadn't meant much to Tim or Tim's men at the time. Pete Cruces had been a slippery *cantina* loafer who had done a job for Tim and then had tried to double-cross him out of ten more *pesos* when he thought Tim was too drunk to notice. Tim Mara, however, was never too drunk to notice, and, when a waiter had thrown the groggy, glass-gashed Pete Cruces out of the *cantina* that night, Johnny had made a private guess that the Indian in Pete Cruces would not forget. He had been right.

"Like to earn a hundred *pesos* tonight?"

Pete Cruces hunched forward, eyes intent. "How?"

Johnny rolled a smoke. The whiskey was stirring his blood but his voice was casual. "I want to see Mara alone. Don't want to meet any of his men before I do. I'll have to know where Mara's staying tonight."

Pete Cruces licked his lips. "You pay hundred *pesos* for that?"

"*Sí.*"

The dark wiry little man exhaled a soft breath. "Pesos oro . . . gold?"

"Silver," said Johnny. "And it's twice too much at that. How about it?"

He expected the nod and gash of a smile he got. "Sure. W'ere I find you?"

"How long will it take?" Johnny asked.

A shrug answered. "How I know? Not so long, I t'ink. You wait in Cantina del Toro?"

"I told you I wanted to keep out of sight," Johnny said shortly. "I'll wait in that alley behind the *cantina* . . . and leave my horse in your shed. *¿Bueno?*"

"*Bueno,*" agreed Pete Cruces, pushing back his chair.

It was dark in the alley behind the *cantina*. Johnny could not see the pale blotch of his gun hand against the oiled holster, heavy and comforting against his leg. The gun was the only comforting thing in the night. Pete Cruces's whiskey had worn away, and the long hard days of riding lay wearily in bone and muscle.

Across the alley, a little to the right, talk and laughter seeped faintly through the back door of the *cantina*. The gaiety would have deceived most strangers in this dry, out of the way country. But Johnny knew the lonely trails through nearby chaparral and desert brush, the narrow dusty town streets. On other visits he had washed the trail taste from his throat with Chihuahua beer in that *cantina* across the alley. And in Cordova tonight he knew men with guns and knives who would kill him on sight. It was not comforting.

Life on foot and horseback passed the alley mouth. And presently two indistinct figures turned into the alley on foot and Johnny faded silently into the low doorway at his back. The thick adobe wall formed a sheltering frame. He moved the gun slightly in the holster and stood taut, listening to the soft, scuffing steps. A woman's soft laugh knifed through the blackness. Johnny relaxed a little. The couple passed close like drifting wraiths, with a man's thick undertone murmuring. The woman laughed again and they stopped a few steps to the right.

The breath of an exclamation touched Johnny's lips. Then he grinned wryly as a key grated in a lock, a door opened, thumped softly shut. And he was again alone in the alley.

Minutes later, the back door of the *cantina* opened, spewing yellow light across the alley dust. Two men stepped out and the closing door plunged blackness about them.

The silence that followed had a solid weight on taut nerves. The two men also were standing still, listening, waiting. But in the brief light striking from the *cantina* doorway Johnny had marked one of them as Pete Cruces, derby hat cocked at the usual jaunty angle. Silently Johnny waited for a sign. It came so unexpectedly that he almost fired the gun that was instantly from holster to hand. A low chuckle had sounded almost under his nose.

"You wait for us?" asked Pete Cruces, the chuckle threading his sly enjoyment.

Johnny swore under his breath. "You'll sneak up on a man once too often. Who's that with you?"

"Name Manuel." Pete Cruces chuckled. "He's leetle dronk . . . but for leetle money he show us w'ere thees Mara e-stay tonight. Pretty good, no?"

"More money, eh?"

"I no have *dinero* for heem. W'at I do? You talk?"

Johnny moved out of the doorway, holstering the gun. "Will he keep his mouth shut?"

"I t'ink so. *Ssst* . . . Manuel."

"Twenty *pesos* now," the man mumbled out of the dark.

Johnny dug in his pocket. Manuel struck a match to make sure the amount was right. He swayed unsteadily, and looked like a cut-throat *cantina* loafer who probably had knifed and robbed more than one victim. He was grinning with drunken satisfaction as the match went out.

"A *caballero, señor.* I like you. . . ."

He lurched against Johnny, hugging him with a familiar arm. Johnny elbowed him roughly away—and whirled suddenly as his gun went out of the holster.

The grab Johnny made caught a coat sleeve whisking back. Pete Cruces had stepped behind him and snatched the gun. As Johnny's fingers dug into the coat sleeve, Pete Cruces whistled shrilly.

Johnny wasted no breath speaking. They had him trapped, as they'd probably trapped many another man carrying hard money in the dark. A knife blade between his ribs would be next. Then the alley dogs would snuffle and bark at one more dead *gringo* who had been too careless after dark.

Rage at the double-cross drove his elbow viciously into Manuel's middle. The man gasped. Johnny stamped on Manuel's foot and wrenched around, grabbing the wrist below the coat sleeve he held.

Manuel wasn't drunk. He plunged in, arms catching Johnny from behind. Pete Cruces almost got the gun with his other hand. Johnny blocked it with his hand over the gun first. But they were two and he was one, a man on his back locking his arms and Pete Cruces trying desperately to tear the gun away. The three of them reeled about the black alley, Johnny too furious to care about the knife that might drive in his back any instant. Then suddenly they seemed to have many more hands. A match flared a step away. Johnny sighted at least three more men around him, and glimpsed the broad hard face behind the flaring match of Denby Frisch.

A gun barrel smashed at Johnny's head. His last bitter thought was that Pete Cruces had guessed correctly he could get more than a hundred *pesos* silver from Tim Mara. . . .

A rough hand was impersonally slapping his face, and, when Johnny moved his head and groaned, a gruff voice ordered: "Get a drink into you."

A bottle mouth was forced between his teeth. Johnny gulped, choked on the raw tequila. When gasping breath came back, his throbbing head had cleared.

He was sitting on the ground, a man kneeling beside him with the bottle, other men standing about him in the night and the restless stamp of horses behind him.

Overhead the sky was an unbroken sweep. In the near distance lights twinkled. He was outside Cordova. Tim Mara's men were around him. Johnny was helped up, a hand holding his arm.

"Where's Mara?"

The smooth voice of Denby Frisch answered. "Tim's busy. Climb a hoss, Johnny. We're ready to travel."

"Where to?"

"What's it matter?" Denby said with the rough joviality that was more dangerous than venom. "You're lucky that gun barrel didn't cave your top. Looked for a while like it had, and we was wastin' time gettin' you out here. . . . Here's your hoss. Climb on."

IV

Johnny swung into the saddle and waiting men roped his legs and dropped a reata loop around his middle. Mara's men knew this sort of business. Johnny Stevens would be all prisoner while he rode with them. They headed west, six of them riding with him, one holding the long, strong reata.

His hands were free. He rolled a cigarette and smoked half of it, pondering in his aching head why he wasn't dead already. This wasn't like Denby Frisch or Tim Mara. Johnny's humorless smile, hidden from them by the dark, was for the advice he had given Frank Watersford and the Thunderbird men, and then had failed to take himself.

"Who's here?" Johnny asked, looking at the dark figures riding close.

"Solano, Garcia, Hancock, Shorty Smith, Ed Wheeler, an' me," said Denby cheerfully. "Like old times, ain't it, Johnny?"

"No," Johnny said. "When you started running off women instead of cattle, you got too low-down for me."

The long lanky Texan, Ed Wheeler, broke the silence, and Ed Wheeler sounded uncomfortable: "You didn't handle Tim right, Johnny. You riled him."

"I should have shot him."

"Might have paid you better," Denby Frisch said genially. "The boys do well when they stick with Tim. He gets a wild idea now an' then . . . but that's Tim's business. You had a place in the bunch. Tim stuck with you an' you turned on him. We'd all hang quick if we didn't stick with Tim."

Johnny spat offside contemptuously. "Boot-licking Tim Mara has kept you riding safe an' easy. Tim likes it. I read your brand the first week, Denby. You'd shoot Mara as quick as any other man if it paid. Hanging's too good for you."

Denby chuckled. "I ain't gonna be hung, Johnny . . . but I may help hang you. Whatever Tim says. He's been anxious to see you."

"Expected me, did he?"

"Couldn't hardly wait till you showed up."

Johnny turned that over in his mind. It made some sense of

all this. Tim Mara knew him as he knew Tim. And Tim had guessed that of all the men in Thunderbird, Johnny Stevens would be the one to come riding out of the far distance to find him. So Tim had been waiting.

Johnny spat again, guessing that the hours to come would not be pleasant. He had seen that side of Tim Mara once or twice before. He had been sickened by the streak of malevolent savagery Tim could exhibit, had tried to put it out of his mind as being flashes of Tim's wild temper for which some excuse existed. Now he knew, if most of the bunch did not, that the hard selfish malevolence was really Tim Mara. The quick smiles, the boisterous good nature that made men like Tim, were only skin deep. And if you scratched the surface right, Tim would turn on you like the wolf he really was.

The town lights of Cordova vanished. They were striking southwest into rolling hills, with higher, rougher country beyond.

"Where we heading?" Johnny asked Ed Wheeler.

"Rancho Prieto."

"I thought so. Old Juan Corvales is the only man around here who'd want Mara's bunch on his doorstep. They're two of a kind."

"Corvales is dead. Tim's buying the place from the widow with the money he meant to use at Thunderbird. Aims to make it headquarters."

"Tim knows you all better stay south of the border after this," Johnny said. "Taking that girl has marked the lot of you. Rancho Prieto ain't your headquarters . . . it's your hide-out from now on."

No one answered him. In another hour they were at Rancho Prieto, Black Ranch. In the pale cold starlight the massive, thick-walled adobe buildings loomed against a black lava cliff thrusting against the sky half a mile away.

They put Johnny out behind the main buildings, in the ranch

cárcel. The windowless walls were heavy logs. The door was foot-square gratings of heavy strap iron. Denby Frisch snapped a padlock and chuckled through the bars.

"Tim's got the key, Johnny. Rest easy till he gets around to you."

"Denby," said Johnny mildly, "I might get my hands on a gun someday. Don't be around."

"Ain't that big talk?" asked Denby genially. " 'Night, Johnny."

When he was alone, Johnny rolled a cigarette, lighted it, and surveyed the room by the match light. The ceiling *vigas* were logs set six inches apart. The floor was scuffed down in spots to other logs buried under the floor. The barred door let anyone passing look in, day or night. Not a chance to break out. The bed was a low adobe platform against the back wall. Johnny sat on the hard edge, feeling the night cold coming between the door bars.

He was finishing a second cigarette when a dark figure appeared outside the bars. "Here's a couple of blankets, Johnny."

It was lanky Ed Wheeler, gruff and brief as he stuffed the blankets through one of the foot-square openings.

"Thanks, Ed."

"You was a damn' fool to come back," Ed said gruffly, and stalked away.

Johnny slept.

A grinning, saffron-skinned Chinaman woke him up by rattling the door.

"You eat?" he sing-songed through the bars as Johnny sat up, yawning. "Coffee hot now! You likee wash? You likee shave? Plenty hot *agua*. Likee clean shirt? Evlyt'ing *muy pronto!* Yes? No?"

"Yes," said Johnny. "But no if I want it, huh? I've got *pesos* gold if you can slip me a gun."

"No gun. Prenty evlyt'ing else. I get."

When the Chinaman returned, Johnny's eyes widened. There was a small pan to wash in, hot water, razor, small mirror, a clean shirt. By the time he was through shaving and in the clean shirt, the Chinaman was back again with coffee, ham and eggs, hot biscuits.

Johnny coldly asked: "What's the idea?"

"You want, you call, I come. Name Hop."

Johnny attacked the food. When he was through, he rolled a smoke and stared out between the iron straps of the door. Rancho Prieto was one of the old *haciendas*. The big house looked as if it had been rooted in the ground since the nearby lava cliffs had writhed with molten rock. Old Juan Corvales had had *vaqueros* and cattle, peon workmen who meekly took the angry slash of his riding whip, and a past that kept him living at bay here on his guarded range. Now Corvales was gone—one hungry buzzard who would not be missed. Tim Mara had taken his place on the buzzard's roost, set to sally out at his leisure and pick the bones of the border country.

Johnny took the cigarette from his mouth and stared intently as Tim Mara and Linda Watersford rode around the corner of the house and headed toward the log cárcel. Linda was slim and prettier than ever in the morning sunlight. Johnny's heart turned over again at sight of her.

Tim was laughing as he said something. Linda smiled back at him. Looking through the bars, Johnny suddenly felt foolish, and then disgusted at the feverish days he had hunted them. He was hard-eyed when they rode up and dismounted.

"Howdy, Johnny," Tim greeted breezily. "Too bad you had to go in there last night."

"Too bad if I hadn't," Johnny told him through the bars. "You've a gun and I haven't. Open the door and take a chance."

Tim chuckled at Linda. "He's still proddy. Reckon we can calm him down?"

Linda smiled uncertainly at the bars. "Hello, Johnny. Tim said you'd be here. Have you seen Father?"

"In El Paso. He was hunting you and he looked bad. He didn't figure you'd be feeling so good."

Tim chuckled again. "You wouldn't have stopped to listen last night, Johnny. Had to cool you off a little, so you could take word back to Thunderbird."

"It ain't the kind of word Thunderbird will want to hear."

"Still proddy," Tim repeated, obviously enjoying himself. "Johnny, that wife quit me three years ago and made it legal last year. I couldn't prove it to you or anyone in Thunderbird. So I brought Linda across the border to see for herself. Linda . . . how about it?"

Linda nodded. "Tim got the papers from Chihuahua City, and a newspaper with the court record printed in it. It came two days ago. Tim wants . . . we want you to take them back to Thunderbird."

"You got here just in time for the wedding again," Tim said, enjoying the moment. "The *padre*'s coming up from Cordova tonight. Satisfied?"

"Satisfied," Johnny said briefly. "Let me out."

"Linda, leave your horse at the corral. I'll talk with Johnny," Tim said.

When she rode off, Tim lost his smile. "You'll get out tonight and see the wedding, Johnny. Then Denby Frisch an' a couple of the men will ride back to Thunderbird with you." Tim spat. He was not friendly now. "I had a hunch you'd show up. Crazy about Linda, weren't you? Crazy enough to bust up that wedding in Thunderbird and then follow her."

"Have it your way. I'd do the same for any woman."

"You double-crossed me," Tim said on an ugly note. "I'd have got you in town last night . . . but I aim to make you ride back and take that mark off my name."

Johnny grinned bleakly. "I knew there was a catch on that Chinaman treating me like the star boarder. You're still a wolf, Tim. When you walked in that church in Thunderbird, you didn't know whether you were married or not. And you didn't give a damn."

"That's right, Johnny. But you'll watch the wedding tonight and ride back and clean up the mess you made. And then stay outta my way. I don't forget a double-cross."

"If you weren't a wolf, you wouldn't call it a double-cross," Johnny said through the bars. "I guess I never belonged in your pack. All I ever wanted was to forget I beat a man to the draw once, and to settle down once more around ordinary folks. And God help that girl, married to you. But if she can't read your brand right, it's her business."

"That's right, Johnny. Just remember it after you ride outta here."

Tim led his horse away.

Flies buzzed and darted in the bright sunshine and the slow hours dragged. At noon the Chinaman brought food. Now and then Mara's men passed in sight of the barred door.

Johnny was glad that Linda Watersford did not appear again. She'd seemed friendly enough, in spite of what he'd done at the Thunderbird church. She'd had plenty of chance to read Tim Mara. She was either blind and foolish, or she didn't care. And if she didn't care, Johnny Stevens didn't care. For old Frank Watersford's sake he'd ride back to Thunderbird with the papers that made so much outward difference. And then he'd ride west on the gun trail.

Dusk came. Lights in the big house made yellow points in the purple shadows. The *padre* rode in from Cordova on a cream-colored mule, sided by two of Mara's men. The Chinaman brought food again, and a lantern.

"Prenty wedding by 'm bye." He giggled. "I make cake, prenty

37

candle. Prenty drunk tonight, you bet, no?"

"Damn your cake and candles."

But he was hungry and ate again by lantern light. He was still eating when a voice drawled at the door. "Here's a bottle, Johnny. You might as well celebrate, too. Put out that light. Tim told the men to keep away from you."

V

The man at the door was Ed Wheeler, the lanky Texan, and he answered Johnny's irritable question. "You'll be let out to watch the wedding, I guess, in an hour or so." Wheeler sounded uncomfortable. "I'm riding with you an' Denby Frisch to Thunderbird. Guess I won't come back. I sorta feel the way you do about things."

"A happy bride shouldn't worry you."

"It ain't her," denied Ed Wheeler. "The world's full of girls. It's Tim Mara and his ways. You seemed to steady him for a time, Johnny. He'd listen to you. Now he's got the bit an' running wild on his own. See what I mean?"

"I saw it back there in Thunderbird," Johnny said. "I saw Tim wouldn't stop at anything he set his mind on. He's black and wild inside. If he'd double-cross a girl, he'd double-cross the rest of us."

"That's right," Ed agreed. "The girl just brought it out. Too bad about her, too. She was heading to the house from the corral this morning an' wiping her eyes."

"She was smiling when she left here for the corral."

"I seen her." Ed Wheeler's voice was biting. "I'll rustle any man's cattle . . . but I draw a line at some things."

"Tim said his first wife quit him and made it legal."

"Guess she did. Tim locked this girl in the house with some of the men watching her an' made a fast ride to Chihuahua and back. What's the difference about another wife? This girl's fought him since the night he grabbed her outside of Thunderbird. She hates Tim's guts . . . an' now she's got to marry him. Nope, Johnny, ain't my kind of thieving. I'm quitting."

"Something funny's going on. I don't understand it."

"Me either, Johnny. Tim offered five hundred if any of the men got you before he did. Then last night in Cordova he changed his mind and told the boys to bring you out here to the ranch safe and sound. Now he's sending you back."

"Ed, lend me your gun."

"Nope. Start trouble around here an' you wouldn't have a chance. Get some of that whiskey in you. Me an' you and Denby are riding in a coupla hours."

Ed Wheeler faded into the night.

Johnny tossed the unopened bottle on the hard bed.

He had more than an hour to wait before a bobbing lantern came to the door and Denby Frisch peered in.

"Ready to start back, Johnny? Tim says you're free to go as soon as he's hitched."

"He told me," Johnny said.

Denby had been drinking. He fumbled with the padlock, put the lantern down to use both hands, and grumbled: "I'd have swore Tim aimed to have your hair. Now he wants you sent safe to Thunderbird an' I've got to ride there with you. You're makin' work for me, Johnny."

"I won't be a worry long," Johnny promised as the barred door swung open and he stepped out.

"Ed Wheeler's saddling now. Come on. The *padre*'s ready to hitch 'em. Tim wants you to see it."

"I'll be there," Johnny said. "But, Denby, you won't."

Denby Frisch read the danger in Johnny's voice. For all his drinking he turned with heavy-footed quickness, giving his right arm a peculiar jerk.

The long-bladed knife slipped into his hand, glinting in the lantern light, as Johnny's fist smashed his jaw. But Denby's head was moving. The blow landed too high up on the solid heavy face. It was like hitting butcher beef and bone that gave a little and was still there. Denby Frisch was still there before the barred door after a lurching backward step.

Johnny knew what was coming when Denby did not drop. The man could fight, and with knife out he always fought to kill. A quick dodge, left arm thrown out, was all that kept the knife from Johnny's chest. He took the blow on his arm, felt it slash through his coat sleeve and cut into the arm. Then his other fist buried deep in Denby's middle. A grunt exploded from Denby. He doubled helplessly. Fully up into the face Johnny hit him, and hit him again. He felt the shock and grind of knuckles smashing Denby's face. Saw Denby's head snap back against the heavy strap iron of the *cárcel* door. The knife slipped from Denby's fingers as he dropped.

Denby lay limply. Johnny dragged him inside. Denby, he guessed, would be helpless for some time.

He took Denby's holstered gun and belt, strapping them under his coat, and locked the iron door and headed with the lantern for the corral, the blood still oozing on his left arm. That, too, could wait.

No one seemed to have noticed the trouble. Men from Mara's bunch were not around. In the big house, probably. But another lantern glowed weakly at the corral. A shadowy lanky figure was swearing at a horse emerging unwillingly from the corral gate.

"Got 'em almost saddled, Ed?" Johnny asked.

Ed Wheeler turned, staring. "Where's Frisch?"

"He's busy."

"Busy, hell," differed Ed Wheeler, stepping close. "You got a gun under that coat, Johnny. What'd you do to Frisch?"

"Locked him up. He'll be quiet for a while. You've got two horses saddled. Tie leather on this other one quick and hold them back of the house. Stay with them. Don't come inside."

"I was afraid of it," said Ed Wheeler almost violently. "Johnny, you know what Mara'll do if you start anything?"

"I've thought about it," said Johnny. "I'll just step inside to see Tim getting married. And then we'll head for the border and stay where we belong."

"Ain't you satisfied to pull out, Johnny, and leave well enough alone?"

"Sometimes," Johnny said mildly, "I think I'm never satisfied. Are we riding?"

Ed Wheeler hesitated while a man could breathe three times, and then he shrugged.

"I'm all fool, too, I guess. If you get outside Mara's house, we'll ride."

Johnny left the lantern there and skirted the lighted windows of the big house. When he reached the door of the big house, it was a little like coming into the church at Thunderbird. He made his decision now as he had then.

Here the audience was all inside, and different from that Thunderbird audience. Tim Mara's men, booted, spurred, wearing guns, and primed with Tim's wedding whiskey. The giggling Chinaman with the cake and candles. And Tim and the girl from Thunderbird, and the *padre* from Cordova.

The door was ajar. He walked into the lighted hall, saw a trickle of blood on his left wrist, and thrust the hand in his coat pocket.

They were in the big room opening off the hall, on the right. From the doorway Johnny saw age-darkened ceiling beams, massive hand-made furniture trimmed with dark leather, shiny brass wall lamps, glowing.

Beyond the watching semicircle of men, beyond the middle of the room, he saw the straight, swaggering back of Tim Mara and the slender straightness of Linda Watersford, facing the

41

brown-robed *padre,* who was droning in Spanish.

The men moved aside, several grinning recognition when Johnny elbowed among them. Some were drunk, others had been drinking. Later they would make a wild, hilarious night of it. But now, washed and shaved, they watched. They had heard Johnny was to be here. His coat hid Denby's gun and the bloody hand was out of sight in a pocket as Johnny stopped out in front and listened.

Tim Mara gave a quick look back, saw Johnny standing there, and grinned his satisfaction as he faced forward again.

Johnny marked a door at the back of the room and one at the side. He noticed Linda Watersford's small white hands tightly clenched at her sides. She stood ramrod-stiff, not moving, eyes seemingly staring straight ahead, with the lamplight making color glints in her soft hair. Johnny was watching her when the *padre's* rapid Spanish brought Tim Mara as far with his wedding as had the preacher at Thunderbird.

". . . knows . . . should not be married. . . ."

Johnny thought he saw the girl taking a deep breath. Perhaps not. She was silent as he reached Tim's side, yanked Tim around for a shield against Tim's gunmen. Denby's gun was hard against Tim's back.

"I thought I'd ask why," Johnny said. "Keep the boys inside and quiet, Tim. Denby ain't here."

Solano Romero was the only one who edged toward the door. Johnny called: "Mara'll be dead when you leave, Solano!"

Tim's voice was shaking with rage. "There'll be time, Solano!"

The *padre* protested weakly: "I do not understand. . . ."

"Neither do I," Johnny answered.

Linda Watersford had moved aside only a step. She was pale. Johnny got the impression that she had passed fear and now was unfeeling. "Why marry him?"

"Why not?" Linda said, strained, close to the breaking point. "It saves your life to carry back the news." Her voice shook suddenly. "You helped me in Thunderbird."

"Quiet, Linda!" Tim raged.

"Quiet, yourself, Tim," Johnny said, prodding with the gun. And he asked her almost wonderingly. "So it helps me if you go through with this?"

"He said he'd let you go . . . afterward."

"Walk out back and call for Ed Wheeler," Johnny ordered, and, when she stood staring, Johnny almost snarled: "Get out! This is between Mara and me now!"

Her quick light steps left the room in a dead silence. The *padre* followed her. Tim Mara's neck was cording with rage.

Almost sadly Johnny said: "You won't let it stop here, Tim?"

"Wait an' see," Tim gritted.

Johnny's thoughts flashed back to that panorama of peace from Kansas City. When you lived by the gun, you had to settle by the gun. Ed Wheeler and Linda would be in the saddle now. Wheeler was man enough to get her back across the border. Johnny holstered his gun with a quick movement and pushed Tim Mara across the floor toward the men.

"Let's settle it, Tim," Johnny said.

It held them frozen, staring in surprise. But Tim had felt the gun leaving his back. He knew Johnny Stevens. Tim had the shoulder gun that never left him day or night. Tim was drawing the gun as he whirled back.

The bunch behind Tim came to life in a wild scramble out of the way.

"Tim!" Johnny called, and it was a call to the man he had sided on the long dry trails.

Tim's teeth showed when he saw Johnny had waited too long to beat the draw. That was Tim's farewell, that and the blast of Tim's gun as Johnny dodged aside.

Tim's bullet drilled the left arm, which was more luck than Johnny had hoped for. And worse than Tim expected. Desperation flashed on Tim's face as Johnny's gun opened up.

But Tim was still all wolf. He fired again as Johnny's shot knocked him off balance. He fired a third time, wildly and helplessly, as the blasts of Johnny's gun drove him back on the floor. And he pulled the trigger a last time as he went limp.

Half the bunch were out the door, others crouching along the walls as Johnny backed, tight-eyed and dangerous, toward the door Linda had used.

"Who's next?" Johnny challenged them.

No one answered. He left the room, ran lightly through other rooms, and out into the night where saddled horses waited.

"Are they coming?" Ed Wheeler rasped.

"Ride!" Johnny panted. "They're out front!"

Linda Watersford could ride like a man. The three horses raced away into the night, circling wide from the lighted house. And presently, when they eased the hard gallop, Ed Wheeler said: "Mara'll follow us across the border!"

"Tim's dead."

There was a gasp from Linda Watersford. Ed Wheeler swore under his breath, and then said admiringly: "Johnny, you're a fool for luck. The boys won't follow us. It ain't their quarrel."

"I figured that."

"You'll do to ride with," said Ed admiringly. "I'd like to throw in with you, Johnny."

"Thanks," Johnny said. "But, Ed, somewhere there's a quiet range where I can raise a few cows and neighbor around with decent folks. I'm looking for that place after I leave Thunderbird."

Linda Watersford spoke in a voice that had new life and hope: "Why leave Thunderbird? It has quiet and cows, and neighbors who will want you to stay."

"I doubt it," Johnny said dryly.

"Oh, yes," Linda said. "You've never seen such neighbors as you'll have. Ourselves, for instance. Will you stay in Thunderbird?"

Johnny looked back at the far faint lights of the Black Ranch, still visible. He was smiling in the dark as he turned.

"Neighbor, you'll be seeing a lot of me from now on," he promised.

★ ★ ★ ★ ★

Herd Hunters Die Young

★ ★ ★ ★ ★

As was the case with the previous short novel, T.T. Flynn's title for this story was simply "Western". He finished it on June 20, 1942. It was submitted by his agent to Mike Tilden at Popular Publications who bought it on July 18, 1942. After his agent's commission, the author was paid $323.00. The story appeared in *Dime Western* (12/42).

I

Steve Harmon was walking along the crooked San Antonio street with Patricia Parker and her father, Major Thad Parker, when the stranger on the tar-black horse upset the present and the future with just two brief words.

He had a sandy stubble on his broad jaw. He wore two cartridge belts, one for rifle, one for revolver ammunition. Steve noted the heavy cowhide chaps, scuffed and scarred by mesquite thickets such as lay to the south and westward, between the Río Nueces and the Río Grande. The man stared boldly at Patricia. Then his glance slid to Steve. "Howdy, kid."

Steve lifted a hand. And as the man rode past, a sudden premonition brought Steve's head around with a startled jerk.

Patricia was amused. "Steve, you get acquainted fast. We've only been here since last night."

"I've never seen him before," said Steve. The incredible premonition must have marked him. Patricia gave him a questioning look.

Major Parker walked beside his daughter with the spare, unbending habit of Army days, which had never yielded to the easier habits of a successful cowman. His manner had the habitual faint disapproval to which Steve had, by now, become accustomed. "He seemed certain of you, Harmon."

"So I noticed," Steve agreed.

The major was as tall as Steve. His glance frowned across Patricia's gay little hat. "He looked like one of the rustlers from

49

the Brasada thickets across the Nueces," the major said coldly. "I'm told this morning that they may be even worse than we've heard up in Colorado. We may have trouble."

"That's one reason I wanted to trail my cattle and horses north with your herd, sir. Our two outfits should be strong enough to handle trouble."

The major, his lips pressed together, walked in silence on the rough cobblestoned sidewalk as they returned to the patio of the Meunster Hotel. The place was owned by a German and built by the Spaniards of an earlier day.

Last night Steve had stood with Patricia and watched the moon pour a silver glow on the fig trees growing in the patio, and on the dark flat stones and the little stream running through the patio like a murmuring silver thread that stitched the old Spanish past to the present and the future.

"It's lovely, Steve," Patricia had said last night. "I'm glad I came."

"Trailing cattle and horses home to Colorado won't be anything like this," Steve had reminded. "I wish you'd go back home on the train."

Patricia had laughed under her breath. "I worked too hard to make Father bring me."

"It's a long trail, and a hard one," Steve had insisted.

"With two big brothers along?" Patricia had reminded. "And my father? And you?"

That had been last night. Now the late afternoon sun spread its hot gold over the second-story galleries above them in the patio, and Major Parker dismissed his daughter abruptly. "You'd better rest in your room, Tricia. I want to talk with Harmon."

Steve's brief smile told Patricia nothing. He did not know what was on her father's mind. It would not, he guessed, be too cordial.

All the way from Colorado on the train, through Kansas and

the Indian Nations, and down through Texas, he had known that Major Parker, and the Parker boys, Guy and Sandy, who were already in Texas, were not too enthusiastic about him. The Parker men wanted too badly to buy his Horse Cañon ranch and water rights.

Patricia vanished into her cool stone-floored room on the left side of the patio. The major spoke stiffly as Steve accompanied him out of the patio. "I'll tilt the price five thousand for your Horse Cañon holdings, and take my chances on finding more of your winter drift still alive down on the Panhandle."

"Still the same answer," Steve refused politely. "The place suited my father to the day he died last summer. And it suits me."

The flush on the major's spare face suppressed temper and irritation, controlled as Major Parker controlled all else in the carefully considered pattern of his life. "I was your father's neighbor, young man. He did not believe you would ever return to live at Horse Cañon. He expected me to buy the place, if it was ever sold."

They reached the street again as an ox-drawn Mexican *carreta*, loaded with prairie hay, lumbered past on great solid wheels that groaned and squealed on ungreased axles.

"I'm sorry," said Steve regretfully. "I thought we settled all this business back home."

But the major testily persisted: "Most of your cattle died in the drift this winter. I'm offering you more than the ranch is worth. You haven't money enough to restock properly. And I doubt if you'll stay with it long, anyway. You and your brother cared little enough for the place, after you were old enough to leave. That much was clear to everyone."

"Let's leave Bud out of it, since he's dead."

"Is he dead . . . or is your twin brother also to be my neighbor someday?" the major demanded pointedly.

51

Steve knew then the major had felt the same premonition that he'd felt when the passing stranger greeted him. Steve stared somberly at the fine hot dust in the street. When he looked up, the major was watching him. So he answered unwillingly, with the tight, unhappy feeling that always gripped him when he thought about wild, young Bud.

"Bud was killed in Arizona before I came back."

"He was shot for a horse thief," corrected the major bluntly. And when he saw the unhappy look on Steve's face, the major added, not unkindly: "I was sorry for you and your father. But Bud was a bad one. I saw it coming on when you two were only boys."

Steve stared again at the dusty street, thinking back through the years, barely aware of the major's next words.

"Folks never could tell you two boys apart. I know Bud's dirt was often blamed on you. Bud thought it was funny. Having you neighbor us at Horse Cañon is one thing. But your brother being there with you is another."

"Bud was shot," Steve repeated. "I talked to men who were with him in the running fight."

"Who found Bud's body?" the major wanted to know.

"He was shot in the back and was hanging over on the horse's neck when he rode away from the others. His horse was found almost a week later, with dry blood on the saddle. I spent almost a month hunting him. It was rough country. I might have been close to his body a dozen times and never known."

"You might be close to him now and not know it," said the major dryly. Then, before Steve could speak, the major stopped him with an impatient gesture. "Bud was always good at covering his tracks. I believed he was dead until that man spoke to you. You're a dead ringer for Bud and why would a stranger speak to you like that? You're twins, you know."

Steve shrugged. He had been asking himself the same question. There was a stern note of finality in Major Parker's voice.

"I don't think Bud died. I think he fell off his horse and pulled through some way. I think he's been seen south of here in the brush country since then. And if Bud is alive, he'll be back at Horse Cañon someday. I don't want him for a neighbor. You'll lose your ranch sooner or later anyway, if Bud joins you. I'm willing to pay more than the place is worth to settle everything now."

"I'll think it over," Steve said, and with a sense of relief he walked away from the stern, level-eyed old man who had known his brother and himself back through the years.

Steve doubted that Major Parker or anyone else had known what it meant to be Bud's double. To have Bud's face and figure and laugh. To have Bud's bleached hair, blue eyes, ready talk, and that warm, fierce feeling of being one with Bud, from birth through life. And to hold the deep and painful knowledge that there was weakness in Bud—a recklessness that Steve had tried to suppress by staying near him, until those last lonely weeks of search in the Arizona border country had left only Bud's unhappy memory.

The major's faint disapproval always suggested that what had been in Bud Harmon might also be in Steve, buried deep and suppressed perhaps, but cast there by the mold that had shaped them one like the other.

At the moment it did not matter. Steve walked the streets, looking for the black horse with the white face blaze, and for the strange rider who had greeted him.

Spain and Mexico had shaped San Antonio, but now the town was Texan, busy and growing, with fine new houses crowding back the old tule-thatched Mexican *jacales*. Wealthy merchants rubbed elbows with lean homesteaders and level-eyed ranch men, with emigrants from Europe, newcomers from the Eastern states, Mexicans from below the Río Grande, bullwhackers, mustang hunters, well-dressed gamblers. Cowmen back from the northern cattle trails swaggered in the streets and plazas.

By deep twilight Steve had searched along narrow, crooked Commerce Street and come a second time into the main plaza without finding the horse or man that he sought. The stranger had probably put his horse in a livery barn or corral and taken a room. He would be out after dark when trade in the barrooms and gambling places picked up.

Two hours later Steve was on the rough stone sidewalk of Commerce Street when he heard a burst of gunfire in the main plaza just ahead.

By the time he reached the plaza other men were hurrying toward the Variety Theater. He joined the crowd around a dead man sprawled in the street.

Excited comments named the victim as Jack Markham, a deputy marshal, shot by two strangers. The deputy had approached the strangers and spoken to them. The next instant guns had been in action. The strangers had walked into the saloon a few steps away and vanished out the back.

On Steve's left a thin, whiney voice lifted importantly: "I seen them! One was a big, sandy-haired fellow. Him an' his partner was in Shorty's barbershop this afternoon."

Steve's mind leaped to the sandy-bearded stranger riding the black horse. The man who would know if Bud were alive or dead. But now the stranger had escaped. Steve edged over behind the man with the whiney voice.

A doctor made a brief examination of the dead man. The body was removed. The crowd broke up. The whining man cut across the plaza. Near the middle of the plaza Steve fell into step beside him and spoke calmly.

"You said that you saw the men who did that shooting in a barbershop this afternoon? Did you see their horses?"

Whiney-Voice wore an old derby hat cocked toward the left eye. He had a seedy, sporty look. His chortle was sly.

"Their horses didn't shoot Jack Markham, stranger. But I sure seen them two hardcases close enough."

"How would you describe them?"

"One of them wasn't so old," said Whiney-Voice. He looked up at Steve, estimating. "He'd be about your . . . your. . . ." There was light enough in the plaza to see the man's mouth gaping in a kind of frozen horror. He stopped, and Steve stopped.

"What's the matter?" Steve demanded.

The answer was laced with stammering fright. "I didn't see nothing! I wouldn't talk, anyways! Ain't any of it m-my business, is it?"

Whiney-Voice would have bolted if Steve had not caught his arm. "My size? Looked like me, did he?"

"You g-got time to get out of town, mister. I won't say a word."

Steve released the man's arm, stood silently, shaken by the knowledge that Bud was still alive. Bud had been here in San Antonio, and was in trouble again. Or rather, Steve was in trouble. For Bud was gone—and Steve looked exactly like him.

Whiney-Voice backed off a fearful step, glancing furtively around. "Wh-what are you goin' to do?"

"Shut up," Steve ordered roughly, and the smaller man sided him with lagging steps. He had seen one man killed by this tall, scowling stranger—or so he believed, and would swear to that the rest of his life.

Two blocks from the plaza, in a crooked, narrow side street, Steve halted at the mouth of an alley. "Walk in there. Keep going. Forget about me, no matter where we meet."

The alley blackness quickly swallowed the man. He would run for help, Steve guessed cynically. And because his peril was great, he walked fast around the next dark corner and headed back to the hotel by the dim, crooked side streets.

He had left his room door unlocked, and was inside, fumbling for a match, before the odor of fresh tobacco smoke warned of a recent visitor. Instantly, silently on his toes, Steve pressed flat against the room wall.

The quiet was absolute as Steve held his breath. Then a low chuckle sounded at the bed.

"Don't get spooky, Steve. It's Bud."

II

Steve swore. "What the hell are you doing here?"

Bedsprings creaked as Bud shifted position and complained: "Now ain't that a fine, brotherly welcome for the prodigal?"

"More welcome than you'll get in the plaza. How'd you find my room?"

"Walked in and asked the Mex porter where my room was. You oughta seen the look on his face." Bud chuckled. "He thought you was blind drunk to forget your room. So you been to the plaza?"

"I'd have been shot or locked up for what you've done, if I hadn't been lucky. They're looking for you."

Bud grinned and shook his head. "Ain't you got it mixed up? You really mean they're lookin' for you," he corrected.

It had always been like this, since Bud had been old enough to sense that strange eyes could not tell Steve and himself apart. And so were unable to tell Bud's guilt from Steve's innocence.

And as always Steve experienced the helpless anger that never was strong enough to cleave deeply between himself and Bud. "You two killed that deputy."

"Why not?" Bud agreed comfortably. "He done me a dirty trick in Austin, and he was fixin' to get a piece of reward that's hung on Brawley. Wasn't anything else to do, was there?"

"Plenty," Steve snapped. "You could have come back to Horse Cañon and settled down. Why didn't you send word you were alive? Me swearing for over three years you were killed in that fight? Father died last year thinking you were dead."

"No!" Bud exclaimed, and then he added slowly: "Maybe it's better. I never was much but a worry to him, was I?"

Silence held them for a moment. Bud broke it. "I guess that's why I faded out. Too many folks worrying about me. Arizona was gettin' too tight anyway. What you doing down here in Texas, Steve?"

"I'm with Major Parker. The northers this winter about cleaned our range. I've got enough cash to make a middling start again. We heard that Texas stock was dirt cheap, so we threw in to buy and drive north together. Guy and Sandy Parker have been down here for a month, near Tornillo, getting stuff together."

"Too bad I didn't know it. I know men who'll get you fifteen-, twenty-dollar horses out of Mexico for five dollars flat . . . many as you want. Good steers and cows as cheap."

"We're showing our brands to the state inspector. Look, Bud, Horse Cañon was willed to me because you were supposed to be dead. Half of it's yours if you'll get in the harness and do right."

Bud slapped his leg, laughing.

"By God, then, I win ten dollars from Brawley. Soon as Brawley said he'd seen me walking with a pretty girl, I knew you were around, Steve. I bet him ten dollars I'd get an offer before morning to settle down and be good. The joke of it is that Brawley thought it was the girl. He said if I got the offer, she'd have to know about me, but if she knew about me, she wouldn't waste breath on the offer. He'd have bet fifty dollars on it."

Always Bud had been like this, with a twist of humor about himself. "You long-legged, outlaw maverick," Steve said helplessly. He struck three matches together, so that the sizeable flame threw light over them both.

Bud sat on the bed, grinning up at the wavering yellow flame. And the old warm feeling came back as Steve thought that strangers who marveled at their likeness would never understand the inner ties that caught them together.

Steve dropped the charred match ends, and the darkness hid Bud.

"How about it?" Steve urged. "Home to Horse Cañon and start all over, the two of us?"

Bud stood up and laughed. "Not me. I'll stay out in the brush. If that was Major Parker who Brawley seen you with today, I'll bet the pretty girl was Patricia. You were soft about her," recalled Bud with amusement. "No wonder you're burring around Horse Cañon. You going to marry her?"

"I haven't asked her. What are you going to do?"

Bud rubbed his stubbled chin. "Killing the town law won't set well with the local folks. I'm going to jump the Río Grande. I stopped in to warn you San Antone won't be healthy by morning, seeing as you're a ringer for me. Better jump the river, too, Steve . . . or, when the shooting happened, was you with folks who can swear you out of it?"

"I was out on the streets alone, looking for you," snapped Steve, and turned blistering profanity on Bud.

At the first pause Bud laughed softly. "That's elegant cussing."

"I ought to take you to the marshal."

"Let's go then and get me hung fast," offered Bud, plainly not worried.

Steve cursed his brother again, futilely, helplessly, as he had in past years for trouble Bud had made. "Get out," he said finally. "I'll do the best I can."

"It'll take some doing," Bud drawled, still amused. "Better

come along."

"No, damn you."

"Going to stay here an' get yourself hung?"

"I'll get out of town tonight and join Guy and Sandy Parker. We're taking the herd over Horsehead Crossing. Maybe I can stay one jump ahead of your poison."

"You'll be a real jumper if you do. Got a horse and saddle? Or a rifle."

"No. I was going to buy them tomorrow."

"Then you're practically naked," said Bud. "Look, Steve, go to Randy's Corral and Wagon Yard. Tell old Jim Randy you want your extra outfit. He'll think you're me. You can trust old Randy up to a thousand dollar reward. But it might be a good idea to get out of his sight before they post the reward for you."

"For you!" Steve corrected bitterly.

"I didn't ask you to stop here in my Texas pasture," reminded Bud blithely. "If you think this is hard luck, cut my trail enough and you'll learn what real hard luck is."

Bud paused, and in the darkness his chuckle was amused. "You can shoot as good as I can, anyway. Keep your gun loose an' drag it quick if a stranger looks like trouble. Because it'll probably be plenty trouble."

"So I'm a damned outlaw and gunfighter until I get out of Texas."

Bud moved close, slapping Steve's shoulder. "It'll be good for you. *Adiós*, Steve. Maybe you'll get an idea why Horse Cañon wouldn't suit me."

The room was still dark when Bud walked out, still highly amused. For long moments Steve stood alone, thinking about Bud and about the dead man sprawled in the plaza street. He began to swear again in the same futile helplessness. And then he lighted the oil lamp in the iron wall bracket and began to

59

yank out his trail clothes, his cartridge belt and his revolver.

The next day Steve rode south and west into thorn brush country. He had ridden all night until daybreak, and had slept off the trail in a mesquite thicket. Last night he had left the hotel after brief words with Patricia at her room door. "I'll see you and your father and your brothers at Tornillo," he'd told her.

She'd asked: "Isn't this rather sudden, Steve?"

"I get ideas. Tell your father about it in the morning. I won't be back this way."

Patricia had known something was wrong. And the bearded, foxy old man at the horse corral also had known something was wrong.

"Must've been something, kid, to clean you down to a side gun an' spurs," old Randy had suggested past the smoky lantern he held up between them.

"Trot out my outfit if you've got it," Steve had snapped, and had been surprised by the hurried fear his irritation had caused.

"Don't get sore about it, kid. I got everything ready."

Now, riding through hot sunlight toward Tornillo, Steve thought of the old man's hasty fear, and wondered glumly what kind of reputation Bud had made for himself.

Guy and Sandy Parker were making headquarters southwest of Tornillo at the ranch of an Englishman named Stoneleigh. They had rented one of Stoneleigh's big fenced pastures to hold their livestock purchases until the trail herd was made up. They also had authority to buy for Steve's account.

Steve knew the northern brush country; he had heard of this brush country of south Texas, called the Brasada, which he was entering. And he began to realize that this Texas brush was deceptive. Stately live oaks lifted above other greenery and bordered broad openings of curly mesquite grass. Birds and wild life were plentiful, with now and then a brief glimpse of a vanishing steer or cow. But close to the brush was a tangle of thorny mesquite and other thorn-covered trees and bushes, mixed with prickly pear cactus, clumps of Spanish dagger, rat-tailed cactus, and endless brush. Steve understood the heavy leather leggings, scarred and scratched, the leather stirrup *tapaderos*, the extra-strong ducking jacket that were part of Bud's riding outfit.

Steve had the oppressive feeling that a living barrier was shutting off the world of great spaces that he knew. The brush hemmed in, swallowed a strange rider. But a fugitive could vanish in that endless thorn tangle.

During the long hot afternoon Steve saw two men riding across the far side of a grassy stretch. They stopped and watched him. On an impulse Steve turned off the trail toward them to talk about Tornillo. He put the horse into a lope, and the strangers rode quickly into the nearby screen of brush. Smiling wryly, Steve reined back toward the trail.

The slap fire of a rifle shot, the whiplash of the bullet was all the warning he had of danger. Steve spurred and swung the horse hard to the right. Then a second bullet scream across his back told how close death had brushed. The two strangers were not warning him back to the Tornillo trail to ride about his business. They were shooting to kill. From Steve's running horse they were invisible. But they could see him and they were still shooting.

Steve yanked Bud's rifle from the saddle scabbard. Hot anger raced with him as Bud's small horse headed toward the nearest brush cover.

They crashed into the thicket. Steve had to weave and dodge wildly in the saddle as the hard-running little roan plunged through invisible openings and interlacing tangles that Steve never would have tried. Thorns stabbed and raked the waist-high leather leggings, tore at the heavy ducking jacket, snagged at face and hands. The wild plunging zigzag through the thicket had borne him toward the concealed strangers. Now, stopping in the sultry quiet, Steve heard the distant crackle of other horses retreating through the brush.

The sounds faded. Steve realized he was sweating, shaken from the anger that had sent him after the men. He thrust the rifle back in the saddle boot and worked slowly out of the thicket, and, as he rode on toward Tornillo, Steve watched the brush and the grassy openings with a new, cold caution.

He reached Tornillo at twilight, riding directly out of the brush past thatched Mexican *jacales,* and then past solid, flat-roofed adobe houses. He had avoided the stage road from San Antonio for the longer back trail, and he came to the center street as a four-horse stage rumbled out to the north through fast-thickening dusk.

There was more business than Steve had thought. Too many saloons for a town this size, more wagons, buggies, saddled horses, and hitch racks than he had expected after the solitary ride. The roan paced slowly along the street and Steve scanned faces and movement on either side. Bud's description might already have been brought fast along the stage road.

Steve dismounted at a hitching bar in front of a small eating place. He wrapped the reins and for a deliberate moment looked around, weighing what he had sensed along the street. Most of the saddled horses that he could see carried rifle scabbards. But what Steve pondered was a guarded watchfulness in every man he had passed. They were more than curious; they had the same cold wariness that he had brought into town. Crosscurrents of threat seemed to fill the purple twilight as he sat down at the wooden restaurant counter.

The sense of impending, unseen danger might come from the thorn brush that held Tornillo against the outer world. But more likely, Steve decided, the threat was in the men who came out of that brush. And when a hand dropped on his shoulder, Steve swung fast to his feet, ready for trouble.

He faced Sandy Parker's welcoming grin. "When'd you get in?" Sandy greeted. "Where's Father?"

"Be a day or so before he and Tricia leave San Antonio," said Steve, and he was grinning, too. Sandy was his favorite of the three Parker brothers.

A year younger than Steve, Sandy was built slim and wiry, with a spattering of freckles and a light-brown silky mustache that Sandy had raised at seventeen with great pride. Here in Texas, Sandy had adopted the brush rider's gear, even to a leather chin strap on his hat. But under the black hat Sandy's face looked worn, strained.

"Tricia came, too?" Sandy asked sharply.

"She wants to make the trip back with us."

"She can't," said Sandy emphatically, then he shrugged. "But we'll settle that later. You coming out to Stoneleigh's place tonight?"

"I'd thought of it. I brought gold in my belt."

"Don't talk about gold here in town!" Then, easier, Sandy said: "I've got to meet a man in the Horn Saloon. Come in for a drink when you're through eating."

A little later Steve entered the swinging half doors and saw Sandy near the back of the bar, talking to two men. They were Nando Watling and Doc Watling, and only in the two names were the two men alike. Nando Watling was the younger and larger, with bull-like power in chest and shoulders and thick short neck. A grin was seldom off his face while Steve was with them.

Doc Watling was Nando's cousin, Steve learned. Doc was a thin, older man, carefully dressed in gray broadcloth. The pallor on his face had a gray, dead look, his black hair was shot with gray, he talked softly in a dead-flat voice.

"We're glad to see you folks from the north. We've got the cattle and you've got the money. Have a drink."

Steve wondered if the gray-faced Doc ever smiled, and, while Steve had his drink, Sandy explained: "I'm riding south tomorrow to look over some cows and horses Doc will sell cheap. Want to come, Steve?"

"I might as well," Steve assented, and Sandy seemed pleased. He told the Watlings that they'd have to be getting along. When they were outside, Steve asked: "Brothers? Doc a real doctor?"

"Sort of, they say. He runs the Horn and has a finger in a lot of things." And for some reason there was weary bitterness in Sandy's added words: "Doc's sort of the big augur for all the Watlings. He's got the brains."

Steve thought over the gray soft Doc as they split to get their horses, and, when they were together again, riding out of town, Steve spoke abruptly. "You look like the riding's been hard. Anything wrong?"

Sandy was silent for a moment, and then he pointed to the round bright moon slowly lifting over the dark wall of thorn brush on their left. "See that moon?"

"Looks nice."

"Think so?" said Sandy, his laugh short. "That ain't a moon, Steve. That's a lamp for the whole damn' Brasada and Mexicans across the Río Grande to rustle and thieve by. Take a good look at it. That moon may cost us all the cash we've scraped up and spent down here."

Steve whistled softly. "Tell me."

"When the moon's out, they can work. Steve, this stretch from here to the Río Grande is the toughest spot in the States and Territories. Back home we heard talk about law getting thin across the Nueces, and some of it sounded like tall talk."

"In a way," Steve agreed, nodding.

Sandy lighted a cigarette and in the match flare his thin face looked haggard and worried. Sandy said emphatically: "We never heard half of it. Not so long ago Mexicans and Indians raided these Texans. Now thieves and killers are in here from everywhere. They're being run out of the Nations and East Texas. A lot of the scum that were in on the big kill of the southern buffalo herd moved down here from the Fort Griffin district. They run cattle and horses over into Mexico and swap for stuff stolen across the Río Grande. The law's a joke here in the brush. A gang can stay hid out and safe as long as they want. The Brasada's crawling with 'em."

"Must be an honest ranchman around somewhere," Steve suggested half humorously. "How about this Stoneleigh?"

"Stoneleigh's too honest for his good," said Sandy promptly. "Around here an honest man has to close one eye most of the time. Take stolen stock hid in a man's pasture overnight, or for a week or so. He'll do better to go blind about it. Talk may get him shot one day while he's out in the brush. Or his own range may be cleaned out. Stoneleigh's trying to hold on until the law catches up. It'll come any year now and there'll be hell to pay while the Brasada's being cleaned out."

"Looks like we'd have done better to buy cattle up north, even at more cost."

"We've got a bull by the tail and can't let loose," said Sandy. "Most of our stuff is bought. Guy and me have been trying to hold it until we can start trailing home. But we've been losing stuff right out of Stoneleigh's pasture. That's why we're going to buy from Doc Watling. Maybe if we spend cash money with the Watlings, we'll have less trouble."

"It's that way, huh?"

"That way," said Sandy grimly. "Dirty work in these parts most probably'll have a Watling mixed in it. You see why Patricia's got to go home by train?"

65

Steve agreed about Patricia, and he told Sandy about the two strangers who had shot at him.

"They might have thought you were the law," Sandy guessed. "Maybe they only wanted your horse and outfit. Or they might have had some stolen beef nearby, or thought you were somebody else. Killing a man ain't so much in these parts."

"They must have thought I was someone else," Steve decided, thinking of Bud, and presently, when they left the main road for a trail through the brush, he was curious.

"We'll short-cut through Stoneleigh's pasture," Sandy explained. "Guy hired four men to ride the fences at night. I want to see if they're on the job."

"Any chance of them taking us for rustlers?"

"Not much. I told them I'd ride home this way two, three hours after dark. One of them'll be looking for me."

The trail struck through the moonlight and mesquite grass of a big opening and Sandy pointed ahead.

"That old dead oak off there is called Dead Man's Tree. Stoneleigh says years ago a raiding party of Mexicans crossed the Río Grande and were cornered near here. Eight were hung on that tree at once. The tree died right after. Mexicans won't come near it after dark. They say the dead men killed it, and are still there."

A few minutes later Sandy said: "There's one of our men."

Steve made out the dark figure breasting the inside of the gatepost, with one hand carelessly on the top gate wire.

"That you, Carson?" Sandy called.

The man did not answer. As they neared the gate, Sandy's horse snorted, whirled off the trail. Steve reached the gate.

"Look, Sandy!" Steve called sharply, and he dropped from the saddle and held the excited horse as he stepped nearer and peered at the gruesome sight against the gatepost.

III

The man stood with his hand on the top gate wire. Seen close, his head was canted over, wide-brimmed gray hat jammed carelessly askew above the temple. A rope had been passed around his back and around the fence post and drawn tight, so that he appeared to be standing there naturally, with the wrist carelessly on the gate wire. But the eye whites were blank and glistening in the sockets. Blood stained the slack mouth, and, as Sandy dismounted and stepped near, Steve thumbed a match into brief flame and saw chest wounds.

"Here's another for Dead Man's Tree," Steve said.

Sandy's voice shook: "It . . . it's Carson, the guard."

Steve touched the limp wrist on the gate wire. "He's still warm." And his voice hardened. "Somebody had a hell of a sense of humor."

"Couple of months ago a buckboard came into Tvevitos with a dead man tied on the seat and the reins wrapped around his wrists like he was driving."

"Makes it worse than murder," Steve said. The hard note stayed in his voice. "We're due to lose cattle tonight. Want to look into it?"

"Might as well," Sandy decided, and he guessed: "They'll probably go through the fence west of here. That'll give a straight push toward Little Angel Creek and not much risk of being seen."

They turned west along the straight fence line, rifles out and ready, no further words between them. Now the threat of the dark brush thickets was real. The softly stepping horses made little sound in the sand.

Three or four miles along the fence, the thin far flurry of gunshots abruptly stopped them.

"In the pasture," Steve said softly.

No other shots followed. Under his breath Sandy said: "Their closest way out is straight ahead and through the fence. If there's enough men, Steve, they'll get us."

"We can worry them some. I keep thinking of that poor devil tied to the gatepost."

"Me, too," agreed Sandy, low-voiced. "Let's go."

Where the fence ran down a steep slope and across a small grassy draw, Sandy halted and listened. Brush crackled faintly in the distance.

"Here they come," Sandy breathed.

"Don't seem to be anyone at the fence," Steve decided. "Most likely they cut the wire and all went in. They'll pass us at a run and keep going. We'd better bust the cattle over into the brush."

They rode fast across the open grass, toward the increasing crash and crackle of cattle coming at a run. They were still in the open when the lead animals burst from the dark brush into the moonlight. Steve spurred toward them, firing a revolver.

The cattle were half wild, and the unreasoning panic of their kind struck the first longhorned cows and steers. They scattered blindly toward the nearest brush. The rest followed; forty or fifty head at least, Steve judged.

He sighted a lick of flame from a revolver off to his left and he swung his running horse toward the stranger, dragging out Bud's rifle. He fired, and the man's horse swerved toward the nearest mesquite, its rider humped helplessly over the saddle horn as he vanished among the thorn branches.

Steve spun his horse in that direction and sighted Sandy charging two more horsemen who had followed the cattle out of the brush. The new men were shooting at Sandy. They turned their guns on Steve as he galloped at them.

Steve heard the high, vicious scream of a bullet passing close. He fired at the rustlers. Sandy's guns were blasting as he converged on the renegades with Steve. Suddenly the two strange riders spurred hard into the brush.

Steve crashed after the strangers. The tangle of slashing thorn branches dragged off his hat. When he pulled up and listened, the strangers were still riding hard through the thickets. Once Sandy joined him, they listened, and could hear only receding movements far off.

"I only seen four," Sandy stated.

"That's about all there was," Steve guessed. "Chances are they're through for tonight. Let's get out of here before one of them throws a bullet at our backs."

Sandy was light-hearted as they rode away. He chortled: "You yelled like I've heard Bud yell in a fight. You get that much fun outta a gun ruckus?"

"Today's the first time I ever mixed in shooting like this," Steve admitted, and he fell silent, pondering the heady excitement that twice today had hit him like fine whiskey, when it was fight or be killed. Steve guessed with a new understanding that it was the same way with Bud.

An hour later they were at Stoneleigh's place on the other side of the big fenced pasture. They found Guy Parker and five men saddling to ride after the rustlers. One of the Parker fence riders had been wounded by the first flurry of gunfire, and they had brought warning of trouble in ahead of them.

Their arrival changed the plans. Guy stayed to talk with Steve and Sandy. The other men rode off with a wagon to bring back the body at the pasture gate. They'd repair the cut fence, try to make sure the other two fence riders were alive, and then return with the wagon.

Stoneleigh was a stocky, pleasant man with iron-gray hair and a practical calm as he worked on the wounded man's arm in the house by lamplight.

"We'll notify the sheriff, for what good it will do," said

Stoneleigh calmly. "Too bad Carson had to get killed. He was a good man."

Guy Parker was an older man than Sandy. In the lamplight Guy looked tired and worried as he watched the wounded man sitting, stripped to the waist, blankly staring at the floor while Stoneleigh worked on a ragged bullet wound above the right elbow.

"If this keeps up, we'll never get away with a trail herd," Guy said heavily.

Stoneleigh looked up from the bloody arm and smiled. "Have to get used to this sort of thing around here, old man. It might not happen to you again. After all, you haven't made any enemies."

Steve put in dryly: "Had this man Carson made any enemies?"

From the corner of his eye Steve saw the wounded man look up quickly. Stoneleigh shrugged. "I can't say much about Carson," he admitted. "He seemed a steady chap, willing to work for wages."

Steve's side glance marked the wounded man staring again at the floor with an expressionless face. He wondered if the fellow knew something about Carson.

Later, with Guy and Sandy and Stoneleigh, Steve sat on boxes out in front of the mud-chinked ranch house and talked while they waited for the wagon to return with Carson's body.

"I'm changing plans. We'll pull out in a few days," Guy decided.

"How about the cattle Doc Watling's got for sale?" Sandy questioned.

"You and Steve look 'em over tomorrow, like you planned," said Guy. "If they look all right, buy 'em. I'll ride into Tornillo tomorrow and see about the trail crew." Guy spat, adding heavily: "Wish we had men here from our own range. I'd feel better."

At sunrise Steve rode southwest again with Sandy to inspect the Watling cattle. They pushed the horses steadily. Around noon they crossed a bare divide, dropped down to little-used wagon ruts, and followed them west several miles to the uneasy bawling of corralled cattle near a mud-chinked, thatch-roofed *jacal*. Waiting at the *jacal* was the gray-faced, unsmiling Doc Watling, the big grinning Nando, and a group of roughly dressed brush hands.

"Climb down an' tear a chunk of meat before you spend your cow money!" Nando Watling hailed with a wave of his big hand.

As they dismounted, a lanky man with a drooping, brown mustache stepped out of the *jacal* doorway. Something was vaguely familiar about the man. Steve turned, looking him over.

He met startled recognition in the man's glance. Without talk or warning the lanky one went for his holstered gun. Steve knew instantly it was to be a killing—and he was the victim.

The trouble caught every man by surprise. Steve's fast jump to one side was the first warning most of them had. Then the lanky man's revolver shattered the peace.

Steve's quick move was all that saved him. His own gun was out before he stopped. He took a split instant to set himself. He'd not have another chance. Then he fired three shots, ripping in one unbroken burst. All three bullets hit the stranger. The first one saved Steve from another shot the man fired. Steve's last two slugs beat the lanky man down into a twitching heap on the sun-baked ground.

Then Steve had his back to the *jacal* wall, his gun searching for more trouble.

Sandy yelled: "Don't anyone move!"

The Watling men scattered out, ringing the spot with drawn guns and ugly looks. A wrong move, and Steve knew that he and Sandy wouldn't have a chance to reach their horses. They were cornered.

Nando Watling shouted a warning: "Don't nobody shoot!"

The drawn-out instant of danger hung ready to snap as Nando Watling plunged between his men and Steve. He pointed to the huddled, now quiet body on the ground.

"Bat walked right out an' hauled his gun. What come over the damned fool?"

The tension slacked. Guns pushed back into holsters as Doc Watling knelt for a moment by the body. He stood up without a change of expression on his gray face.

"Mister, that was good shooting," he said dryly. "How come it happened?"

"Ask him," said Steve shortly. "I never saw him before."

Steve said that—but he wondered. Something about the man still seemed familiar. He could be one of the two strangers who had ridden into the brush yesterday and started shooting.

Doc Watling's pale cold glance looked Steve over. "Bat's been in San Antone for a few days. Just got back last night. Couldn't be you tangled with him there?"

"I'd remember it."

Doc Watling shrugged. "Bat sure took a dislike to you on sight. Serves him right. Let's have a look at them cows you come to see."

That seemed to settle the matter. One of the men grinned and said that Bat must have brought back a hangover, the way he was slow with his gun. Steve walked to the nearby corral with a new idea of how lightly a killing was regarded in these parts. He was sure now that more of Bud's past was catching up with him. It was worse than being Bud, for this way danger came without warning.

After inspection of the cattle inside the dusty pole corral, Sandy said: "It's up to you, Steve. You need this many more head to top off what we've bought for you. Doc said yesterday he'd sell for nine dollars a head, delivered to Stoneleigh's pasture and road-branded there for us if we're short of help. He'll guarantee they'll pass the state inspector."

"Sold," decided Steve.

The dead man was still on the ground under a cloud of flies when Steve and Sandy rode off. "Funny, the way that fellow went for you," Sandy commented, frowning.

"Maybe he thought I was somebody else."

"Must be some tough-looking characters in the Brasada." Sandy grinned.

Steve let it go at that. He still didn't want to talk about Bud, and, when they got back to Stoneleigh's place, after dark, Sandy made it easy for him. Major Parker and Patricia had arrived.

Before entering the house, Sandy suggested: "Maybe we better not talk about that shooting just yet. No use to worry Tricia and Father."

"I was thinking the same," Steve confessed. But inside the house he came under the major's probing stare.

"Young man, you left San Antonio almighty suddenly," Major Parker stiffly greeted. "I couldn't make sense out of the reason you gave Patricia."

"I didn't give her much of any reason, I guess," Steve admitted.

"You might have been in trouble, by the way you left."

Steve chuckled at that, but the major's annoyance seemed to sharpen to antagonism. And a little later, when Steve stepped out in front of the house with Patricia, he learned the reason.

"Steve, there was a killing the night you left San Antonio," said Patricia under her breath. "That wasn't the reason you left, was it?"

"Why, now, you know I didn't shoot anyone that night."

But Patricia was unhappy. "I know you didn't. But the next morning Father had heard all about the killing before I told him you were gone. He wanted to know how you had acted. Steve, the description of one of the men who did that killing could fit you. And the way you left so suddenly. . . ."

"Looks bad, doesn't it? The major didn't tell the law where it could find me, did he?"

"You know he wouldn't . . . even if you were guilty."

Steve patted Patricia's arm. "I'm not so sure about that. The major doesn't approve of me, and he's a stickler for law and order. But I didn't shoot any man that night. . . . You're going back on the train, aren't you?"

"Guy and Father want me to, but I won't," said Patricia promptly. "Father's cows may be in danger . . . but his daughter isn't."

The moonlight reminded Steve of Sandy's warning on the Tornillo road last night, and of the dead man standing his gruesome watch at the pasture gate. In the moonlight at his side Patricia looked very small and lovely. Steve looked down at her and thought of the man he had killed this day, huddled unnoticed under a buzzing cloud of flies.

"You heard about the rustlers we ran into last night?"

"There's always been rustling, even at home," Patricia countered. "Don't try to scare me, Steve. I'm going home on the trail."

The next day Steve would have talked to Major Parker about it, but the major's new curt aloofness persisted. Steve had the angry, helpless feeling that, if the major heard all the truth about the killing in San Antonio, and the killing at the Watling corral, their relations would grow even worse.

In the afternoon the Watling men came in with Steve's cattle.

Nando Watling was in charge. A branding fire was lighted. All afternoon the hot, dusty work of branding went on. The Watling cowpunchers were as hard-working a group as Steve had ever seen. Three of them, Steve noticed, had not been at the corral the afternoon before.

Late in the afternoon one of the three—a stocky, bowlegged man called Hoop—stepped back from the branding fire, wiped a sleeve over his sweating face, and grinned as he rolled a cigarette.

"All the way to Colorado with 'em, huh?"

Steve nodded.

Hoop had a broken nose and a chin scar showing through a rough beard stubble. He pulled on the cigarette and squinted at Steve through the smoke. "Ever been down this way before?"

"Nope," denied Steve, calm and instantly wary. Here was Bud's trail again.

Hoop inhaled again. His squint had no particular expression. "It's a nice country around here," he said. "Don't have no winters to fight." Hoop scratched his jaw behind the scar and pulled the cigarette from his lips. "I'd've swore you been around these parts before, from that old brush jacket an' scratched-up brush leggin's you're wearin'."

Steve looked down at Bud's heavy leather leggings. He hadn't thought about Bud's clothes. Too often in past years he'd traded clothes with Bud. The Parker boys, Stoneleigh, and the major hadn't seemed to notice, either.

"Borrowed 'em," Steve said briefly.

Hoop nodded, apparently satisfied, and went back to his work. He had, Steve guessed, left the fire on purpose to ask questions. Any way you looked at it, the questions cut back to Bud—and probably meant trouble.

IV

The rest of the afternoon Steve stayed wary, sharp-eyed. Little things he would have missed now had meaning. He saw Hoop talking with Nando Watling, caught the burly Nando looking toward him.

Again, Steve turned, and saw Guy Parker staring at him. "Anything on your mind?" Steve called.

Guy shook his head, unsmiling.

The last O Bar trail brand was burned into the last tough hide. Stoneleigh had food ready for all hands. Before eating, Steve went into the house with Nando Watling to settle the tally. Doc had not come with the others.

"Hundred and fifty-seven head, I made it," said Steve, leafing through the grimy tally book.

"That'll do," said Nando, grinning.

Steve had put gold pieces from the specie belt into both coat pockets. Nando counted with him as the bright yellow coins dropped on the table beside them.

"Seventy!" said Nando as the last gold piece dropped. He was grinning as he scooped the money together with big hands. "Any chance for some of us brush poppers to get a sackful of this if we head north?"

"Hard to tell. There's money up north."

"You oughta know," said Nando gustily. He winked. "It's give Doc an idea. Them fool Texas Rangers been raising hell over in Gonzales an' De Witt Counties, an' down into Refugio an' San Patricio. They'll be around here next. Doc thinks a smart man ought to pull out before he has to fight Rangers for a living."

"Depends on the way a man makes his living, doesn't it?"

Nando's grin broadened. "There was a Ranger in Tornillo yesterday." He watched Steve closely, and, when Steve made no comment, Nando let the subject drop. But he was still grinning his wise, sly grin as they went out to the cook house to eat.

After the Watling men rode away, Steve lingered outside in the night, wondering if the Ranger in Tornillo had been working on the matter of the dead San Antonio deputy. For the first time Steve realized how close he was to being shot or hung for Bud's desperate ways. And he couldn't take to the brush like Bud could; he had to stay here and start the trail drive back to Colorado.

Carson, the dead fence rider, had been buried out in the pasture. Today Stoneleigh and Major Parker had ridden to Tornillo to talk with the sheriff.

When they returned, Stoneleigh was bluff and cheerful. "The sheriff says he'll do what he can about Carson, which won't be much," he stated. "But he says the governor is recruiting another troop of Rangers. That deputy marshal who was killed in San Antonio has brought an outcry for a clean-up. Honest men may have a chance around here before long."

In the low-ceilinged, lamp-lit living room, where they had joined Guy, Sandy, and Patricia, Major Parker regarded Steve coldly.

"The sheriff says a Ranger was in Tornillo yesterday, asking questions."

That was all the major said. Guy's look settled sharply on Steve. Patricia, sitting to one side, looked suddenly unhappy.

"The Rangers may help us get away from here without trouble," said Steve calmly.

"I hope so," said the major stiffly. "We should be ready to leave in three days. Wagons will be here tomorrow. I didn't hire men for you, Harmon."

"How many men will you need?" Stoneleigh asked Steve.

"Three and myself ought to carry my share of the drive."

"I can give you names of men who might be interested," Stoneleigh offered readily. "You could ride fast and see them all tomorrow."

"Thanks," said Steve gratefully, and he asked the major: "Will Patricia be going over the trail?"

"I'll arrange Patricia's plans for her."

In the morning Steve left early. Stoneleigh had given him six names, with directions how to find the men. Two of them, Ben Holland and Carty Smith, were the pick of the six, Stoneleigh had advised.

Holland and Smith were partners who had been rustled flat. They were disgusted with the Brasada. Taciturn men who minded their own business, they were honest and good cowmen, with plenty of nerve.

By midafternoon Steve had located three of the men. Only the third man was willing to leave at once on a northern trail drive. He was a thin, cheerful, young cowpuncher named Slim Polk, whose boss had been killed a few days back. Steve found Slim Polk and another man working mossy-horn steers out of a brushy bottom.

"Yup, I'll go," Slim Polk readily agreed. "Got three horses I'd like to take along."

"Bring them along to Stoneleigh's place tomorrow." Steve looked at the sun. "How's the quickest way to get to Holland and Smith's place?"

Steve memorized the rough map that Polk drew on the ground, and before it was dark he rode up to the small mud-chinked log cabin where the partners lived miles from a neighbor.

A spotted hound barked. A windmill was pumping. The partners were not around. Steve decided to wait, so he watered his horse, unsaddled.

When he heard the dog barking, he stood up in time to hail two approaching riders. They were Holland and Smith.

By lamplight in the cabin both men were long, lanky, and

deliberate in movement. Holland had a black beard and a broad Texas drawl. Smith had a long black mustache and seemed reluctant to speak at all.

"Your proposition hits me," Holland drawled without hesitation. "Carty, how about it? Won't never be a better chance to git outta this damned brush."

Smith looked at his partner. Some silent message passed between them. Ben Holland nodded to Steve.

"We're hired," he said briefly. "Git some grub with us an' shake down here tonight. Ain't no sense startin' out now."

In the morning at breakfast Smith looked across his tin plate, cleared his throat, and spoke for the first time.

"You could've saved a ride by speakin' to us when you was in Tornillo yesterday."

Steve gulped the food in his mouth. "I was in Tornillo yesterday?"

Ben Holland said: "We was in Doc Watling's bar while you was buyin' drinks. You must've sobered fast on the ride out here."

"Was I in Tornillo when you left last night?"

They regarded him solemnly. Ben Holland replied briefly: "Nope, not if you was here when we rode up."

Steve hurriedly finished eating.

"I'll see you at Stoneleigh's," he told them, and he saddled and left, riding fast.

So Bud hadn't gone to Mexico. Yesterday Bud had been drunk in Tornillo.

The dusty, rutted main street of Tornillo was almost deserted when Steve rode in. Doc Watling's Horn Saloon was empty of customers. Steve had never seen the red-cheeked, plump bartender now on duty. But he got a smile of recognition as he breasted the bar. And a cheerful greeting.

"How you feel this morning, mister?"

"All right."

"Wonder you ain't got a head. You sure was flyin' high yesterday. . . . What'll it be?"

"What did I do yesterday?" Steve asked.

"Well, nothin' much." The bartender shook his head. "But you oughta know better'n to play poker with a skin full."

"So I played poker? Who with?"

"Don't remember things next day, huh?" The bartender chuckled. "Sometimes that's best. You got in a poker game with Doc Watling, if you got to know the worst."

"Was it that bad?"

"It's always bad playin' poker with Doc." The plump man chuckled. "An' it's twice as bad playin' poker with Doc when you're drunk. Doc's always sober."

Steve nodded. He could believe that after twice meeting the gray-faced, unsmiling man.

"How much did I lose?"

"Well, I dunno about that." Reserve veiled the bartender's manner. "I keep busy here at the bar. Have a drink on the house. You got it comin'."

Steve nodded, and he put down the whiskey and stood considering for a moment. "Where's Doc Watling?"

"Couldn't say. He rode outta town early. Seems like I heard Doc say he'd see you at Stoneleigh's ranch this morning. Maybe he went there and you forgot all about it."

"Looks that way," Steve agreed, and he went out to his horse.

Bud obviously was not in Tornillo this morning. No telling where Bud might be. Bud's memory had never been too good after drinking. If Bud had said he would meet Doc Watling at Stoneleigh's place, there was slight chance that Bud would be there. But he might be.

Once more Steve silently damned his twin brother. It was like

Bud's sense of humor to enter Tornillo and pass himself off as Steve. It had been an old trick of Bud's when they were kids.

Steve wondered as he rode what Doc Watling would say if he reached Stoneleigh's place and suddenly faced two Steve Harmons, so alike no stranger had ever been able to tell them apart. It might jar Doc Watling out of his gray-faced reserve.

Stoneleigh's ranch house looked quiet enough. There was no sign of Doc Watling. The wounded pasture rider, arm in a sling, was loafing on a box.

"Doc Watling been by here this morning?" Steve asked the man as he rode up.

"Yep. He's out in the pasture, I guess."

Stoneleigh came out of the house just then with a bridle and a saddle blanket over one arm, and saw Steve and lifted a hand in greeting. "How d'you feel this morning, old man?"

Steve grinned a little. "All right. I see Doc Watling has been talking about yesterday."

"You might say he has," Stoneleigh agreed, and he shook his head. "Too bad. A lot of queer things happen at Tornillo."

"I wouldn't be the first man who got drunk there," Steve reminded, smiling wryly.

"No," assented Stoneleigh. He looked uncomfortable. "Perhaps I should have warned you." Stoneleigh paused, then shrugged. "You didn't seem to need warning."

"Maybe I didn't," Steve said, and he thought that Stoneleigh was looking at him queerly. "I suppose Doc Watling usually gets strangers in a card game," Steve ventured.

"Usually," Stoneleigh agreed, still looking uncomfortable.

Steve dismounted, liking the Englishman for his obvious regret over the card losses. Before anything more was said, Major Parker came out of the house. Steve braced himself for the major's disapproval.

Then something new, strange about the major riveted Steve's

81

attention. The major had never looked more stiffly unbending. His cheeks had a hard pallor. His face had never been so set and stern.

Steve waited for the older man to speak. It was going to be unpleasant. Once more he could thank Bud for the way the major felt about any little slip Steve seemed to make.

The major stopped in front of Steve. His pallor was even deeper than it had seemed at first sight. A jaw muscle was jerking, as if the major were under heavy nervous strain. But when he spoke, his voice came as precise and cold as the cut of a blade.

"Harmon, you never were any good. I should have decided so years ago. It will please me if you take your things and get out. I hope never to see you again."

Steve pushed back his hat. "That's a little rough, for a few drinks."

"Rough?" said the major, his voice suddenly shaking. "What do you call gambling away your ranch, your cattle, and your horses? You refused to sell Horse Cañon to me and to my sons . . . and yet you throw everything away to scum like this Watling crowd. Now I'll have *them* for neighbors."

For a moment Steve's mouth opened soundlessly. Then because he knew Bud and what Bud could do, the impact of it hit him. "You're sure about that, Major?"

"This man Doc Watling showed me the papers. They have the signatures of sufficient witnesses."

"My name signed to the papers?"

"Yes."

Steve drew a shaky breath. He understood Stoneleigh's pitying regret, the curious sardonic look on the wounded man's face. "Where is Doc Watling?"

"Out in the pasture with his men and ours," said the major savagely. "They're cutting out your share of the drive. The

Watlings wanted to drive north with us. I told them it was impossible."

"Why do they want to drive north?" Steve muttered, and then he remembered big Nando Watling's remarks the day before.

The Texas Rangers would probably be in soon to clean out the Brasada. Doc Watling had decided it would be safer and more profitable to move. Doc must have had the Colorado ranch in mind when Bud rode into Tornillo and got drunk. Doc Watling had worked fast, steering Bud into a crooked card game, and now had ranch, cattle, horses, everything the Watlings needed to settle far from the Brasada.

The major's shaking anger continued. "We'll have no peace at the home ranch. Stoneleigh has told me all about the Watlings. To a man they're thieves and killers. You've thrown them on our doorstep with your worthless, irresponsible ways. And after refusing the more than fair price I offered you."

"It looks bad," Steve muttered agreement.

The major was not appeased. "We wouldn't have a cow left by the time we reached home if they trailed with us. They're getting what they own. I wish it were the last I were ever to see of them. And of you, too, Harmon. I can't order you from Stoneleigh's place . . . but I resent your presence from now on."

The major turned on his heel and walked back into the house. And Steve silently watched him go.

Stoneleigh spoke awkwardly: "I say, it's too bad. I understand how the old gentleman feels. But a man doesn't lose his ranch on purpose. Just want you to know there's a welcome here."

"Thanks," said Steve gratefully, and it took an effort to smile at the stocky Englishman. "I'll ride out in the pasture and talk to Doc Watling."

"Be careful," warned Stoneleigh bluntly. "I know how you must feel. But Doc Watling has six or seven of his Watling tribe with him. They evidently came expecting trouble. They'll think nothing of shooting you if you lose your head."

"I won't lose my head," said Steve, and he swung into the saddle.

Riding out into the big fenced pasture, Steve somberly turned it all over in his mind. The papers Doc Watling held were not legal, with Steve's name signed by Bud. But that couldn't be proved now. Bud was not here. And even if Bud showed up and told the truth, it might not help. Bud could not prove that he had signed the papers. Only one man could back up Steve's oath that Steve had not signed the papers. That man was young Slim Polk, who had directed Steve to Holland and Smith's place the afternoon before. Even with Slim Polk's testimony, it might be impossible for Steve to prove that he had not ridden straight to Tornillo from the talk with Slim Polk. That did not help now, anyway. Doc Watling and his relatives were not going to surrender what they now had. They'd kill Steve or Bud or Slim Polk if the threat of a court hearing seemed to promise trouble.

The roundup was not hard to locate. Guy and Sandy, with their men and Stoneleigh's men, were helping comb the brush thickets and head all cattle and horses toward Stoneleigh's home corrals. Behind a running group of steers Steve found two of Stoneleigh's men. They told him the Watlings were working the west side of the pasture. Two miles west Steve found Nando Watling and two of his bunch hazing a mix of horses and cows.

Nando Watling rode over with a broad, sly grin and greeting. "You sure made us a present yesterday. We're pullin' stakes for that gold-piece country."

"Where's Doc?"

"He's sorta been expectin' you," said Nando. "I'll ride with you." And as they sided each other at a fast trot, Nando slid a calculating look over another grin.

"Doc had an idea you'd be pawin' the dirt this morning.

Where'd you go last night? We hear you didn't come home."

"Had other business."

"You look like you slept out." Nando chuckled. "Red-eye'll get you down. I slept twenty miles in the saddle one night afore I fell off in a patch of prickly pear. What kinda ranch did Doc win from you, anyway?"

"Supposed to be a pretty good one," said Steve briefly.

"We'll do with 'most anything for a headquarters," Nando stated cheerfully. "Us Watlings all stick together an' get along."

They found Doc Watling and two more riders leisurely crossing a broad open stretch of mesquite grass. The two riders moved in close to the graying Doc, and Steve knew they were there to guard Doc against any trouble.

Doc Watling's soft-voiced greeting was almost friendly. "We didn't wait for you to show up, Harmon. We want to make this cut in a day so we can leave."

"I'd like to see the papers I'm supposed to have signed," Steve demanded.

"You can see 'em . . . but you can't touch them. The boys'll have guns on you while you're looking. We don't mean to lose these papers."

Their horses side-by-side, Nando and the other two men ringing them with drawn revolvers, Doc Watling took the papers from inside his broadcloth coat.

"You signed the cows first . . . then the horses, and finally your ranch," Doc said softly. "There's your writing, and witnesses under it. Them witnesses are businessmen in Tornillo. Satisfied?"

"I'll have a lot of argument explaining it away," said Steve colorlessly.

"More than argument," agreed Doc Watling as he put the papers back in his coat. He looked Steve over. "I offered to drive north with old Parker. He didn't like the idea. We'll pull

85

out a day or so after him. Want a job with us? You'll come in handy helping us get settled on that Colorado place."

"You've got a hell of a nerve."

"Call it that," said Doc softly. "The offer'll stand for a while. You'll probably be heading out of these parts." Doc started to roll a cigarette. His soft voice did not change. "The Rangers are looking for a fellow called the Nueces Kid. They think the Kid shot a man in San Antone the other day. If he's smart, he'll hit the brush."

"Any reason for telling me?"

"There's liable to be a man or so around here who's seen the Kid before. No telling when the Rangers might hear about him. That is, if the Kid raises any trouble. That mean anything to you?"

"Why should it?" said Steve, and he left them.

V

Patricia was standing outside Stoneleigh's house. She had been waiting for him, Steve guessed. They knew each other too well to waste words.

"How did it happen, Steve?" she asked when he dismounted beside her. "When have you been really drunk?"

Steve smiled a little. "Yesterday, wasn't it?"

"When, before yesterday, did you ever get in a card game with strangers while you were drunk?"

"Never did," Steve admitted.

She nodded, satisfied. "That man, Slim Polk, rode in a little while ago. He told me you left him in the middle of the afternoon yesterday, Steve. You were a long way from Tornillo. You were headed for a ranch still farther from Tornillo. What they say happened after that doesn't make sense. I know you, Steve."

"Thanks," Steve said. He looked down at Patricia, wanting to take her in his arms and give comfort and take comfort.

He put the wish aside, perhaps forever. He had stopped being Steve Harmon, with a future on the Horse Cañon ranch that included a wife, a family, and happiness. For he was Bud's double, with all of Bud's wildness, guilt, trouble on his shoulders. He had no ranch, cattle, or future that promised more than a hangman's rope.

Patricia pleaded: "Steve, can't you explain?"

"Afraid not. I wish you'd promise to go back on the train."

"I will . . . if you'll go back on the train with me," said Patricia.

"I can't do that."

"Then I'm going with Father and the boys. . . . Steve, what are you going to do?"

"I don't know. Stop worrying about me," said Steve almost curtly.

Patricia flushed, and just then the major stepped out of the house and settled anything else they might have said.

"Patricia, go inside at once," ordered the major in his iciest manner.

The girl hesitated, and, when Steve said nothing, she went silently, angry pride in her straightened shoulders and head. The major stalked after her.

The wounded pasture rider had moved to the shady side of the bunkhouse. Steve led his horse back there. "Where's that Slim Polk I hired?"

"Out'n the pasture. He'll hire with Major Parker if his job with you has blowed up. I should've told him he'd be a damn' fool to go with the Parkers' herd."

"Why?"

"Takin' a herd over to the Pecos is bad enough any time. What'll it be with the Watlings trailing close behind? And their herd road-branded the same as the Parker herd? Hell, they're apt to kill off the Parkers an' take everything."

"You get ideas," said Steve slowly.

The wounded man shifted on the box and grinned thinly. "You better not get ideas. Look what happened to Carson. He had a little feud with Nando Watling. Tyin' a dead man up like that is Nando's mark."

"Sandy Parker and I left Nando Watling in Tornillo."

"There's a handful of short cuts outta Tornillo this way if you know the brush. Nando was probably laughin' at you while he was talkin', and figurin' how many of your cattle he'd have before morning. He was probably foggin' out of Tornillo one way while you two went out the other way." The wounded man spat. "I'd hate to be in your boots. You think them Watlings mean for you to get outta this alive? And maybe show up in Colorado to make trouble over your ranch? Hell, they don't work that way. Doc's sittin' purty now. He'll cut all the hay in sight while he's got the chance."

"I wouldn't be surprised," Steve agreed, turning his horse.

The first cattle were coming in sight when Steve stopped by the house and called to Stoneleigh.

"I'm riding on some business," Steve told the Englishman. "I'd like you to tell Slim Polk he's on my payroll until I tell him different. That goes for Holland and Smith, too."

"Glad to tell them."

Steve hesitated. "You might warn Major Parker to change his road brands. He might lose a good many head if the two herds cross the Pecos together."

"That's a fact," Stoneleigh agreed shrewdly. "Anything else I can do?"

"Nothing," Steve decided. "I'm on my own now, I guess."

It was past noon when Steve once more rode into Tornillo. Bud was on his mind. Bud hadn't come to Tornillo merely to get drunk. Bud had had some reason for not riding fast across the Río Grande into Mexico. Bud had not gone to Stoneleigh's ranch. Sober, Bud might come back into Tornillo for another drink.

But the fat bartender in the Horn Saloon merely asked: "Find Doc Watling?"

"Had a talk with him," Steve said, and he had a whiskey and walked out under the stares of several men who must have seen Bud drinking yesterday.

The whiskey was no help to the baffled resentment as Steve searched for Bud in the other saloons. He had no appetite but he stopped at the restaurant where he had eaten the day before. Among the horses at the hitch rack was a big, tar-black horse like the one Bud's friend had ridden along the dusty San Antonio street. Bud had called the man Brawley. When Steve walked in, Brawley was eating at the back end of the counter. He looked up as the door opened.

He picked up the rifle leaning against the counter, and came toward the door, speaking one word out of the beard stubble, for Steve's ear alone.

"Outside."

In the street Steve spoke first: "Where's Bud?"

"Don't know the feller. Dammit, Kid, you played the fool yesterday. Let's get outta here!"

Brawley did not know Bud's real name. He thought Steve was Bud. At the moment it was better to let him keep thinking so.

"Go where?" asked Steve.

"Back to camp. You know Bat Sanders is thick with these Watlings. When you didn't come back last night, I was sure they got you, an' come into town this mornin' to see. And what do I hear? A feller of your description was on a big drunk yesterday . . . an' a Texas Ranger has been in town lookin' around. Let's get back to camp."

"Suits me," said Steve, certain now where he would find Bud sooner or later.

Brawley made a comment as they left town. "Where'd you get that roan? I thought you left him with old Randy, in San Antone."

"Friend rode him to Tornillo."

Brawley nodded, and only Brawley could have headed into the brush, following only vague cow trails, and come in miles of riding to a grassy opening beside a sluggish thread of water.

A pack horse and a saddle horse were staked near smoldering campfire embers, and Brawley yanked out his rifle and suspiciously muttered: "There's your other horse, Kid. Who rode him here?"

Steve lifted his voice. "Come out, Bud, damn you!"

"Coming," answered Bud's voice cheerfully, and Bud walked out of the brush with his rifle.

Brawley dismounted, grumbling: "No tellin' about strangers. He could've shot. . . ." Brawley broke off, took a good look at Bud, and his head swiveled to Steve. "I ain't been drinkin'," Brawley gasped. "But, by God, there's two of you!"

Steve's pent-up anger burst out at Bud's chuckling. In front of the dazed Brawley, Steve damned Bud for what Bud had done the day before, telling Bud everything.

For once Bud was taken aback. He remembered little of what had happened in Tornillo. "I'm sorry, Steve."

Steve threw back savagely: "What good does that do me now? Why didn't you keep going into Mexico?"

Bud poured coffee from a pot on the smoldering embers and gulped the black liquid.

"I got worried about you," said Bud across the empty tin cup. "This Tornillo country ain't healthy for me, Steve. I thought I'd better stay close to you."

Bud put the cup on the ground and looked down at his hands.

"They've made me plenty of gun trouble. I never thought they'd do it with a pen." And frowning, Bud continued: "These Watlings are mean. Doc Watling's a snake. I hear another snake named Bat Sanders has thrown in with 'em. I made Bat walk yellow in San Antone, but he's laying for me. I was afraid you'd run onto him."

"I did, at one of the Watling corrals. Sanders is dead. He didn't have time to call your name to the Watlings. But if I read sign right, a bowlegged, broken-nosed rider with the Watlings knows the Nueces Kid. Doc Watling thinks I'm the Kid."

"I remember that Hoop Chase from Mexico. He's snaky, too," Bud grumbled. "Steve, I'm sure sorry. Want me to ride into Tornillo an' swear to the truth about them papers?"

"You think that'll do any good now?"

"Nope," decided Bud more ruefully. "Texas Rangers after either one of us they ketch first, an' the Watlings are set to hold what they've got. It's a purty deal, ain't it? I'll have to kill Doc Watling, take them papers away from him, and tear them up."

"Which is what he's expecting," snapped Steve. "You'll get shot by the men around him. Use your head."

"I still got a headache," grumbled Bud.

Steve said: "Major Parker's pulling out soon. If I read sign right on the Watlings, they mean to follow on his heels with the same road brand. If the major gets to Colorado alive, he'll be lucky. If he gets there with half his herd, it'll be a miracle. Patricia is going with them. God knows what may happen to her with the Watlings on the prowl."

Bud looked at Steve and then spoke softly: "Can't let her or her folks get hurt, can we? What can we do?"

"Ride into Tornillo with me. We won't need Brawley."

"You're the boss," stated Bud promptly.

On that ride the years rolled away, and they might once more have been boys on the Horse Cañon ranch. But when they rode into Tornillo, Bud's face became a mask, his eyes studying every man who moved on the street. And when Steve led the way into the Horn Saloon, Bud paused in the swinging doors and made certain who was in the long shadowy room.

"What'll it be?" inquired the pudgy bartender, and then he saw Bud breast the bar at Steve's side. His jaw dropped and his pink face took on Brawley's stunned look.

"Whiskey," ordered Steve briefly, and he ignored the barman's wildly questioning expression.

They drank. Steve paid, walked out with Bud before the bartender or any of the customers had courage to question the two armed strangers who looked exactly alike.

"What now?" Bud asked.

"Go back to camp and wait, if you're helping the major get north. That's all I want now."

"Have it your way," said Bud. "We'll be at camp."

Night was dropping when Steve reached Stoneleigh's ranch. The Watlings were gone with Steve's share of the trail drive. Ben Holland and Smith and Slim Polk were there, and riders were holding Major Parker's cattle and horses in close to the ranch house. Supplies were being loaded on a chuck wagon. Bed wagon axles were being greased. Hurried preparation for the trail was visible on every side.

Stoneleigh explained to Steve: "Major Parker decided to leave in the morning." And then he added: "He's not taking time to rebrand."

"It may not matter," said Steve, and he unsaddled the jaded roan and called together the three men he had hired. "Working for me may be dangerous," he told them. "You're free to hire with Major Parker."

Ben Holland stroked his black beard. "What kinda danger?"

"The Watlings."

Holland looked at his silent partner, and again some message passed between them. Holland drawled: "The Watlings have already cleaned us out. We ain't afeard of them. Sure you need us? You ain't got a herd to drive now."

"I can buy another. How about you, Slim?"

"Major Parker don't exactly need any of us," said Slim Polk. "I got an idea who killed that rancher I worked for. He was a nice feller, too. I feel mighty sorry for his wife. You hired me. I'm with you. I ain't a bad shot, either."

Steve grinned at the three. "Can't tell you what might happen. Slim, do you feel like riding to Tornillo tonight? You can come back in the morning."

"Sure. What'll I do?"

"Stay sober. You might drop word around Doc Watling's bar that you've hired out to me for a trail trip north, and you're waiting while I see about another herd. Don't speak about Major Parker leaving in the morning. But let drop I'm riding to your old boss' ranch tomorrow to see if his wife's got cattle for sale."

Holland and Smith looked at each other and studied Steve with sharpened interest. Slim scratched his ear, grinned uncertainly. "That all?"

"That's enough if you do it right. Be back early and tell me what's happening in town. Here's five dollars to eat on."

Carty Smith dug a gold piece out of his vest pocket and spoke briefly: "Here's ten. Bring me 'n' Ben both kinds of cartridges."

"Good idea," decided Steve at once. "Here's another ten for the same thing."

VI

Late into the night preparations for leaving continued. Sandy Parker stopped for an awkward word with Steve.

"I hate it to turn out this way, Steve. What are you going to do?"

"Can't say," Steve said truthfully. "I hope you folks get through all right."

"We'll do all right if the Watlings aren't at our heels. Don't know what we'll do when they settle on your Horse Cañon range."

"That's a long way off," said Steve, and it was all he could say.

Later Patricia came out. "Will I see you in Colorado, Steve?"

"Don't know."

Patricia looked up at him. "I've been talking to Father. Is Bud still alive?"

Steve waited before he said: "Yes."

"Oh, Steve! Bud did this, didn't he?"

"Doesn't matter. It's done."

"It does matter!" Patricia reached for his hand, held it tightly. "Always it's been Bud. Don't try to protect him now. Something can be done."

Steve held her hand, and he was positive. "I can't do as much with the Watlings as your father can do. And the best he can do is get away from them fast."

"Isn't there any law here?" demanded Patricia rebelliously.

"Not much that can help me."

"Because of Bud," she burst out resentfully. "Now I know who must have shot that man in San Antonio."

"Forget it," Steve advised almost gruffly. "What's done is done."

"It's always been 'forget it' when Bud does it," said Patricia in a stifled voice, and close to tears she left him.

The feel of Patricia's small hand stayed on in Steve. Her memory would always stay with him. But he had to let her go. A broke cowhand or a dead man was nothing to offer Patricia Parker.

He was still alone, outside, when Major Parker came to him.

94

"So it's Bud, Steve? And you'll do nothing about it?"

"Bud has his good points."

"So has the devil, they say," stated the major. "Come home with us."

"I've business here."

The major dropped a hand on Steve's shoulder. They stood in silence. "I'm sorry," the major said finally. "Good bye, Steve. And good luck."

That helped a little. . . .

In the dawn Steve watched the trail drive leave Stoneleigh's pasture and head for the endless horizons. Major Parker and Patricia drove off in a two-horse buggy. The last dust drifted away and they were gone.

Stoneleigh spoke to Steve as they turned back to the house. "I wish them luck. They'll need it."

"How many honest men live in these parts?" asked Steve reflectively.

"Quite a few. When the Watlings clear out, they'll have a chance. Doc Watling has held the bad ones together around Tornillo. Once Doc is gone, with Nando Watling and a few of the worst ones, honest people will show their hands."

Steve nodded, and a little later, when Slim Polk rode in, Steve met him at the corral.

"I sure got noticed when I let out I was workin' for you." Slim chuckled. "Doc Watling come over primed with questions. He wanted to know what you aimed to do with hired hands."

"Did you tell him I was going to see the rancher's widow today?"

"Uhn-huh. He acted like it was something to think over. The Watlings are aimin' to get a trail herd together fast and pull out. Nando an' some of the others was havin' a last big drunk. Nando's takin' the first herd. Doc aims to stay behind and follow

95

later with another herd. Nando was totin' a quart of whiskey an' singin' about the land of gold and honey waitin' for the Watlings up north." In the early sunlight Slim looked queerly at Steve. "Doc wanted to know if there was two of you around the ranch here. He says two of you was in the saloon yesterday." Slim reached for tobacco sack and papers. "Nando was mighty interested in when the Parkers aimed to leave. I told him four, five days."

"Good. Get some grub, Slim, and saddle your best horse."

The sun was not two hours high when Ben Holland, his silent partner, Slim Polk, and Steve rode away from the ranch. Smith broke his silence with a drawling remark.

"So we're lookin' at cattle today?"

"If nothing happens," Steve replied.

They rode to a trail striking off south through the brush, and Steve reined up.

"Here's your way to the place. You three tie your horses out of sight of the house and lay low until I get there and call for you. Keep your eyes open. Don't be seen by anyone."

Steve continued on some miles, and cut off into the brush toward a hogback ridge. In another hour he had cut the sluggish thread of water that he sought; he followed the water up until, without warning, he rode into the grassy opening where Bud and Brawley were camped.

The horses were staked, ready. Bud and Brawley had stepped out of sight when they heard his approach. They came back into the open, uncocking their rifles, and Bud said: "You'd been easy if we were looking for you."

"I'd have Injun-walked on you if you were looking for me," Steve retorted, dismounting. "All right, Bud, let's go. Brawley, too, if he's willing. You won't need that pack horse."

"Where we going?" asked Bud, turning for his saddle.

"Going to look at some cattle a widow woman's got for sale."

"You're buying all over again, huh? I'll buy for you, Steve. I got money."

"I won't want your money, Bud. The major started north this morning, trying to keep ahead of the Watlings. They'll be after him fast when they find out."

Bud shrugged, but, when they rode from the hidden camp, Bud hopefully suggested: "Maybe you aim to hustle off a few head on the side."

"I don't. This is an honest ride."

Brawley looked disappointed and grumbled: "I figured there'd be some kind of trouble, mebbe with the Watlings. But they got all they wanted from you, didn't they?"

"It'd seem that way," agreed Steve. "But a smart man like Doc Watling looks ahead. He's heard that Bud and I were in his bar yesterday and a man couldn't tell us apart. Doc's brainy enough to wonder what'll happen if he has to prove which one of us signed those papers. He might figure it was easiest to beat the law to an argument and settle everything by killing Bud and me before the Watlings pull out."

Bud slapped his leather leggings. "So that's why I rode into town for one drink an' rode out? Steve, a hundred dollars gold says Doc has heard where you aim to look at cattle today."

"A man who works for me did say something about it in Tornillo last night," Steve admitted gravely.

Bud's laughter was carefree as he drew his rifle from the saddle boot and made sure the magazine was full.

"Hear that, Brawley? He laid the bait where Doc'll hunt him up and start trouble. Steve don't mean for the Watlings to follow the Parkers. We're riding into a wolf fight that'll be something."

"You're guessing," corrected Steve mildly. "We're looking for cows. If there's any law-breaking, we won't start it."

"Sure," agreed Bud, grinning. "Steve, if you'd stay with me, we'd run the Brasada."

Steve told Bud and Brawley about the three men he had sent ahead to the widow's ranch.

"I don't know much about them," Steve confessed. "They're the best I could hire. Keep your eyes peeled for them. I'll ride ahead and talk with the widow. You two stay back out of sight unless I call for you."

Bud protested: "If the Watlings catch you riding out alone, they'll cut you down like a lame rabbit."

"They'd want both of us first," Steve declared positively. "One of us won't do them much good. I'll see if the widow has had any visitors. Chances are the Watlings aren't bothering with us today."

Bud grumbled, but he dropped back with Brawley and let Steve push on ahead.

Like Stoneleigh, the dead rancher had built of upright logs, mud-chinked, low, with corrals out back. When Steve surveyed it from the edge of the brush, pale wood smoke drifted from the cook house pipe. As Steve rode to the house, he noticed gay flowers the widow had planted, and he wondered how much happiness this lonely thorny brush ranch had repaid her work and hope.

He knocked, and smiled as the door opened. For an instant he remained smiling as he looked into Nando Watling's broad grin and the double-barreled shotgun that Nando was centering on his chest.

VII

Nando said jovially: "Step in. We been waitin' for you. Don't drop your hands or I'll blow you in chunks."

Doc Watling was there, and eight other men, including the bowlegged Hoop, and with them was the gaunt, unsmiling widow whose husband had probably been killed by these same men who had invaded her house. One man was watching her.

Still jovial, Nando closed the door. "We left Tornillo early. Get his guns, boys Hold his arms. He's tricky."

Doc Watling, still wearing neat broadcloth, had no particular expression as he stepped close, eyed Steve narrowly, and shook his head.

"Can't tell which is which," Doc said, baffled. "If half a dozen men hadn't seen them together, I wouldn't believe it was possible." And he asked Steve: "Where's the other one?"

"Other who?"

Doc Watling hit Steve's mouth with the heel of his hand, smashing lips against teeth so that they bled. Two men held Steve's arms.

"You listen to me," said Doc softly as ever. His eyes had an unblinking stare that lacked even anger.

Steve spat blood. His smile was gone. He felt hard and ugly as he answered Doc. "Keep talking, damn you."

Doc hit him again, grunting with effort. It mashed Steve's nose, drove his upper lip between the upper teeth. Groggily Steve saw the widow open her mouth as if she had cried out in silent pity.

"I don't know which one of you is which," said Doc, breathing harder. "But I mean to have the man who played cards with me and signed them papers, and the other one of you, also. Which is which?"

Steve shook blood from his face. "I'd have more sense than to play cards with a crook like you. I didn't sign any papers. If you think the Rangers can do anything about it, call 'em."

"We'll do better than the Rangers," Doc promised.

"Lemme work on him," said Nando in the same jovial manner. "He don't know how I got my mind set on that Colorado land." Nando's slap on Steve's shoulder might have been friendly. "We mean to have us a time up north there. First off, we'll put on plenty of fat meat outta that Parker herd." Nando winked at Steve. "I aim to put my private brand on one little heifer in that herd. I sized her up yesterday. She'll do to take along."

Steve spat blood in Nando's broad face. "You low-down dog! You man enough to take me on alone?"

Nando's big fist knocked Steve against the men who held him.

"Leggo him!" Nando yelled, smearing the red blood off his face with a sleeve and jerking a horn-handled knife from his belt. "I'll cut his damn' throat!"

Doc Watling's colorless voice dropped across the big man's rage like a cold, sharp blade. "Nando, you ain't killing no one until we get both of them together."

Nando stepped back, breathing hard, still holding the knife, and Steve knew he had never been closer to a slit throat. And still was. Bud and Brawley had watched him enter the house, evidently thinking he was safe. Ben Holland, Carty Smith, Slim Polk should be out there, too, waiting for word from him, unless they had blundered into the Watlings. Steve was wondering about them when he heard the gunshots.

He was instantly forgotten as Nando Watling jumped for the door, swearing. "That's Pete with the horses! Somebody snuck up on him!" Other men followed him, and, outside, Nando roared: "Here comes Pete, all shot up!"

Doc Watling spoke harshly to the two men holding Steve. "Keep him in here. Kill him if he makes any trouble."

Another rifle shot stabbed the sunlight outside, then another, and the Watling guns crashed back in answer. Doc Watling cursed and ran out.

The man holding Steve's arm wrestled him across to the side window, swearing, demanding: "Who's out there?"

Gunshots were coming from the brush. A bullet dropped the

staggering Pete. The Watlings were dodging across the open, shooting as they moved. And as the two men guarding Steve wrenched him away from the window so they could look out, a shaking voice ordered: "You two get away from him! Let him go!"

They had left the ranch widow unguarded. She had caught up the shotgun Nando had abandoned for a rifle. She was gaunt, pale with desperate purpose as she aimed the shotgun.

The man at Steve's left arm snarled: "She wants the same thing I give her old man an' she'll get it!"

Both shotgun barrels erupted in a blast that shook the low-ceilinged room. The full charges struck the man's chest. He was dying as he plunged against Steve.

Steve's right arm was released. The gun muzzle against his back went away, and then at Steve's side the gun spat.

Steve was already moving as the woman stumbled and dropped the shotgun. He wheeled, slapping his right hand on the big Colt still leveled at his side. His thumb jammed in under the gun hammer as it dropped for a second shot. The metal gouged into the thumb and Steve got his other hand on the gun and wheeled on around, tearing the gun away.

He took a blow on his face as his shoulder drove the Watling man back into the window, shattering the glass. The man made a wild grab and yelled with fear as the gun muzzle went hard into his middle. Steve thought of the woman this man had shot, and the husband she had already lost, and he pulled the trigger twice.

The woman was on her knees in the middle of the floor, both hands against her side where the bullet had entered. Graying hair straggled over her gaunt face and she was smiling.

"Ain't going to be so hard living, now that I shot the right man. . . ." She fainted.

A bullet tore through the mud chinking. Outside, a man

shouted: "Back in the house, boys, get your breath! They're all around us!"

Steve shoved fresh cartridges in the gun and shouldered out through the doorway. A bullet grooved Steve's shoulder, shocking, numbing—and he yelled with high satisfaction as his own lead drove the Watling man reeling against the house.

Bud's whoop of encouragement lifted from the brush. Steve grabbed the dead man's six-shooter and ran to the corner of the house, gun in each hand. Three of the Watlings were down. Two more were down inside the house. Five were left, still out in the open, where they met cross shooting from the brush front and from the back. The horses had stampeded out of sight. Big Nando and Doc were among the five men starting back to the house.

Nando saw Steve first and opened fire with his rifle. Doc Watling looked thin and pallid with rage as he halted, started hammering with his side gun. Steve cut loose with a yell as he saw the broken-nosed Hoop Chase drop his gun and fold. The hot excitement of it again was driving through blood and nerves. Big Nando rocked as a bullet found him, then he started a lurching run toward the nearest brush.

Doc Watling hesitated only an instant and followed, and the other two men broke and ran, too.

Steve took careful aim, resting the gun barrel on his arm, and dropped the rear man, and then both his guns were empty. He was feverishly reloading when the Watling men disappeared into the brush and he saw Bud run across the clearing.

"Stay back, Bud!" Steve shouted.

Bud waved his revolver and kept on. With one gun loaded, Steve started running, too. Bud vanished in the brush a hundred yards from where Nando and Doc had entered, and Steve ran directly after the two men.

Bud was somewhere off to his right, angling through the

brush to head off Nando and Doc. Off to the left, toward the back of the clearing, would be Ben Holland, Carty Smith, Slim Polk, who had evidently stampeded the Watling horses and opened up when the Watlings ran out of the house.

Nando and Doc were trying to lose themselves in the thorn thickets ahead. Steve heard brush crackle ahead and kept on. Then he burst through a tangle of thorny bushes into a high mass of giant prickly pear. And there big Nando Watling was waiting for him with a leveled rifle, behind the thick cactus. Nando's face and hands were thorn-slashed and bleeding. Not grinning now, his broad face was dark with fury as the rifle lined on Steve.

The rifle bullet drove just over Steve's scalp as he dived forward into the thorn-studded cactus. A second bullet smashed wet cactus pulp over his face and struck the ground behind him. They were not twenty feet apart, the thorny barrier rising between them. As the second bullet missed, Steve heaved up through the thorns and faced big Nando who was plunging through the cactus toward him.

The rifle must have been empty, for Nando hurled the weapon at Steve and snatched the short gun from his belt.

"Hold it!" Steve warned harshly, and only wasted words. Thorn-slashed, too, and bleeding, he drove lead through the cactus leaves into the renegade's rush. It did not stop even as Nando's handgun opened at him. Then the big man threshed down in the cactus.

In a crouch Steve heard his name shouted off to the left. He answered, moved back into the brush. Ben Holland and Slim Polk came to him, their fingers on gun triggers.

"Carty's dead," said Ben Holland. "Them men got here before we did. Carty heard the horses back in the brush and we eased over to look. That Pete Watling shot Carty without no warning, and then run for the house when we opened up on him. Soon as I seen who it was, I knowed trouble had busted. When all them Watlings come outta the house, we knew what to do." Ben Holland looked askance at Steve. "I thought I seen two of you at one time, back there in the open."

"My brother," Steve said. "He was hiding out across the clearing with a pardner. He's ahead of us somewhere. Doc Watling's ahead. Nando's down in a patch of prickly pear just over there. I think he's dead. Didn't want to look until I was sure. You'll have to be right over him before you see him."

"If he ain't dead, he will be," promised Ben Holland with flat determination. "An' a cactus patch is just the place for him."

Some distance to the north a gun went off, a flurry of shots followed, died out.

"Bud's found Doc Watling," Steve guessed. "Wait'll I make sure Nando won't be after us."

The prickly pear was quiet. Gun cocked, Steve edged in, sighted a motionless boot, and a moment later saw Nando Watling, face down and still. Steve left him there, led the other men at a run toward the sound of the shots.

He risked shouting to Bud and got no answer. More warily they spread out and advanced. Slim Polk, off to the right, suddenly called: "Here they are!"

Steve was with Bud a moment later, in a grassy opening in the thorn brush. Doc Watling was there, too, and the story could be read. Doc Watling had crossed the opening and, like Nando, had waited with cocked rifle for the man following him. Doc had shot Bud, and Bud had run at him, shooting. Doc Watling had turned to run. One of Bud's bullets had struck Doc's back and dropped him. Bud had collapsed a few feet away and clawed through the grass and dirt until he reached Doc.

Bud had lived to search Doc's pockets. Bud was lying there now beside Doc, quite peacefully, with the hint of a smile on his face and one blood-smeared hand holding papers he had taken from Doc's coat pocket. Steve knelt by Bud, looking down in Bud's face, and thinking back through the years. A lump crowded into his throat. Bud had laughed his way through all the wildness, and now Bud was smiling, as if to say it was all right.

Steve took the papers from Bud's hand, and looked at his name Bud had written on them for a joke, while drinking. Slowly Steve thumbed a match and watched the papers burn, and he put a hand on Bud's quiet shoulder for a moment.

Steve was calm as he stood up in the silence.

"One of them shot the widow woman," Steve told Ben Holland and Slim Polk. "We'll have to get back to her. You feel like riding, Ben?"

"Sure."

"Ride to Stoneleigh's and tell him to get the sheriff and a doctor, then spread the word around among honest people that they've got a real chance to take hold now."

Slim waited while Steve looked down at Bud for a last moment, then they started back to the ranch house.

Steve said: "Ride and catch the Parkers. Tell them what happened and that the Watlings won't trouble them now. Tell them I'll be following them up the trail to Horse Cañon."

$\star$ $\star$ $\star$ $\star$ $\star$

Renegades of the Rimrock

$\star$ $\star$ $\star$ $\star$ $\star$

T.T. Flynn didn't know where this short novel was to be sent by his agent when he finished it on July 30, 1942, so as with the two previous short novels he titled it simply "Western". Marguerite E. Harper, his agent, sent it to John Burr at Street and Smith, editor of *Western Story,* who wanted as many stories as he could get from her top writers of Western fiction: T.T. Flynn, Peter Dawson, and Luke Short. Burr bought it and the author was paid $283.50 after agent's commission. It was titled "Renegades of the Rimrock" when it appeared in *Western Story* (1/2/43).

I

They were only four, and they had been ten, far back there in the north, beyond the smoky-blue peaks that raked the brazen sky. The bony steers, cows, and staggering calves strung painfully across the harsh dry flats might tally four hundred. They had been seven times four hundred back there where the wind whispered in the high pines and white water leaped and sang down through rich green mountain graze.

They were headed south, and the hot south wind dusted caked faces with gritty welcome and the dry land reached into dry shimmering distance. An hour past noon, Tom made his decision and told it to big Basco Sweet, who pointed the drive into the wind.

"We've got to make sure whether that Indian told us right about Bone Lake. If the water ain't there. . . ."

Basco was a big man, short-legged, long in the waist, great shoulders humped and bowed with lumpy muscle. Riding bowed and tireless, hat pulled forward, red silk neckerchief screening nose and mouth from dust, he made a lumpy, sinister figure. But when one great hand pulled the red silk down in dusty folds around the thick neck, the face of Basco Sweet was that of a huge placid child who had no worry or thought beyond the day.

"Be bad if the Indian lied," said Basco slowly. He rubbed blond beard stubble sprouting raggedly on his jaw and plaintively wagged his head. "Too bad none of us ever come this

109

way before, Tom. We took a mighty long chance on what we'd find."

"We came the only way we could," said Tom. "Maybe we'll find a spot on that Bone Lake range . . . if we make it."

"Mighty dry, Tom."

"Four days more to the lake, the way we're going. Maybe enough water ahead to get us there," said Tom as he had been thinking through the morning. "Basco, I'm afraid if we don't find the range we need at Bone Lake, we're through."

"Them cows'll be through, even if we ain't."

"Still time by tomorrow night, or next morning to swing east toward the mountains," Tom said thoughtfully.

Basco spat. "Indian land east, Tom. Be near as bad as what we left. They'd throw us back this way on the dry land or rustle us clean for trespassing." Basco swept a long, powerful arm to the west, where the red and yellow strata of eroded hills and sheer-sided buttes made ragged breaks in the sweep of shimmering distance. "There're the front steps of hell . . . an' no water or graze in the back room, if we could haze a few head that far."

"Got to be Bone Lake if it'll hold us," Tom decided. "And we've got to know about the lake quick. Basco, I mean to ride on today and tonight. One extra horse ought to get me there sometime in the morning, and back again. You and Cass and Dink can keep 'em coming."

Basco spat again and nodded. "Easy, Tom. The critters is too wore out to worry about straying. Take that sorrel of mine. He'll stay with you an' bring you back."

Tom reined back to tell Cass and Dink and to get the sorrel. Cass was riding swing and watching the scanty remuda. Dirty jaw bandages framed Cass's thin, feverish face, a face that had not smiled for days. Cass shrugged when he heard Tom's plan. He could talk only in a mumble past the bandaged jaw.

"Ride it out if you like, Tom. Can't make things any worse than they are now."

"Things will get better, Cass."

Cass rode, sagging in the saddle, without energy or interest. All the youthful fire had left him, and he mumbled without interest: "You know dang' well nothing'll get better for us."

Tom Gannett looked at his younger brother. Cass missed the brief compassion in the look. Luke and Jed Gannett were dead. Ogle Svenson, the Gannetts' big cheerful Swede partner, was dead. Lou Grady, Wahoo Jim, Long Sam Summers were dead. The past, when Cass had been light-hearted and merry, was gone. The fever of grief and fury, of pain, defeat, flight had burned Cass Gannett thin and hopeless.

Tom tried to strike the spark that must still be there. Roughly, out of the hard, stubborn certainty that had never left him, he said: "It'll get better! It has to. We've still got cattle. We've got a chance. What more do we want? We got licked and run out. It won't happen again. Good men don't stay down."

Cass's face between the dirty bandages had the look of wasting fever that had burned and gutted the spirit inside. Cass's reply was gutted, flat, dead, final with proof for which Cass had abandoned argument. "Jed and Luke, Svenson and the others were good men. They stayed down . . . under the dirt I helped pile on them."

"I know," Tom said, gentle now.

Cass was nineteen. Those older brothers, Jed and Luke, strong, confident, sure that the Gannetts were on top and would stay on top, had been part of the confident horizons bounding Cass's life. In his sleep Cass still mumbled the grief and shock of their passing.

"Jed and Luke went out fighting," Tom said. "They'd still be ready to fight if they were here, kid."

"They aren't here."

Tom drew a breath. "They weren't licked, Cass. They . . . they. . . ."

"They were just killed," Cass supplied leadenly. He looked at Tom, licked dry, cracked lips. "I ain't licked. I'm just tired of it. Tired of fighting. Tired of thinkin' about Jed and Luke, Svenson and the others."

He pushed the stained and dusty black hat back on the jaw bandages that were tied up in his black hair. He rubbed his grimy forehead. For an instant Cass looked wistful, hurt, his face much younger than nineteen between the red-spotted face bandages.

"Seems like they come back in my head at night, Tom. Seems like they're alive an' we're the dead ones, blind-stubborn to keep pushing on when we ought to rest an' forget."

"It's the fever working in your head," Tom said quietly.

"It ain't in my head. It's down deep inside . . . I'm sorry, Tom."

"It'll come out all right," Tom promised, and he rode on back to Dink Hawkins, knowing the words he left with Cass were only words. Not hope. Not a promise against the memories that roiled in Cass's head at night and burned through the dry, blazing days.

Dink Hawkins was riding the dusty drag in the mule-drawn chuck wagon. Dink was a top hand, small, shrewd-faced as he hunched cheerfully on the wagon seat, with a bandaged foot resting on a folded blanket and his saddled horse siding the wagon on a lead rope.

"If my maw knowed I'd grow up to ride a trail drag behind two ornery mouse mules, she'd've throwed me in a cactus patch an' dusted her hands in good riddance," Dink greeted, and his black eyes snapped humor.

"I had a feeling you'd turn out a muleskinner," retorted Tom, grinning, and then he sobered. "I'm riding on to have a look at this Bone Lake range."

Dink nodded. "Only thing to do. We'll make out. When you get to the lake, Tom, if there's water, walk out an' waller in it. Take a big mouthful and spit it out, an' say that's fer Dink, who's spittin' dust, cussin' mules, an' a-comin' after you."

"I'll do it," Tom promised, grinning again. He walked the horse beside the lumbering wagon. "Brighten Cass up a little, if you can. He's off his feed."

Dink nodded. "Do what I can, Tom. I been noticin'."

Hours later, Tom could still see them when he turned in the saddle and looked back. For a time they had been diminishing miniatures of riders, cattle, and tarp-topped wagon. Finally only a pale streak of dust against the low blue sky gave sign that men and beasts were plodding painfully into the south. Then the sun was setting, blood-red, huge, malevolently hot upon that far western horizon.

Basco Sweet's sorrel horse loped easily on the lead rope. The gray horse Tom rode was still strong under the dust-caked sweat. Two hours before dark they paused at scummy water in a drying tank. When the sun was gone, clear stars bloomed out, the wind turned cool and brought the far yelp and wailing of coyotes roving the vast and lonely world. For a little the past came back to Tom Gannett and rode the dry miles with him.

Jed and Luke, Ogle Svenson and the others. Each one tried, true, tested. Each one sure of himself, sure of the others. They had had no doubts. Tonight the memories closed in, mile after mile, and brought no doubts and left no doubts. Luke Gannett had died, shot through the chest. Bloody froth had bubbled on Luke's lips as he'd said: "Wish I could stay to see you come out of it, Tom."

On another day, Jed had been shot through the face, dropping instantly. But Jed's lips had been smiling a little when they found him, as if Jed, in death, had not been worried about what might follow. Ogle Svenson had died in pain—shoulder, neck, belly ripped and torn by blasting lead. But Ogle had died with eyes clear, mind working, fading voice confident.

"Yust give 'em hell, Tom."

Three men had died when Wahoo Jim went down, with gun empty and smoking in the open street of Rimrock town. More would have died if Wahoo Jim could have lived to reload.

They were gone. They were dead. Good men who quit because they died, and only then. Tonight they rode with Tom Gannett, and they were strong and sure.

Dawn blotted the fading stars, left the moon pale and lonely to meet the new strong sun. Tom was riding the sorrel now, leading the jaded gray horse, and, as light pushed back the night, he scanned intently this new country into which he had ridden.

The land was rolling now, more broken, a little higher. Bunch grass was thicker, stunted juniper and gnarled piñon pines were scattered here and there and getting thicker ahead. Tom rode down into the great raw gash of an arroyo that headed somewhere in the east, toward the mountains. Here and there in the damp bed were skim-deep pools of upward seep from the underground flow.

Stretched flat, Tom drank by the leached-dry horses, and, when he rode on, the country still lifted a little with each rolling swell and the sparse dry life became stronger in the soil. The sorrel horse snorted, threw up its head. Tom caught the smell of death and, looking upwind, saw a dead horse some hundred yards away, beside low junipers. The dead horse was saddled.

Tom stopped, peering from tired, bloodshot eyes into the new blaze of sunlight. He swallowed brackish water from the battered saddle canteen, rolled a cigarette, and lighted it before riding to the horse.

Coyotes had been feasting. The dry dirt had taken prints of

high-heeled boots striking hard as the rider went out of the falling saddle and ran with the rifle from the empty saddle boot. Tom guided the sorrel along the footprints, certain of what he would find.

Any horse might stumble in full run, drop, stay there. But the rider would not light running with his rifle, and keep running unless danger was close and great. The saddle left there on the dead horse told what had happened.

Tom picked the spot before he reached it. A higher knob of ground held tilted slabs of eroded sandstone rock. In danger, Tom, too, would have run to the rocks to fight. The stranger had made his run, reached the rocks, fought, and died.

He was still there and the coyotes had been there. The sandstone slabs were pocked, gashed by flying lead. The early sun glinted on empty brass shells beside the body. Rifle, revolver, and gun belt were gone. The man had been beardless, blond-haired. He had fought and died and been left here.

"Too bad, stranger," Tom said absently, aloud. "Couldn't have been a sheriff's posse. They wouldn't have left you and your saddle like this. Bet you got one of them at least."

Tom lined the bullet marks and walked stiffly from the long ride downslope until he found hoof marks and sign where men had dodged and bellied to the ground behind scant cover that was handy. Five, six, seven men, he judged. The empty shells they had left were treble the scattered empties around the dead man. There was blood upon a rock, blood dark-caked in the ground where one man at least had been hard hit. That was all. It had happened three or four days ago. A man might puzzle out their tracks and trail them down, if minded to. Tom rode on.

The empty country was not the same. Death had passed and its threat remained. Tom Gannett's bloodshot eyes were sharper, more alert, and weariness faded before tightened nerves, wary senses. Basco Sweet, Dink, Cass were plodding after him with the gaunt, footsore cattle that must have free water, free range quickly. It had to be the Bone Lake range, if the lake was there as they had heard.

By midmorning the rolling slopes were dropping, flattening out. The grass was still better. When Tom saw wild horses break and run in the distance, he grinned, reined up to watch the long-tailed, long-maned stallion take his mares to safety. Horse tracks had been growing plentiful. Where wild horses ran and grazed there would be water.

Miles on, a low ridge broke away in a last slope. On the great plain beyond, some miles away, the lake lay, blue, placid as the Indian had said. Not big. Not deep. The gently sloping land drained water to Bone Lake from all four directions.

White, dry bones were there, where generations of cattle and horses, and perhaps deer, had mired, died, been killed beside the water. Not half a mile away two riders were heading up the slope.

They saw Tom and stopped, and he checked the sorrel and the gray horse that would have broken into a run toward the blue water beyond the strangers. The men were wary of him. They had been riding with rifles out and ready. They studied him and scanned the long low ridge over which he had ridden. They waited—and, after waiting a minute, Tom rode slowly toward them.

II

He left the rifle in the saddle scabbard. But he went forward thinking of the dead man at the sandstone slabs. Tom Gannett could die the same way if the cards fell right.

They were young men, hats pulled low against the sun glare. Each one wore two side guns and held a rifle. Their horses were middling, the saddles old, boots, overall pants, blue shirts hard-worn. Both of them had a hard-worked look. That much Tom saw with narrowed, focused eyes. Their faces were impassive, watching him. Tom weighed their faces and relaxed. He was twenty-six, older inside, and hard and rough inside, too. These two were men like Cass, about twenty, watchful and ready. But like Cass they lacked the hardness that would make them dangerous to a peaceful stranger.

"Howdy," Tom hailed them first.

He got back—"Howdy."—and he grinned easily at them and reined up with tobacco sack and papers in hand. He was rolling a cigarette, lounging easily in the saddle as he jerked his chin, Indian fashion, toward the lake.

"Nice water out there. Pays a man back for a lot of dry riding."

He saw that one man was taller than the other, looking a little the older, with black hair, a smooth, good-looking face that was thin and somehow feverish-looking from inner fires. Like Cass. This one said laconically: "How much dry riding you been doing?"

Tom grinned again and lighted the cigarette easily before he answered. "From up north beyond high Lonesome Peaks. Never been down this way before."

They were not convinced. The other one, slightly younger, with reddish hair, scant reddish mustache, a look of wariness on his chunky face, said: "Where's your outfit? How come you're riding light with two horses, no blankets or anything to grub with, all the way from the High Lonesomes? What brands you got on them horses?" He walked his horse in a quarter circle, the better to see the brands.

"That's a lot of questions for a stranger," Tom said, still easy, still smiling. He had seen the dead man. These two had reasons for their talk. He got answer bluntly from the same one.

"No offense meant . . . and it ain't all the questions you'll get from us. Like it or don't like it. Jack, I make it Rafter X on the sorrel and Four BRS on the gray. You heard of them brands?"

"New ones to me, Shorty."

"Four BRS is mine," said Tom calmly. "Up north it's the Four Brothers brand. Been on a lot of hides in its day. It'll be on a lot more. Fire your questions and I'll fire mine. I've been riding all night and I mean to wallow in that lake water pretty quick now."

"Where's your outfit?" Shorty asked again.

"Coming."

"When?"

"Day or so back. I rode on ahead to scout the lake. Wasn't sure there'd be water here. I'm turning back soon as I soak up some of that lake."

"What kind of outfit you got?"

"That," said Tom amiably, "ain't any of your business. This is free range, isn't it?"

The two exchanged glances.

Shorty nodded. "It's on the books that way. Free range. Free water and grass."

Jack, the taller, black-haired, slightly older man, asked with a trace of irony: "Your outfit wouldn't have cattle in it, by any chance, heading for this free range?" His irony deepened. "All this free water and grass?"

"Might," Tom granted, and he regarded them curiously. "Wouldn't matter to you two, would it? No objections?"

"None," said Jack with the same irony. "Move right in. Make yourself to home. Free water, free grass, free air. She's yours . . . if it's us you're asking."

"Well, well," Tom mused, eying them. "That's friendly. Free water and free grass and you're making me a present of it. Wouldn't have anything to do with the fact that nobody's cattle seem to be using the water or the grass right now, would it?"

"A stranger wouldn't know about that," Shorty said, "and a man who wasn't a stranger wouldn't bother asking. Huh, Jack?"

Tom broke in, studying them: "This wouldn't have anything to do with the dead horse and dead man I found a few miles back there this morning, would it?"

Both were instantly alert. Jack leaned forward. "What'd the dead man look like?" he demanded sharply.

"Not much now. It happened several days ago. Coyotes have messed things up. His horse went down and he must have shot it out from a pile of rocks. They left him there. Left his saddle on the horse. I guess they took his guns and belt. He had blond hair and a shaved face. Coyotes didn't leave the brand on the horse. Stirrups had short taps and a manila rope was still tied on the saddle. All that make any sense to you?"

Jack's searching look was taut and burning. Shorty drew an audible breath, looked at Jack, shook his head.

"Couldn't be anyone but Soapy. They got him, Jack. I was afraid they had, when he didn't come back next day."

"Yes," Jack said without shifting his look from Tom. "What I'm asking is whether this man knows more about it. He's got all the answers down too pat. He rides south from the High Lonesome country . . . and out of a thousand ways he could have come riding, he goes straight to Soapy and finds out all he'd know if he'd been there when Soapy was shot."

"Easy," Tom warned, not smiling now. "Questions are one thing. Talk like that is another. When I find a dead man, I want to know how he was killed. The sign is all there. He put up a fight. Hit one of them at least. I don't know who Soapy is and I don't give a hoot. Maybe he had it coming to him. I don't know who you two are or what's on your minds. But if I was siding against the dead one, you make it plain I'd be against you. That right?"

"That's right," agreed Shorty.

"If I was against you," Tom said curtly, "I wouldn't be fool enough to ride over the hill and down to meet those two rifles you toted ready. I'd have stayed back there out of sight until you rode a little closer. There wouldn't have been any talk. I'd have made coyote meat out of you and let you lay like this Soapy was left. Think it over . . . and then, if you like, I'll guide you back after I get my face in that lake water. Or you can backtrack on me from here and find him."

"I kind of like the way he talks," Shorty told his companion.

"Can't trust anyone," muttered Jack. His head came up, and he short-reined his horse as the thin report of a rifle blended with the soggy slap smack of lead on flesh.

The gray horse gave a startled lunge, whistle of fright, and tore the lead rope from Tom's hand. The animal's front legs were buckling in the first steps.

Tom reined the sorrel around, swearing with surprise as he caught rifle from saddle boot. Too late he thought how this would look to these suspicious strangers. The side of his eye marked Jack's rifle muzzle swerving to cover him. Jack's sudden accusation was savage.

"He was holding us here while the others got set to trap us!"

"Wait, you fool!" Tom blurted.

Then he knew he'd never stop it. He drove spurs cruelly deep into the sorrel, reined the animal around, and threw himself hard over in the saddle.

At that he almost died when the rifle crashed a killing shot. The bullet grooved the smooth-oiled leather of Tom's gun holster. His shout sounded futile against the report echoing in his ears.

"They got my horse! I don't know who it is!"

The outraged sorrel squealed, bucked. The gray horse was down, kicking on the ground. Other guns were speaking from the ridge crest.

A hammer blow struck the rifle Tom gripped. The shock numbed his hand, drove up to his shoulder. When he looked down, the gun stock was shattered, gun slipping from his nerveless hand. He heard Shorty's warning shout.

"Hold it, Jack! They shot him!" Then Shorty blurted: "They're comin'! Get goin' or they'll have us out here in the open!"

Tom fought the bucking sorrel with one hand and looked back up the slope. Horsemen were riding hard into view toward them. They were cut off from the ridge and the rolling country to the north.

"We can reach the *malpaís!*" Shorty yelled, and led the way, slashing with the rein ends.

Tom followed. He'd been caught with these strangers. He'd get their trouble if cornered out here in the open with them.

When he looked back, Jack was close behind. The pursuit was not gaining. Over a shoulder, Tom counted seven riders in the strung-out pursuit. Sporadic shots they fired went wild. For that matter the first shots from cover had been a long chance at dropping a horse or two before the men rode into view.

Chances had lessened that the three of them could bear right over the ridge into uneven range and some hope of cover. Ahead the slightly rising open plain looked bleak, but Shorty seemed to know where he was going, what he was doing.

Numbness passed from Tom's arm and hand, but his rifle was gone and the jaded sorrel was unfit for a run like this. If the horse gave out, went down, putting Tom afoot without a rifle, he'd have the chance of a bushed rabbit cowering in the open. Jack still rode behind him. By now it was plain that Jack still did not trust this stranger, wanted him in sight. Tom smiled thinly at the double danger. It was like him that the smile topped growing resentment, anger at riding peacefully into a tight like this. The dead man and words that had been said back there outlined trouble that only fanned the anger.

The sorrel horse was big Basco Sweet's pride, and now the sorrel proved itself. Full out, the sorrel raced up the long slope of plain when another horse would have staggered and dropped. Shorty, on a short-coupled, powerful roan, was still ahead when they galloped over the last quarter mile of rising ground.

Shorty had yelled—*"Malpais!"*—when he started the run. Suddenly there ahead to the west was *malpais*. It was as if the great bowl of grassy plain and the water of Bone Lake had taken all the good, and the bad had been hurled aside here to the west in harsh, uninviting badlands.

A lava belt had come from south to north, following the lower contours. Off in the southwest were several low dark cones that must have spawned the lava. The sullen black lava flows had pushed north in thick fluid destruction, spreading out in low spots, pouring on in narrower lava dykes that crossed and criss-crossed the uneven land, later flows on top of older flows. The weather of ten thousand years had eroded uncapped rock and soil, leaving lava-topped ridges, cut by tortuous arroyos and small cañons as the land fell away to the west. And all this had been hidden when a man rode in from the north toward Bone Lake.

Looking back, Shorty grinned, lifted an arm in salute, and bore left downslope toward a sullen black lava dyke that abruptly ended, high and narrow, like a ship's prow. They galloped past the prow, where lava chunks big as a house room were piled in frozen confusion on the steep slope.

Shorty swung to the right along the base of the dyke. A quarter of a mile over to the left another lower dyke formed a narrowing cañon that writhed out of sight less than a mile ahead. Tom would have stopped at the prow of the big dyke, where the great lava rocks gave cover, and shot it out. But Shorty seemed to know what he was doing. His partner came riding hard behind. The sorrel still seemed able to run. Tom went with them, helpless without a rifle.

The pursuit had been closing in a little. Now they were shooting without pause. The lava dykes held in the gunshot echoes, the whip-like scream of passing lead, some of it close now, dangerous.

Jack ranged up alongside, quirting his long-legged black horse. His thin burning face was set.

"Ride it out!" Jack yelled at Tom.

"Pull on! My horse is about done!" Tom marked the angry suspicion his words drew. Jack still did not trust him at their backs. Jack scowled at the sorrel and was swearing to himself as he dropped back again.

Tom's hard grin promised a settlement if they got out of this. He wanted less of them than they wanted of him.

If they got out of it. The sorrel was weakening. There was a limit to blood, flesh, bones, and fighting heart. The horse was at his limit and still running. When he dropped, he would be dying. It fanned Tom's helpless anger. A man who killed his game horse might be right, but the killing was a crime. This one especially, for there had been no reason for Tom Gannett to be caught in this trouble.

Still the pursuit was gaining. Ahead, the cañon narrowed, bearing sharply to the left out of sight. Jack galloped up abreast again. Shirt sleeve on his left arm was blotched with new blood and his wrist and hand were red-streaked as he made a stiff gesture to ride faster.

Tom pointed to the lathered sorrel, shook his head. Two hundred yards or less would put them around the sharp turn. But that promised small help. The lava dykes were growing sheer, hemming them in. They'd have to keep riding. Back over his shoulder Tom studied the pursuit.

Two men were riding the lead, the others scattered back.

They were still shooting. Tom ducked involuntarily away from the keening lash of a bullet past his ear. He was grinning thinly at himself for dodging, and still looking back, when the long-legged black horse went down, catapulting Jack from the saddle.

III

Without thinking, Tom checked the sorrel and reined back. Jack had rolled and slid, and now sprawled, motionless. The black horse was trying to get up. One front leg was broken and it was wounded.

"All right, Gannett, you dog-goned fool!" Tom said savagely, and he spurred the lathered sorrel back.

Jack's rifle had fallen off to one side of the wounded horse. Tom made a flying drop from the saddle, wasted a span of seconds to shoot the black horse. Then he scooped the rifle off the ground, dived back to the dead horse, making certain the rifle muzzle was not dirt clogged. Panting, on one knee behind the dead horse, he made his stand, sighting on the lead rider racing toward him.

The first shot missed. Swearing, Tom levered in another cartridge, then stared as the horse under the second rider went down. He had not shot at that horse. He looked back. Shorty had wheeled where the cañon turned and was galloping back toward him. Shorty's rifle was still in the saddle leather. Shorty had not dropped the horse, either.

Tom lined the front sight on his first target, a big bearded man with hat brim turned up in front. The man was firing a rifle skillfully at full gallop. Tom squeezed the trigger, grunting as the bearded man jerked upright, swayed over, grabbed at the saddle horn, and desperately sawed the reins to turn his horse back.

The other man was afoot, horse down. He suddenly staggered and went down to a knee. He came up without his rifle and broke into a lurching run back up the cañon. Tom had not fired the bullet that had hit him. When Tom looked back, Shorty was returning at full gallop and just drawing his rifle from the scabbard.

Already heart had gone out of the pursuit. The other riders were scattering out, pulling up. One of them brought his plunging horse to a stop and helped the limping wounded man up behind him. The man Tom had wounded spurred on past them, shouting something as he passed, and kept going. Another horse began to jump and buck as if it had been hit.

This time Tom was certain a rifle had blasted from somewhere behind him, beyond Shorty, where the lava rocks rose steeply at the cañon turn. He shot twice, winged one man. Shorty galloped up and launched from the saddle with a whoop.

"Got 'em on the run! Burn 'em down!"

Shorty fired, fired again, fired a third time. The retreating riders were uncertain targets. Tom lowered his empty rifle and stood up.

Shorty gave it up, too, and turned a broad grin on him. Shorty's scant reddish mustache bristled with satisfaction. "They'll learn to stay out o' this *malpaís!* That's twice we've curried 'em close!"

Behind them an unmistakable gunshot raised a distant spurt of dust beyond the last retreating rider. Shorty turned, snatched off his hat, waved it jubilantly.

"Had a trap here?" Tom questioned.

"Nope. Kind o' hoped we'd find a little help, though." Shorty grinned. His face clouded as he turned to his partner. "How's Jack?"

"Hit in the arm. Don't know what happened after he landed on the ground."

Tom had the queer feeling that time had turned back to the High Lonesome country. Once more it was ride and fight. He

125

shrugged the feeling aside and went to Shorty's partner.

The arm wound was not bad. The headlong plunge from the rolling horse had knocked Jack cold. Brackish water remained in the battered canteen. Tom sloshed some of it on Jack's face. They worked on him a few moments. Jack stirred, sat up, shaking his head groggily.

"You cut it close," said Shorty cheerfully. "I was hightailin' on ahead and didn't see you. The stranger here rode back and held 'em off with your rifle."

Jack put out a hand for a pull to his feet. He wagged his head again to clear it, and stared at Tom, narrow-eyed. He looked at his dead horse and back at Tom. A slow smile lighted his face. "I had you wrong. Thanks."

"Forget it. They must have been following my tracks and caught us all together."

Jack took a stiff-legged step and grimaced with pain. "Things are kind of unhealthy around here."

"Kind of, it seems," Tom agreed. "Who's making it unhealthy?"

"Couple of old curly wolves by the name of Samshu Peyton and Gregorio Garcia."

"They ain't even curly," corrected Shorty cheerfully. "They're scabby, flea-bitten, and full of worms. 'Specially Peyton. An' when you take old Samshu's son, Buck Peyton. . . ." Shorty shook his head. "Words fail me," he said.

"We were talking about Bone Lake water and free grass," Tom suggested.

"We were talking," agreed Jack. He jerked a thumb up the cañon. "They were doing something about it. Mister, your business is your business. But if you've got cattle headed for free water and free grass in these parts, they'll graze and drink quicker in that High Lonesome country where you started."

"Might be your idea," Tom said dryly. He rubbed his stubble-covered jaw. His eyes were tired. The long night ride lay leaden in bone and muscle. But the rough, hard certainty of the Four Brothers was in him, fanned strong by the wild ride and the fight. "There's other ideas," he said, still dryly.

"He still don't understand," Shorty decided. "Mister. . . ."

"I'm Tom Gannett."

"I'm Shorty Case. This is Jack Hyde. You got a welcome back there that won't get any better. You seen bones at Bone Lake. Old Samshu Peyton and Garcia have got their own private bone yard for a hundred miles through here."

"All free range?"

Jack Hyde ripped the bloody shirt sleeve from his left arm and answered Tom. "Free range for dead men. You just had your sample."

Shorty grinned. "Take a look at us. We're samples, too. This country is the tag end of nowhere. Peyton and Garcia have run things so long they figure it's law and right. They got water rights and land of their own. But they keep the free grass an' water handy for their own use when they need it. Anybody else gets a different idea, gets treated rough."

"What's the law say about it?"

Shorty scratched his head. "Seems to me I've heard that word before. Jack, you know anything about it?"

"Tie this piece of sleeve around my arm," Jack Hyde ordered. Inner fire lighted his thin face once more. "There ain't any law in these parts," he said bitterly to Tom. "Most folks don't even like to hear the word. Too many of them came in on the jump from the law. Top dog is who can stay on top, and it suits 'most everyone."

"Except you and me," asserted Shorty cheerfully.

"There's a law if you ride a couple of days south to Caliente to find it," Jack explained. "At Sabrino, over at the foot of the mountains, there's a one-eyed deputy who locks up a drunk

Indian now and then."

"Sabrino jail is a tree post planted in the street," Shorty said, grinning. "Gig Haines, that one-eyed deputy, handcuffs his prisoners to the post till he gets around to collecting fines." Shorty spat, winked at Tom. "That's drunk Indian law. It ain't the law you'll get, drifting in for free grass and water."

Tom had rolled a cigarette. He nodded up the lava cañon as he smoked. "Whose men were they?"

"Samshu Peyton's men. They mostly ride north of Bone Lake. Old Gregorio Garcia hires Mex hands an' they stay south of the lake. And Garcia's Mex hands are tough, too."

Tom smoked a moment, and nodded. "Top dog is the one that stays on top? Suits me, if that's the way it is."

Jack Hyde inspected the crude arm bandage and reached down for the remains of his shirt. His comment held cynical bitterness.

"He still don't understand. But we tried, anyway."

"Here comes Miss Jeanie," said Shorty suddenly. "What do you know? I thought it was Pop Skivvy or Slim helpin' us from the top of the lava. Jack, you got to tell her about Soapy. I ain't got the nerve. She won't like it."

Tom would have thought the rider coming at a hard gallop from the turn of the cañon was a man. Forewarned, he saw it was a woman in man's overall pants, man's shirt and hat. A rifle was in her saddle scabbard, a man's gun belt with holstered gun around her waist. She should have been a powerful woman, strong-faced, rough, to match the outfit. Instead, she was a girl, slender, pretty. Tom thought of a willow wand, supple, strong, whipping angrily in the wind, as this girl swayed on her blowing horse, her cheeks flushed, eyes snapping, voice unsteady.

"Jack, I thought you were dead this time."

"I'm not."

"You're wounded."

"Just a scratch. Forget it."

"You know I won't. I can't. I thought you two would ride out and find trouble today. I was up on the lava, watching for you, when I heard the shooting. I saw what happened. They almost killed you this time. It was too far for me to help much with my gun." Her cheeks were an angry red as she spoke hotly to Shorty. "You're as much to blame as Jack."

Shorty looked meek, chastened. "I git the blame for everything. We were just lookin' around."

"Looking for trouble! I wish Jack had never hired you, Shorty Case. You back him up and egg him on."

"Yes, ma'am," agreed Shorty meekly. "I'm low-down and no-account. It's all my fault."

"Jeanie, stop hazing Shorty," Jack said flatly. He was a year or so the older. He acted older, with authority. "I meant to ride over toward Sabrino to look for Soapy. Wait'll I get my saddle off and we'll go back with you."

"We never did git to Sabrino to find out about Soapy," said Shorty quickly. "We met Tom Gannett here, riding in from the north to get his fill of water at the lake. We were passin' the time of day when that bunch of Peyton hardcases bobbed some shots from the ridge for luck and come jumpin' at us. Wasn't anything to do but git back here in the lava. We didn't want trouble. . . ."

"You never want trouble, do you?" Jeanie flared angrily.

"No, ma'am," said Shorty, red-faced even to his ears.

"Then why don't you get out of here? Jack might leave, too, then."

"Yes, ma'am," said Shorty vaguely. "That's what we were tellin' Gannett. This ain't a healthy country to stay in. He'll tell you that's what we said. I better help Jack git his saddle off." He suddenly recalled Tom. "Gannett, this here is Miss Jeanie Hyde, Jack's sister."

Tom remembered to snatch off his hat. He had been standing bemused, watching Jeanie Hyde's anger, thinking of her cool, accurate shooting from the high lava dyke.

"Howdy, ma'am," he said, and for no reason his face felt red, like Shorty's face.

"I saw you turn back for Jack," Jeanie told him. "You saved his life. They would have killed him."

"Not that bad, I guess, ma'am. Anyway, he'd have turned back for me."

Remembering the fresh bullet gash in his gun holster, Tom had to suppress a slight smile as he wondered what Jeanie Hyde would say if she knew how close her brother had come to killing him. He guessed why they had not told her about the dead man he had found. Her anger as she rode up was the mark of her fear, deep inside, for her brother. The dead Soapy would increase that fear.

Tom had questions about them all. He put the questions aside, content for the moment to look up at Jeanie Hyde, dressed like a man, armed like a man, supple, sure of herself in the saddle. Some part of him back through the months and years had been empty, hollow, unfilled. Jeanie Hyde, in her man's pants and hat and gun belt, was reminding him of that emptiness of which he seldom thought.

Shorty had to take his rope, dallied to saddle horn, and drag the dead black horse away from the saddle.

"I'll tote it," Shorty said, getting down. "Jack, you better climb up behind Miss Jeanie. Her horse ain't been run out."

Jack nodded and spoke to Tom. "We've got a camp a couple of hours away. Water, grub, and a chance to sleep. Like to have you come with us."

Tom cocked an inquiring eye at Jeanie Hyde.

"Please," she said. "It's only a camp. I do the cooking, but you can eat it."

"I wanted to be sure about the grub," Tom said gravely. She caught the glint of humor in his eyes, and smiled. Tom was smiling as he went to the sorrel.

IV

A stranger could easily have gotten lost wandering in that lava *malpais*. Two good gunmen could stop a dozen following them. The *malpais* formed endless traps of frozen rock, writhing, spreading, piled helter-skelter, gutted, gashed, eroded. The four of them rode between lava dykes where hands could touch rock on either side, through grassy sweeps hemmed in by lava. The horses picked their careful way over glassy-smooth sheets of lava and followed the white sandy beds of tortuous arroyos.

Tom noted cattle and horse tracks. The sense of black, brooding lava desolation began to leave him. Grass, bushes, cactus, stunted trees grew on and among the old lava flows.

"Any water back in here?" he asked Shorty.

"Little . . . if you know where."

"Free water?"

"An' grass. What there is of it. Nobody claims it." Shorty looked around and grinned. "It'd be a job to hold it. Old Samshu Peyton an' Gregorio Garcia never got that hoggish. They know it'd be a mouthful that'd gag them."

Tom nodded agreement. Strange riders could fade in and out through the lava, could fight and run, and turn and fight and vanish. A cow outfit would find it costly to face all that while their cattle scattered on the scanty graze. He let questions pile unspoken in his mind, content for the moment to be guided deeper into the lava, while he watched Jeanie Hyde riding straight and easily on her big horse.

They came to another knife-like break through a high lava dyke. A voice hailed them from the top.

"You're bringing 'em back quick, Miss Jeanie. Where's Jack's hoss?"

Jeanie looked above, toward the invisible speaker. "Where you would expect, Pop! They got into a shooting. I don't think anyone will be following us."

They were in the cut, stirrups all but scraping the sides when the voice again came hollowly down from the strip of blue sky above. "How many'd you kill, Jack?"

"Didn't see the end of it, Pop. None, I guess. Wounded a couple."

"Better luck next time," said the hollow voice from above.

Jeanie's answer rang up between the dark lava. "Come down from there and have some coffee, you bloodthirsty old terror!"

"Pop, you'll git more'n coffee for that talk!" Shorty called up. "Miss Jeanie's on the warpath!"

"Shucks!" came back from above. "I seen her on the warpath when she had pigtails an' dolls. I seen her paddled an' squall. I'm too old to worry about Miss Jeanie Hyde's warpaths."

Tom was smiling as they rode out of the cut. These strangers were close to one another, like a family. Their salty humor was leavening for a grimmer side that brushed death and violence. He felt at home with them.

They rode out into the bright white sunlight, and Tom suddenly realized why he felt at home with them. They were like his own Four Brothers outfit, each tried, each certain of the others. Then he stared across the sun-drenched open into which they were riding to the right. High lava dykes bounded an opening a full mile by half a mile. The grass was good. Trees had rooted around the edges. Ahead of them the park-like opening narrowed to a point. Trees grew there and scrub bushes. A small pole corral had been built against sheer lava rock. Several hobbled horses grazed nearby. A chuck wagon stood beside the trees, bedrolls near, blue drift of smoke lazing from the ashes of a cook fire.

Shorty rode close to Tom and gestured ahead. "Headquarters of the Box H. Ain't it snug and cozy?"

"Wouldn't have believed it," Tom said truthfully. "Don't I see water, too?"

"Sweet water," said Shorty. "Comes from under the lava on one side an' goes under it again on the other. Used to be a camp spot for Indians comin' through the lava. Still is, only they don't move around so much."

"Got cattle?"

"Few," answered Shorty. "We keep 'em out o' here much as possible to save the grass. There's a few other places they can water."

The camp was deserted. Jack Hyde swung off the horse. His sister dismounted lightly.

"Build up the fire, Shorty, for coffee," Jeanie said. "There's cold meat and bread if anyone is hungry. Jack, let me see that arm."

The water was a cool, slow flow about a yard wide, across ten yards of open where the lava dykes came together. A small tarp tent for Jeanie Hyde stretched between two trees. Tom watered the dead-beat sorrel and turned him out to graze. He ate cold meat and bread, drank hot coffee without asking questions or being questioned. He was yawning when he stood up and smiled at Jeanie Hyde.

"That sets mighty good, ma'am. If nobody minds, I'll lay back under the trees for a few hours, and then get on my way."

"Stretch out on Soapy's bedroll," said Shorty. His face was blank as he explained to Tom: "Soapy went off on some business and he ain't back yet. He won't mind."

"Then I won't," Tom said, pokerfaced, too.

Back under the trees, boots off, stretched flat on the open

bedroll, he thought of the dead man who had owned the tarp and blankets under him, and he thought of the close finish with death back there toward Bone Lake. But he was thinking of Jeanie Hyde when he went to sleep in short minutes.

He timed the sleep for four hours. It was about four hours, and midafternoon, when he rolled off the blankets. He walked to the running water, sloshed its cold comfort on his face. He was running fingers through his hair as he turned to the chuck wagon and met Jack Hyde, Shorty, and a tall, stooped old man who could only be Pop Skivvy.

"Feel better?" Jack asked.

"I could use a lot more of it."

The younger man nodded understandingly. He was unsmiling, serious. So were the other two. "We figured a little advice wouldn't hurt you," said Jack.

"It never did," Tom invited.

"You didn't say how big an outfit was behind you," said Jack. "You got a fair sample this morning of what you're up against. If you aren't sure you can handle it, better turn back."

"We've got about four hundred head. Counting me, there's four of us left. The rest were good men. They're dead now. We got licked and run out. Can't go back where we started. The cattle won't make it back over the dry country they're in now," Tom told them calmly. "We've got to have grass and water quick."

"Four of you," Shorty muttered dolefully. "Man, it'll be murder if you stop on that Bone Lake range. Might be you could make a deal to trail over it fast and keep going."

Tom was building a cigarette absently as he looked at them.

"Free grass is free. Top dog, you said, is the one who can stay on top. I was wondering if there's a place back in this *malpais* where we can throw our herd while we think it over."

Shorty chortled. "I told you, Jack! It stuck out all over him.

You got a wolf neighbor who means to howl."

"I hope so," Jack said. He had that look again of fire burning deep inside. "There're five of us, not counting my sister. Soapy made six, but they got him. We got licked, too, and run off our place. Only we didn't run far. We stopped here in the *malpaís,* and we mean to stay here until we're back where we started."

"I see," Tom said, and what he saw most was the stubborn fire of purpose in this younger man. Jack Hyde had been licked, but he wouldn't stay licked. He had put his back to the lava rocks and was making his fight, win or lose, live or die.

"This *malpaís* will hold four hundred more head for a time, if they're scattered out right," Jack said. "If your herd can trail one dry day, there's a way in from the north that'll miss all the Bone Lake range and Peyton's riders."

"I was wondering," Tom said. "We ain't in any shape to trail straight into a fight. Tell me the way in here. I'll head off my bunch."

"Son," offered Pop Skivvy, "I'll side you there an' bring you back." The oldster's leathery face was a mass of wrinkles, eyes deep-set, shrewd, humorous. "I've killed Injuns all over this country when I was younger. Know 'er like I do my saddle. You ready to top a fresh hoss an' ride?"

V

Three days later, at dusk, the thirst-maddened cattle came off the dry trail to stagnant rock pools on the northwest fringe of the lava. Grass was scanty, but Pop Skivvy was reassuring as he watched the animals plunge to the water and drink.

"They can drift easy now until we get 'em scattered out."

Pop Skivvy's hair was white, his deeply wrinkled face as old as the lava flows. He lounged in the saddle, high-crowned hat pushed back, leathery skin and stringy muscles hung on a big-boned frame. Pop Skivvy's old eyes had the humorous glint of youth. Tom Gannett had been hard put to keep up with him on the fast ride north.

"What you aim to do now?" the old man asked abruptly, squinting at Tom.

"Rest a couple of days and think about it."

"You'll have thinkin' to do," said Pop Skivvy bluntly, and he rode off toward the other side of the pools.

Tom sat in the saddle, watching dying color on the western horizon. He knew now exactly what Pop Skivvy meant. On the north ride, the old man had talked freely about the Box H brand, started over against the mountains, south of Sabrino, by Ben Hyde, now dead.

"Ben Hyde was a good-natured kind of dreamer," Pop Skivvy had said. "He read books an' was stubborn, in a kind of smilin' way. Had water and grass back in a couple of them small mountain valleys. Minded his own business an' was satisfied with his small bunch of cattle. Samshu Peyton an' Garcia seen all that an' never bothered him much. Peyton said once he liked a good pinochle player like Ben Hyde handy. Wasn't no trouble to speak of until after Ben Hyde died, two years ago."

"Jack Hyde didn't play pinochle?"

"Wasn't that. Old Samshu is crippled up now an' poisoned with his own meanness. His son, Buck Peyton, runs most of their business, an' Buck likes a pretty face better'n cards. Buck's mean, like his old man was, loud-takin' an' bull-headed. He went for Jeanie Hyde . . . and run into a bull-high fence with her. Last time Buck called around he'd been drinkin'. Jack run him off the Box H. I knowed what was comin' then, an' it shore came, with Buck Peyton's meanness behind it an old Samshu just as mean because Miss Jeanie had fenced Buck out o' her pasture. Free mountain grass around the Box H went first. The Peytons moved in a big herd an' cleaned our free graze to the roots. Box H cattle was rustled, too, while that was going on.

Couldn't prove where they went even after Buck Peyton boasted in Sabrino he'd have the Box H busted before he was through."

"You don't make me like this Buck Peyton," Tom had said. "What else did he do?"

"That was enough. The Box H never did own enough land to hold its cattle the year around. Jack seen what grass he owned going fast, feeding it this time of year. Rustling hadn't stopped, either. We tried moving the cattle toward Bone Lake to save the home grass. Got into a ruckus with the Peytons over that, lost a man an' some more cattle. We talked it over, Jack, me, an' Shorty, an' decided to throw the cattle over here in the *malpais* the rest of the summer an' save the home grass for winter. Hadn't been over here three weeks when we found that the home fences had been cut an' Peyton cattle had et most of our winter grass. Buck Peyton figured that'd finish us. He sent word he'd be needing the *malpais* next. Jack sent back word the *malpais* was the deadline. Peyton cattle or Peyton men'd be shot on sight if they showed in the *malpais*. And that's the way she is."

"How does the sister like it?"

"She's pulled her part. But she's a woman. Can't see it the way a man does. Jeanie wants to sell out."

"This Gregorio Garcia in it?"

"So far he's been keepin' out, except to claim grass south of Bone Lake. He'd think it was funny that Buck Peyton got run off by Jeanie. All old Gregorio aims to do is raise cattle an' hold all the grass in sight. I don't guess the Peytons figure they need any of his help, anyway, against Jack an' Jeanie."

All that was in Tom's mind as he watched the last daylight wane in the west. He looked through the dusk at Cass, still wearing the dirty face bandages. Somberly Tom wondered how right Cass was in wondering if they were the dead ones, blind-stubborn to keep pushing on against trouble. The past came back again through the hazy dusk, the bawling, tramping of the cattle. Jed and Luke, Wahoo Jim, Ogle Svenson, and the others. Cass was right and Cass was wrong. They had not died. Death had stopped them, but they had not quit. Tom smiled, strong himself again, certain what to do.

Next day they worked the cattle deeper into the *malpaís* and scattered them. They brought the trail wagon to the Box H camp and rested, and Jeanie Hyde was not glad to see them.

Tom knew why. It was two days later before Jeanie said it, face to face. Tom had ridden in early, dragged up wood for the cook fire, cut it to length with the axe while Jeanie mixed biscuit dough on her work board at the back of the chuck wagon. They were alone.

Tom leaned on the axe, perspiring, smiling faintly with pleasure as he watched Jeanie's flour-dusted arms work the dough. Jeanie turned her head and her look was level and questioning.

"You're feeding us fine grub," Tom said. "Means a lot to us to rest a little and get grub like this."

Jeanie punched the dough as if it could feel the thing she felt. Tom sensed it, stormy, rebellious, seething in her since they had pulled into camp.

"I ought to feed you poison," Jeanie said, and she added: "Not because you're not welcome. Because you mean trouble to us."

"That's plain talk," Tom said soberly.

Jeanie punched the dough again. Color was in her cheeks; her eyes were dark and stormy as she dusted flour from her hands and faced him.

"It's time for plain talking. You men are planning trouble and trying to keep me from knowing it."

"Well, now, not exactly that."

"Exactly that!" said Jeanie flatly. "I've been talking to your brother Cass. I know what happened before you started south.

138

Fighting, killing, until the last of you were almost wiped out."

"Cass is taking it a little hard."

"Why shouldn't he?" Jeanie demanded. "His two brothers meant something to him. The rest were his friends. They'd be here alive if they hadn't tried to fight three big outfits that combined against them."

"They wouldn't be here if they were alive," said Tom mildly. "They'd be proving that they'd never quit while they were right." Tom groped for words to explain. "It's hard for a woman to see, but. . . ."

"Any woman sees plainly enough," Jeanie cut in passionately. "Getting killed doesn't settle anything. I want my brother Jack alive, not dead to prove he isn't afraid. I know he's not afraid. But when he hasn't a chance, it's time to quit. Fifty years from now he'll have those years. He won't be long forgotten like Soapy will be . . . oh, yes, I know Soapy is dead. Like Jack will be dead if he keeps on."

"Fifty years from now," Tom said thoughtfully, "a man would be looking back and remembering that he quit. Every one of the fifty years he'd know he quit. When he quit once, he'd quit easier the next time, like dry rot working through a timber. He'd know it was in him and . . . and"—he gestured helplessly—"he wouldn't be the man he'd like to be. Can't you see?"

"I can see Soapy and John Strong, who was killed before we came here in the *malpais*," said Jeanie. She was pale now. "I can see your brothers and the other men who were killed, and Cass and Dink Hawkins who were almost killed. I can see it's not worth it. I could have stopped Jack if you hadn't come here."

"Could you? Maybe you don't know your brother like you think you do. He's a man his father would be proud of."

"Pride!" cried Jeanie furiously. Her clenched fist struck the work board. "Don't talk to me about pride! Talk to me about happiness and hope for the future, Mister Tom Gannett." Jean-

139

ie's lip curled. "If you can find any hope with two out of your four men crippled . . . and Buck Peyton and his father hiring more than twenty hands."

"You don't understand."

"You won't understand!" Jeanie charged angrily.

They faced one another across Jeanie's hot anger. Tom made another helpless gesture. "I didn't come here to make you feel this way. If pulling out would help you, I'd leave. But it won't. Jack's mind was made up before I met him. Will it make you feel any different if I promise that I'll help him, but I won't ask him to help me?" Tom lifted the axe, looking at it soberly, and then at Jeanie. "I'll move our wagon to another camp in the morning if it'll make you feel any better."

"It won't," said Jeanie, and her stormy emotion went away. She smiled wanly. "I worry. But I think I'm really glad you're here. Now we're not so alone and helpless out here in the *malpaís*." Jeanie groped for words. "In this Sabrino country there isn't much law. If you're not the strongest, no one cares much what happens to you. When trouble comes, you're alone."

"I know," Tom said. "It's that way 'most everywhere." A smile etched in around his eyes. "That's why it pays to stay strong."

Jeanie smiled, too, refusing further argument by turning to her biscuit dough. "You promised about Jack," she reminded over her shoulder.

"I promised," Tom agreed.

VI

That night the stars were bright, the small campfire glowing when Jack Hyde brought up the future. Jeanie was in her tarp tent back among the trees. Pop Skivvy and Basco Sweet were on guard at the two breaks in the lava dykes. The rest of them were sitting, sprawling in the firelight and shadow.

"Pop Skivvy was scouting the edge of the lava today and saw

some of the Peyton men riding this way," Jack said. "He turned them back with half a dozen shots."

"I'd have let 'em come closer an' put the lead in them," said Dink Hawkins cheerfully from sprawled comfort on his blankets.

Jack sat, cross-legged, near the fire, light and shadow shifting on his thin, frowning face. "They might have been heading into the lava for trouble. My guess is they were just making sure we stay back in here." Jack looked through the firelight at Tom, who was smoking thoughtfully. "We've got to make a move before water and grass play out on us."

Tom looked around at them—Cass, moody, silent; Dink Hawkins still lame but ready for anything; Shorty Case, cheerful like Dink Hawkins, and no less a fighter; Slim Wiggins and Cal Moore, two lanky, middle-aged men, short on talk, who had worked for Ben Hyde and were sticking with his son. They had all become more alert, eying him.

"Lease me your Box H Ranch for a month," Tom said, squinting across the fire.

"What good will the Box H do you?"

"It'll give the Four BRS brand a right to be around here. I've got some ideas."

Shorty Case chuckled wryly. "The ranch wasn't enough for us. You'll have to sprout ideas. Big ones."

"Big ideas come easy as little ones. We're strangers. Maybe that'll help."

"It won't help the way you want it," Jack said, frowning at the fire. "But if that's what you want, take the Box H lease for a month. What'll you do with it?"

Tom grinned and yawned as he stood up. "Sleep on it first, then ride around and get acquainted. I always did like to know my neighbors."

In the morning Tom took Dink Hawkins, whose foot had healed

enough to ride. Dink asked no questions until they were out of the lava, southeast from camp.

"You asked a lot of questions before we left, Tom, but you didn't say much. Are we just ridin' around?"

"Seems so."

Dink's black eyes were shrewdly questioning. "You was all-fired particular to have me along, with Basco wanting mighty hard to come."

"Basco's built too much like trouble. You're a deceiving little cuss."

"Sounds like a slap an' a pat," said Dink suspiciously. "Who we going to deceive?"

"Maybe no one."

"Near as I can see, we're heading toward this Garcia's place."

"We are," Tom said, and let it go at that.

Jack Hyde had traced a map on the ground. Rolling land lifted gradually toward the mountain foothills. Arroyo Largo was easy to recognize when they reached its half-mile wide cut, with cottonwoods along the banks, silver-gray *chamiza* thickets in the center sands, and an inch-deep, yard-wide flow of clear water out of the higher land to the east. They followed the arroyo up, and the earth-colored adobe buildings and pole corrals of Gregorio Garcia's ranch appeared on a wide grassy flat, half encircled by the arroyo and backed by low hills.

Dogs bolted toward them, barking. At small adobe huts beyond the corrals children stopped and stared. The men in sight were Mexicans. Tom rode toward the biggest house, long, low, with a shaded, dirt-floored portal across the front, and he said: "I'll do the talking."

An old man sat on the portal in a rawhide-covered chair. A barefooted, fat woman brought a pitcher and glass to a hide-covered table beside the chair and hurried back in the house as the two men rode up and dismounted.

"Howdy," Tom greeted.

He got back a mumbled: *"Buenos días."*

The old man was small, shriveled, wrinkled, eyes bright and watchful. By Jack Hyde's description he was old Garcia, sent across the plains to a St. Louis school in his youth, speaking better English than most Americans—when he chose.

"I'm looking for Gregorio Garcia," Tom explained.

"Garcia? *Qué quiere con* Garcia?" the old man mumbled. He drank from the glass while bright watchful eyes surveyed them.

Tom grinned. "I don't speak much Spanish, *Don* Gregorio. It'd be a help if you'd use your good English. Those men inside the windows can put up their guns. This is a friendly visit."

The dark, deep-wrinkled old face split in an answering grin. *"Por diablos* . . . who are you?"

"Tom Gannett. Hawkins here works for me. I've leased the Box H Ranch."

The glinting humor in the bright old eyes might be mockery. They were bright, but they were old—old with the shrewdness of long years. Gregorio Garcia drank from the glass again and held it up. *"Atole,"* he mumbled. "Goat's milk and maize. Every day until he died my grandfather drank *atole.* He was one hundred and four years." Silent mirth shook the shriveled figure in the big chair. "You will not need *atole.* You will not live so long, young rooster."

Tom chuckled. "I heard about Buck Peyton. I was wondering how you felt about the Box H."

The old man sat still, like a shriveled mummy. "I am old. What is this business to me?"

"Might be a lot if Buck Peyton gets you to fight for him."

Once more the silent mirth shook the wrinkled figure. He mumbled in Spanish, then brought it out in English: "The rooster looks behind the roost before he flies up, *qué no?*"

"You might say it's that way," Tom said, grinning. His smile lingered while he met the shrewd old eyes. "I thought I'd tell you I'm not interested in anything south of Bone Lake."

Old Garcia emptied the glass, filled it from the pitcher. Tom noted that the dark, claw-like hand was strong, steady as it held the pitcher. He guessed that old Garcia's shriveled helplessness was as deceiving as Dink's short-statured mildness. He'd be a man to direct a fight, old, canny, knowing the country and men and tricks. Smiling, watchful, Tom waited while the old eyes studied him, and filmed a little with what seemed memory and regret.

Old Garcia drank more *atole*. He sighed and moved restlessly. "I would give my *atole*, my chair, my ranch, to be a rooster, again, too," he said dreamily. "*Señor*, I am too old to care what happens north of the lake."

They were riding away before Dink broke his silence. "You reckon that old coot meant it?"

"We'll have a hard time if he doesn't."

"Meaning it'll be easy if he keeps his men off our backs?"

"Ought to be a little easier."

"How easy?"

"I don't know," said Tom. His face had settled into bleak lines. "I promised the Hyde girl I wouldn't drag her brother into it."

Dink whistled softly. "How come?"

"She thinks he'd have quit. She'll blame us if he's killed."

"*Mm-m-m*," said Dink. Sarcasm edged his voice. "Can't have her down on us, can we?"

"Go to the devil!"

"Looks like you've gone," said Dink dryly. "Shucks, there's only four of us an' Cass ain't got any heart for it. What chance'll three of us have against that Peyton outfit?"

"I'm riding to Sabrino to see. You coming with me?"

Dink gave him an outraged look. "I'm here, ain't I?"

They rode easily, saving the horses. The Sabrino road was over against the first foothills; they struck it and followed the dusty ruts past taller trees, the higher loom of the mountains on their right. Twice they overtook and passed slow freight wagons. From a rise in the road they saw three horsemen well ahead of them, heading toward town.

"People everywhere you look," Dink said cheerfully. "Gives me a crowded feeling."

Tom's smile was a thin slit of humor. "Get used to it. With luck we'll meet a lot of folks."

Sun slanted hot in midafternoon as they rode in among adobe houses and log cabins to the dusty open space that formed a rude plaza in the center of Sabrino. Dink pushed back his hat and looked around.

"Livery stable, barbershop, stores, liquor. There's a Chinee eating place across there. I want a whole cow, fried with a sack of spuds an' onions."

"You might as well," Tom said. "Two drinks apiece is the limit if we stay here all night."

"That," guessed Dink, "means trouble."

They rode the horses to the livery barn for water, feed, rest. "No telling how hard they'll have to run," Tom decided.

The liveryman was red-headed, talkative as he stumped on a peg leg. "Four BRS brand," he commented. "That's a new one around here."

"We just rode in," said Tom, pulling off his saddle.

"Here, lemme put it up. . . . Strangers come through here a lot. It's healthy country for strangers."

"How healthy?" asked Dink. He got back a sly grin and wink.

"The mountains is healthy for some, and, if a man takes a notion to leave quick, there's the lava strip an' the dry country on the west. No worries at all, you might say."

"Any big ranches around here?" Tom asked.

"Biggest one is old Samshu Peyton's PX Ranch. You aim to hit 'em for a job?"

"Might."

"You can find out about it quick today," said the red-headed liveryman, grinning as he reached for Dink's saddle and stumped to put it up. "Peyton an' his son Buck come in town with some of their men not more'n half an hour ago."

"Seems like this is our lucky day," Tom said to Dink. To the liveryman he said: "We'll saddle up again."

The liveryman's jaw dropped.

"They ain't that far away. Old Samshu's likely to be at Cole Hunford's store. He hangs out there when he's in town. Owns part of it. If Buck ain't around the Navajo Bar, he'll be along. Does most of his drinkin' in there."

"Might have to follow them out to the ranch," Tom said blandly. "Come on, Dink, top your leather. A little water's the best we can give these horses right now."

When they rode out of the barn, Dink almost wailed: "Don't we get them steaks?"

Tom grinned thinly. "Got to press our luck while it's with us. I'll do the talking here, too. You sure you can jump around fast on that foot?"

"Middlin' fast. What kind of talking you aim to do?"

"It'll be short and sweet. Come on, let's have a drink."

"It won't fill my hollow like steak," Dink grumbled, but when Tom led the way across the rude plaza to the Navajo Bar, Dink became quiet, watchful. Which was like Dink. He was little, but deadly in trouble.

The Navajo Bar had a slant sun roof in front, a half-filled hitch rack. Men were talking, laughing in the dim, cool interior. Tom tied his horse at the end of the rack and gave a quick look at handgun and rifle. Dink dismounted, also, saw him, and did the same, eyes narrowing. Dink was the smaller man, quiet, inoffensive, still limping a little as he followed Tom inside.

The bar was on the right, running back from the door. Nine or ten men drinking, talking, quieted as Tom and Dink entered, and looked them over.

Tom spoke to the bartender. "Two whiskeys," and he added: "Nice town you've got here."

The fat bartender was bald, amiable-looking. "Best little spot in a long ways. You two strangers around here?"

"Mostly. I've heard the name of Buck Peyton. Maybe you know him."

The fat man looked startled. His uneasy glance slid down the bar, where talk had stopped.

The fourth man down the bar stepped out. "I'm Buck Peyton. What about me?"

Tom turned, arm resting on the bar edge, face thoughtful as he sized up the man. Buck Peyton was not quite like Pop Skivvy's talk had made him. He had a big, self-confident swagger, hat pushed back, vest open, thumbs hooked in cartridge belt. He was black-haired, his broad face a little too heavy and unpleasant, and now slightly sneering. His voice had come a little too loud. The thick under lip looked as if it sneered easily and often. He had the edgy challenge of a young man sure of himself, always on top, used to having his own way.

"Pleasure to see you," Tom said thoughtfully. "My name's Gannett. I own the Four BRS brand, that's called the Four Brothers brand. We've leased the Box H Ranch. I rode into town to beat you down to the yellow dog you are, and tell you to keep out of my way."

VII

"*Oop!*" Dink blurted in stunned surprise, and then, like a striking rattler, he was suddenly out from behind Tom, six-gun cocked, rifle in other hand, voice a whiplash of warning. "Hold still, strangers!"

Buck Peyton was caught by the same surprise. He stood with startled rage spreading darkly on his broad face. One man looked as if he were going for a gun, but that man froze at Dink's command. The rest gaped wordlessly, holding quietly before the threat of Dink's guns.

Tom spoke to the bartender. "Don't you get any funny ideas." He stepped away from the bar, gun still holstered. "How many of you are Peyton men? Tally out, quick!"

Five admitted it. They were hard-looking men, all armed. Tom grinned at them.

"Takes a lot of you to gun-nurse this yellow skunk, don't it? Everybody turn around and shuck guns to the floor. You won't get hurt if you keep out of this. Game's open if you mean to sit in."

One of the Peyton men, with a drooping mustache, tied-down gun belt, and cold direct eyes, spoke gruffly: "No chips in my hand to play. Sounds like a deal for Buck to ante." He turned around. His unbuckled gun belt thudded to the floor. The other men followed his lead.

"You, too!" Tom said to Buck Peyton.

"A hell of a chance you're giving me, ain't you?"

"How much chance did you give that boy and his sister on the Box H? Twenty gunmen to two youngsters minding their own business. Grab that belt buckle quick!"

Peyton licked his lips, glaring. His heavy belt and holster thudded to the floor.

"Get away from it," said Tom, and to Dink: "Get the rest of them over against the wall." Tom tossed his own gun belt over by his rifle that leaned against the bar. The move he made next was quicker than Dink's move with the drawn gun. Open hand cracked loudly across Buck Peyton's broad, rage-flushed face.

"You too yellow to fight alone?" Tom asked.

The slap and question were like a match flaring to gunpowder. Buck Peyton's wild oath was thick with rage as he lunged forward.

Tom was already going back out of reach, smiling thinly. His final taunt was derisive. "Somebody should have whipped the yellow out of you long ago!"

He had the big man frenzied, wild. "I'll kill you!" Buck Peyton yelled. His hand slapped back on his hip. A horn-handled sheath knife flashed out in his hand. He lunged again, striking with the knife.

Tom dodged, throwing up an arm. The knife had been back there on Peyton's hip, out of sight. The furious slash of the blade would have gutted a steer. Tom's outflung arm hit up against Peyton's wrist behind the knife. It knocked the blow up; the knife came back across Tom's arm, slicing shirt sleeve and flesh. Tom grabbed the wrist as it struck again. The knife point raked across his shoulder. Holding the wrist, he drove his full weight forward, so that Buck Peyton staggered back off balance.

"Want me to stop the skunk, Tom?" Dink yelled. His voice sounded far away through the straining effort humming in Tom's ears.

"No!" Tom gritted explosively. He took a wild blow on the side of the face, jumped back suddenly, and slapped his other hand to the knife wrist also, and jerked and savagely twisted. Buck Peyton was somewhat bigger and heavier than Tom, but little stronger. He grabbed for the knife with his free hand as he was jerked off balance forward. Still twisting the wrist, Tom bore the knife to one side out of reach. For a span of seconds, Buck Peyton's corded muscles checked the twist, then Tom's savage strain brought the wrist on around and back. Peyton groaned as muscles neared the tearing point. He dropped the knife.

They were both panting, sweating from the brief, furious effort. Tom caught a hazy glimpse of strained faces watching them from the left side of the barroom. His own face was rock-hard as he released the wrist, shifted half a step, and slugged Buck Peyton with left fist, right fist, left fist, right. . . . The blows drove the bigger man back, blood starting over mashed lips. Buck Peyton threw up an arm and tried to dodge around. Tom smashed under the arm to the heart and followed him.

Peyton stumbled back in a half circle so that his back was to the door. Past him Tom caught another hazy glimpse of men in the doorway. He heard faintly someone shouting outside, warning Sabrino plaza of the fight. Buck Peyton was trying to stand and fight. His big fist struck high on Tom's forehead. It hurt. Tom shook it off, caught another blow on his guarding arm, and smashed to Buck Peyton's face again, flattening the nose. Then Tom crowded forward, striking, striking, taking blows that now came a little clumsier.

Buck Peyton's mouth was bloody from lips and mashed nose. His face had a mottled swollen fury. He lurched back, swiping a hand across nose to clear his breathing. It smeared the blood and the hand came away red, and Tom's fist passed the hand and smashed soddenly against the jaw.

Peyton went back, throwing up both hands in guard as his head shook groggily. Tom followed him, striking under the arms, striking over them. Buck Peyton turned away, stumbling toward the bar. Tom caught his elbow, yanked him around, and hit him again fully in the face. Peyton staggered half around and fell to his hands and knees. His head was toward the doorway, packed now with staring men. He tried to scramble up toward the doorway. Tom reached out after him.

"Get up!" Tom panted, and, when Buck Peyton came blindly up to hands and knees, Tom grabbed him by collar and silk neckerchief and dragged him to his feet.

Tom was close to staggering himself as he hit Buck Peyton the hardest blow of all on the jaw. He felt bone give in his fist. The soggy shock of it went back up his arm. But it was the end. Buck Peyton sagged back into the doorway among the men crowded there. They gave way before him, tried to catch him. His heavy weight went down among them, full length on the hard-packed dirt outside the door.

Tom was sucking mighty gasps of breath. He fought the weakness, the urge to stagger as he turned back, shaking his head to clear the haze that had fallen around him and Buck Peyton's swollen, red-smeared face. The salty taste of blood was on Tom's tongue. He looked in the bar mirror and saw his cut lower lip. Left shirt sleeve was bloody from the knife slash. But his eyes were clear, face hardly marked as he caught up his gun belt and strapped it on with shaking hands.

Dink Hawkins had moved back into a half crouch, facing the door, his gun covering the men against the wall. Still sucking great drafts of air, Tom looked at the Peyton men.

"With plenty of guns to back him up, he's good at running a woman off her ranch. You hardcases sure picked a man to fight for. This is a new set-up. I'm hiring good men at the Box H Ranch tonight, before my outfit pulls in and takes over. But they better be good men. We don't use any other kind." Tom caught up his rifle. "Ready, Dink?"

"Lemme get these men away from their guns first."

"They can have our backs to shoot at if they feel like it," Tom said, drawing his handgun.

Dink shrugged and followed him to the door.

The silence inside the barroom spread outside and men moved back as Tom came through the doorway. Buck Peyton still sprawled on the smooth hard dirt. Tom looked down at him and swept a look around the silent faces.

"I'll bet some of you were afraid of him," he said, and

grinned. Then he looked out toward a big two-horse buggy careening across the open plaza toward them. "Who's that?"

A broad-shouldered, bearded man said: "It's Samshu Peyton, his old man."

Tom thrust his rifle back into Dink's hand. He stooped and with a grunt of effort heaved Buck Peyton's heavy form off the dirt, carrying Buck through the break in the hitch rack to meet the buggy that whirled up in a flurry of dust. Across the heavy burden Tom measured the driver in the buggy, rifle leaning on the seat edge beside him. Tom thought of a bony, huddled old rattler. Old Samshu Peyton was not as old as Gregorio Garcia. He lacked the ancient timeless look of that bright-eyed, shriveled old man huddled in the hide-covered chair, sipping goat milk and ground corn in the custom of his grandfather. Samshu Peyton's mustache was a gray smear on a long thin upper lip. Skin stretched tautly in unhealthy pallor from cheek bones to jaw. He huddled on the buggy seat like a man grown old inside faster than the years had aged him. Hard, bitter, tricky, ruthless, and now betrayed only by the body that held all that. Eyes muddy gray and glass-hard flamed at Tom, and a rasping querulous anger demanded: "What happened to Buck?"

"I beat the daylights out of him, and, if you were his age, I'd do the same to you. Take him an' get out of town with him!"

Old Samshu Peyton's bony hand caught at the rifle. "PX men, git here!" his shrill rasping voice shouted.

Tom grunted mightily as he heaved the dead weight in his arms. He heaved it over the buggy wheel, soddenly onto the buggy seat and floor, against the rifle and Samshu Peyton. The buggy creaked and rocked heavily under the impact.

"Git with him, you blasted old buzzard," Tom said savagely. He fired a shot across the nervous team of bay horses and they bolted into a run.

"Looks like the one-eyed law runnin' to your back, Tom,"

Dink's voice warned.

Tom turned from the buggy dust with smoking handgun. Hitched horses were at his right and Dink was standing there in the hitch rack opening, watching the small crowd. Shorty Case had named the one-eyed deputy as Gig Haines. The man wore a black patch over one eye. The face under the patch was puffy, loose, and Haines was wheezing as he trotted up. He rolled his old eye uncertainly at Tom's gun. "What's wrong here?" he demanded.

"Nothing to worry you," Tom said. He holstered the gun. "I just beat Buck Peyton down to size and sent him off with his old man."

"B-Buck Peyton?"

"I own the Four Brothers cattle brand that'll be on the Box H Ranch from now on. I see you're the law. You make sure we get our share of the law. If that ain't plain to you now, you'll have time to think it over. Let's go, Dink."

VIII

No one stopped them as they rode leisurely away from the hitch rack. When they were out of earshot, Dink let out an explosive: "Satan's sister! Whyn't you warn me, Tom?"

"You might have talked me out of it," Tom said. "Don't look back."

"My back is crawling and saying . . . here it comes, Dink! Here it comes! They've got their guns now!"

"Mine, too," Tom admitted, grinning faintly. "I'm gambling they won't shoot. It'd spoil everything to get nervous and look back. I'm going into this store ahead and get some boxes of shells. We'll probably need 'em. Stay out on your horse and don't look back across the plaza."

"You ain't gambling. You just went crazy. Two of us coming in here and calling it war."

Tom walked leisurely into the store, and, when he came back out with pockets bulging and sagging with cartridge boxes, Dink was lounging in the saddle.

"I ain't looked," said Dink. "But my neck is stiff on one side from keepin' my head still. Let's get out o' here and back to the lava."

"We're going on to the Box H Ranch," Tom said as they headed leisurely out of the plaza.

"Just the two of us?"

"Yep."

"You sure are crazy," charged Dink viciously. "I ain't had my steak. You lit off the powder before that barkeep even got my whiskey poured. Now you're headin' the two of us to an empty ranch where the Peytons will come lookin' for us as sure as skunks give off stink."

"I told Basco to meet us there tonight."

"Three of us," Dink said bitterly. "Don't make me laugh. You know we ain't got a chance."

"Didn't have a chance, anyway," Tom declared. "Top dogs stay on top around here, and the Peytons were sure on top. I promised Jeanie Hyde I'd keep her folks out of this. Cass is still feeling low. You and me and Basco weren't much to crowd the Peytons back."

"We still aren't."

"There's a chance old Gregorio Garcia will stay off our backs now."

"There's still only three of us against the Peytons," Dink reminded sarcastically. "Next time you promise me a short, sweet talk with strangers, don't pick out our lucky day." He snorted. "Lucky day. That's one to hang over the fireplace."

Tom smiled grimly and looked at the slashed arm, which had closed up and stopped bleeding. "Jack Hyde and his men haven't got a chance, Dink. They're game, but they won't whip the Peytons."

"I seen that right off."

"We didn't help them. Our cattle are only eating them out of the lava faster."

Dink nodded.

"Free water and free grass," Tom said slowly. "We've got to have some of it. The Peytons are hogging free range they can't use. They're on top and they mean to stay on top and they've got enough guns to wipe us out."

"Tell me somethin' I don't know."

"I'm showing you," said Tom, somber again, face set hard over the rough hard purpose inside. "It'll have to be short and sweet and quick if we stand a chance. Old Garcia may let us alone now. The quickest way to stop a rattler is mash his head. After that he only squirms."

"Why didn't you gut-shoot young Peyton then an' get it over with?" Dink asked morosely.

"I can't walk in and kill a man who never heard of me before. It'd have made things worse, anyway. I'd have been marked as a dangerous killer. Old Gregorio Garcia would have been set against us. The law might have taken a hand. Every Peyton rider would have made it his quarrel. Old Samshu Peyton would have had just what he needed to run us out."

"I suppose so," Dink conceded glumly. "I was only talkin'. So we get run out, anyway."

"Maybe," admitted Tom. "But I gambled that this Buck Peyton wasn't so big inside, after all. He couldn't be to run over the Box H because Jeanie Hyde wouldn't have any of him. I took a chance I could whip him."

A satisfied grin lighted Dink's face. "That fight was a whing-dinger. But I dern near shot Peyton when he yanked that knife."

Tom smiled ruefully. "He fooled me. That knife looked as long as his arm when he jumped at me. Maybe it's a good thing he did. I wanted some of these tough Sabrino gunnies to see a stranger walk in and slap Buck Peyton around. They needed to get the idea he had a yellow streak and wasn't so much. I took a chance and got by with it. I mashed his rattler's head out in public the way they'll understand. He won't be the same man again to any of them. Old Samshu Peyton won't look any bigger because of it. Top dog has run things around here, and they've had a look at who means to be top dog. They know the Four Brothers brand has come to town and is hiring good men at the Box H from tonight on. My guess is some of the hardcases would rather draw Four Brothers pay now than let Buck Peyton egg them on in this fight."

Dink spat expressively. "You're hirin' good men tonight, before your outfit gets here. If Basco rides over to the Box H tonight, that'll leave Cass as the rest of the outfit. You sure got nerve."

Tom grinned. "We're short on cards, so we'll need bluff. Nobody around here knows how big our outfit is. We might have forty gun hands coming. I set up as top dog and they saw the game open. Every good man that joins us is that much help. Every one we can bait away from the Peytons helps a little more."

"It's a whiskey dream. All Hades is due to pop as soon as Old Man Peyton gets his wits workin. You let 'em know our outfit ain't at the Box H yet. Old Peyton and his pup will come foggin' around to take charge before we get help."

"No doubt of it," Tom assented. "We might as well get it over with. They'll be fighting us around the Box H instead of running Jeanie Clyde and her brother out of the lava."

Dink's look was sharp. "You're doing a lot of worryin' about them folks."

"I promised Jeanie Hyde we'd keep our fight away from them."

Dink spat again, more expressively. "When a man gits to promising a pretty girl, he'll say the dangedest things." Dink looked over his shoulder. "Two men follering us fast. Reckon it's trouble?"

"Might be," admitted Tom, turning to look.

When the galloping riders were closer, Tom reined up and waited. He recognized the bearded man who had answered his question about Samshu Peyton in front of the saloon. The other rider was the Peyton man with drooping mustache, tied-down gun, and cold, direct eyes who had unbuckled his gun belt first in the saloon. They galloped to the spot and stopped. The bearded man spoke brusquely.

"I'm Gid Smith. This is Rock Ryan. He worked for the Peytons. I didn't. He's sent word to them that he's quit. We like what we seen back there in town. You hirin' now?"

"You're hired."

"You'll need us," Smith commented as the four of them rode on. "When's your outfit coming?"

"Can't say, exactly."

"You'll need all your men. Samshu Peyton an' Buck'll give you a fight now."

Rock Ryan spoke, as coldly direct as his look: "Old Samshu don't get around much. Buck has been running the PX. But Samshu still thinks like a wolf an' twice as fast. Look out for him."

"They'll visit the Box H tonight," Tom guessed. "Buck Peyton won't rest now until he's even with me. He'll be wild as a slapped grizzly when he gets some gunmen behind him."

Rock Ryan nodded. "If he ain't wild, Samshu will be. That old lobo'll have at you before you get a chance to dig in with your outfit."

"We had it figured that way."

"Who you got at the Box H now?"

"No one."

Rock Ryan stared without expression. "Two of you headin' there alone, where the Peytons can find you?"

"Four of us now."

Rock Ryan looked baffled, then he shrugged. "Maybe a few more of the PX boys will ride over. Buck Peyton don't set too well with some of them. But you'll still be short-handed for trouble."

"You can turn back."

Ryan's baffled look deepened. "Buck an' his old man will kill if they can. But you won't hold back out o' sight until your men get here. Mister, I don't read your sign."

"Don't try. If Buck Peyton wants a killing, he and his men will fill a gunsight quick as we will."

A rumbling chuckle came out of Gid Smith's beard. He slapped his leg. "Rock, that's sign any man can read. It's gun sign an' guts."

Rock Ryan smiled thinly and fell silent. They were riding south out of Sabrino on the wagon road. A weather-faded board nailed to a roadside tree, Box H and arrow burned into the wood, sent them southeast into the foothills on a narrow, little-used ranch road.

IX

The country lifted gradually, trees grew taller; the road swung in beside a shallow little stream, clear and hurrying over gravel and stones.

"Purty water," commented Dink as the horses drank. "If there was good grass, it'd be something."

"Seven, eight miles to Box H grass," Gid Smith informed him.

They followed the water around a low forested shoulder of the mountains, passed through a wire gate, and in front of them two mountain valleys came together.

"Finest spot I ever seen for a small spread," said Gid enthusiastically. "There's enough water down each valley. Snow don't drift bad. Three or four hundred head can do here the year around if they feed high up in summer an' save the bottom grass for winter."

"Not much grass now," Tom remarked.

"Buck Peyton put almost a thousand head back through here," Rock Ryan told him briefly. "A low-down trick, but he was givin' the orders."

"That free range north of Bone Lake will pull us through."

Rock Ryan gave him another cold, probing look. Tom was casual. The baffled look passed over Ryan's face again as they rode on.

A mile up the left-hand valley they found the log ranch buildings and pole corrals on a sunny flat against the rising, forested slope behind. Hollowed-out split logs brought spring water off the slope to the main house and carried water on to corral troughs set down in the ground. Jaybirds were noisy about the deserted buildings as they rode up.

"There's grub inside," Tom said. "We might as well eat while it's peaceful. Dink, you hungry enough to worry with it?"

"Just gimme the padlock key an' watch me."

"I'll ride around and see what we've got," Tom decided.

He rode alone up the valley. Graze on the higher slopes was perfect for summer. The sheltered sunny valleys were perfect for winter. Tom rode up in among trees and found the fence line. Beyond the fence wire he saw visible evidence of the Peyton cattle that had grazed the higher slopes. The valley grass also had been badly eaten.

The sun dropped to the mountain shoulder as Tom turned back down the gently sloping valley. A good three miles away he could see the pale-blue drift of smoke over the log ranch house.

Purple shadows were reaching out through the quiet. Gold and rose colors crept over the high, lazy clouds. The quiet, the peace were rare with promise of content, happiness.

Tom thought of Jeanie Hyde, and in this hour he understood better her frantic, almost fierce intent to find again the peace, the happiness she must have known in these quiet valleys. It made him think of Jed and Luke, Wahoo Jim, Ogle Svenson, and the others, who had missed this rich full peace Jeanie Hyde had possessed.

The trampled valley grass caught Tom's eye. He thought of the higher slopes grazed clean, and of the Box H cattle that had been rustled. Looking down the valley again at the cook smoke above the ranch house, he thought of Jeanie Hyde at her cook fire in the lava *malpaís,* while Buck Peyton swaggered in Sabrino with his gunmen. All this Jeanie had lost. She would not have it again by running away. Wahoo Jim, Ogle Svenson, Jed and Luke Gannett would have fought for this as they had fought in the High Lonesomes. They would have died fighting the Peytons without regret. Jeanie was wrong. Her brother was right. Thinking of Buck Peyton and old Samshu, Tom's face hardened again. The rough, hard certainty grew strong inside, and he rode to the cabin planning what had to be done.

Dink had opened beans, cut into a ham, found coffee and canned milk. The four of them were eating when the sound of an approaching horse sent Tom into the open with his rifle.

It was Basco Sweet. Jerking a thumb at the four saddled horses, Basco rumbled: "Who's here, Tom?"

"I hired a couple men."

Basco's broad, placid face split in a grin as he dismounted. His loud rumble was gratified. "We can use 'em. Four of us ain't enough, even out there in the lava with young Hyde an' his men."

Tom's warning gesture silenced the big man. They walked

away from the house and Tom told what had happened during the day. "Our outfit is supposed to be coming. Just keep quiet about it."

Basco was astonished, then grim. "I should've brought Cass."

"He'll do better out of this."

"He's a Gannett, ain't he?"

"He's young," Tom said. "Get some grub under your belt and we'll get ready for tonight."

Dink came out of the log house and met them.

"You ought to keep a fistful of hay in that big mouth!" he growled under his breath to Basco. "We heard you plain in there hollering that only four of us was in the lava with the Hydes."

Basco looked troubled. Tom said: "I hoped they hadn't heard." Then he shrugged. "Might as well go eat."

The two new men made no comments during the meal. But several times Tom caught Ryan's cold, estimating look on him. The man was thinking.

They went outside into the thickening evening. Their guns were with them. The tightening feel of trouble was closing in with the night. Rock Ryan was smoking a cigarette as he walked over and caught Tom alone.

"I heard your man," Ryan said coolly. "Four of you, eh? I'll bet a month's pay there ain't any more. Want to bet?"

"I didn't hire you to bet."

They measured one another in the dusk. Ryan said: "Buck Peyton would give a lot to know there was only four of you taking over here. What if I quit now an' ride on?"

"I wouldn't like that tonight."

"Think you can stop me?"

"I'm willing to try. Make your move."

They were still measuring one another, hardness clashing against hardness. Suddenly a thin smile gashed Ryan's face.

"There was only two of you when I hired out. No talk about more help comin' tonight." Ryan shook his head; he was no longer baffled, but he was wondering. "I can read your sign now. You tackled Buck Peyton alone because that was all you could do." He drew on the cigarette and echoed Dink's words: "Mister, you sure got nerve."

A far faint shout down the valley drew them quickly around. They joined Dink, Smith, and Basco in front of the log house as another faint shout drifted through the dusk.

"Three or four riders," Tom said, peering. "Wouldn't be warning us if they meant trouble."

Basco Sweet had cat eyes at night. "Five of them," he counted.

The five riders approached at an easy lope. Rock Ryan abruptly said: "There's Tennessee Red. I kind of looked for him." As the men came closer, Ryan called other names. "Latigo, Joe Ring, Cap Haynes, Bill Sandler." He said—"About like I thought."—and lifted his voice. "What about it, Red? You mavericks lost your way?"

Tennessee Red was tall, lean, grinning as he made a running drop from the saddle and faced them. "We drawed our pay and went to town for a drink. Then it seemed like a good idea to rustle up another payroll. Who's the hiring man who messed up Buck Peyton's face? Buck looked like a calf herd had stampeded on him."

"I'm hiring," Tom said. "There's liable to be trouble."

Tennessee Red shoved black hat back on his head. His grin broadened. "You'll get trouble, all right. It's comin' just about daybreak when you figure it ain't gonna happen tonight after all."

"You sure about that?"

"Old Samshu said it. Joe Ring here rode into Sabrino just as the rest of us was fixin' to head here. Joe played smart. He stayed back on the ranch until he heard what was gonna happen. Joe says Samshu give orders for everybody to get some sleep, because they was gonna be up in the middle of the night an' surprise the Box H at daybreak."

"That was fast thinking," Tom said admiringly. "Ring, what'd old Peyton say when you drew your pay?"

Joe Ring was a small, lean, sharp-nosed man with a ready answer. "Thunder, what could he say? He cussed me out an I cussed him out an' took my pay an' rode off."

"Let's see your money."

"What for?" asked Joe Ring, suddenly sullen.

"Never mind. Let's see it."

"I got it here. Ain't that enough? You don't like the way I do, I'll git back to Sabrino."

Tom drew his gun. "Show the money you got from old Peyton."

"I was thinkin' the same thing you are, Gannett," said Rock Ryan at Tom's elbow. "Old Samshu never would have paid him off an' let him go after hearin' the plans. The old man thinks faster'n that. Joe's done plenty of dirty work for him. I was surprised to see Joe here." Ryan's cold voice said: "Lemme take Joe over to the corrals. I know how to loosen his tongue."

Tom looked at Joe Ring, who was uneasily eyeing the hard faces.

"I'm a stranger to him," Tom said mildly. "Maybe he thought it was all right to run a little sandy on me. I'll give his tongue a chance right here. I won't kill him if he tells the truth."

Joe Ring licked his lips. His voice was hoarse. "I come here to help an' I get this."

"You haven't got anything yet," Tom said in the same mild manner. "But you aren't even a good weasel crook or you'd have thought up a better story. You much of a gambler?"

"Little," said Ring with sullen uneasiness.

"Then gamble that I won't kill you when I count to twenty if

163

you aren't talking straight and fast. One . . . two . . . three. . . ."

The hard faces ringed them in sharpened, watchful silence and the dull gloom filling the valley grew more somber. At the count of ten Tom cocked the heavy revolver.

Joe Ring's eyes fastened on the slight thumb movement with fascination. Sweat started on his forehead. His fists slowly clenched and opened, and then closed again.

At fifteen Joe Ring stopped moving even his fingers. His head was thrust forward a little, eyelids had stopped blinking, and, if he breathed, it was not visible.

"Eighteen," Tom counted. "Nineteen. . . ."

X

Joe Ring's pent-up breath burst in a sobbing groan: "Wait! Old Samshu thought it up! Five hundred if I killed you before I left here! But he was payin' a hundred if I came here an' made sure you thought he'd be after you tonight or in the mornin'!"

"So he's not coming here," Tom said, and read his answer on Joe Ring's sweating face. "What's he going to do?" Tom demanded. His mind leaped over the possibilities, and he had the answer before Ring could reply. "He's got a reason to want me expecting him tonight. His men are riding tonight, aren't they? To the lava, after the Hydes, I'll bet!"

Joe Ring nodded. He was still hoarse.

"Couple of the men recognized you in Sabrino as one of the men they jumped the other day by Bone Lake. Buck an' the old man are goin' after the Hydes tonight. They'll take care of you later. PX men have been scoutin' the lava at night. They know where the Hydes are campin'. Tonight, when there's a good moon, they'll jump the camp."

Tom spoke to Rock Ryan at his elbow. "You were right. Old Peyton thinks like a wolf and twice as fast. First he'll jump where he isn't expected. And if he can get me shot in the back tonight, he's that much ahead. Are you men ready to make a hard ride?"

"We hired out," said Tennessee Red without hesitation. "You going after the Peytons?"

"We'll out-wolf him and be there when he jumps. Couple of you men tie Ring up so he'll be here all night." And to Joe Ring, Tom said: "You won that gamble. I'd have killed you at twenty."

It had to be this way, iron-willed purpose, no weakness. The hard, cold drive of it went with Tom through the foothills to the west. The men who rode with him had the same rough purpose.

They had chosen sides when they left the Peyton ranch. They had known what they were doing. They had not been greatly surprised at the move old Samshu Peyton was making. They had come ready to fight and they were ready now as the steady trail lope of nine horses beat against the night and the long, black-shrouded miles fell behind.

Tom had decided to enter the lava south of Bone Lake. The men he had hired knew the shortest, easiest way across country. Tom let them find the way while he chafed at the easy trail gait they held to save the horses.

Any time after the moon was up the lava camp might be attacked. Someone would be watching on the lava near the camp—Pop Skivvy, Cass, or some of the others. But Jeanie Hyde and the rest would be asleep. They would not have much chance against all the Peyton men. They had not expected a cold-blooded wipe-out as long as they stayed back in the lava and off the free range. They might have been safe if Buck Peyton had not been whipped in Sabrino today. Tom swore with soft bitterness as he thought that he had brought this on them after all. If Jack Hyde was killed and Jeanie lived through a bitter night fight, he'd have to face her grief. If Jeanie lived—one target was as good as another in the moonlight. . . .

The sky paled little as the glowing moon rim pushed up over the eastern mountains, and the night had substance and form. They did not pass within sight of Bone Lake. To Tom, fretting at the slow pace, the ride seemed endless. And then, abruptly, the first lava was ahead of them in dykes sinister and black under the climbing moon.

Tom took the lead, riding harder. Hoof beats drove back in muffled echoes from the lava through which they raced. Once Tom lost the way. Dink straightened him out.

Now the night seemed one blaze of moonlight hatched by black ground shadows from the lava dykes. Tom had never cursed moonlight, before. He did now, and trained his ears for gunfire that did not come. Then, suddenly, Tom reined up, topping the others. Over the blowing horses, faint, sharp gun reports came out of the night ahead.

"They've jumped the camp!" Tom blurted harshly, and he spurred and slashed with the rein ends.

He was racing in the lead rounding a shoulder of the lava when a horse whinnied loudly just ahead. Then another horse whinnied, and in the moonlight ahead a close-held bunch of saddled horses began to plunge and pull away from two riders who held them.

"Scatter 'em!" Tom yelled.

The empty saddles ahead told how the Peyton riders had slipped close to the lava camp on foot, leaving their horses here. One of the guarding riders fired a shot. Tom saw the red lick of muzzle flame and his horse dropped.

He kicked boots out of stirrups and was hurled from the saddle. He thought of the riders behind as the ground came up and hit him. He rolled, slid, with hoofs driving all around, and overhead men shouting, guns blasting.

A horse leaped Tom's rolling body. One hoof slashed across his shoulder. Then the last of his men was past and he heard the heavier pound of the PX horses stampeding. He staggered up dizzily and saw one of the PX riders being dragged by a boot that was caught in a stirrup. The man was dragged a hundred yards in the wild mêlée of stampeding horses before the foot pulled loose. He lay there without moving. Tom's shoulder hurt. But bones were not broken. He could move, could limp back to the rifle he had dropped as he went out of the saddle.

"You all right, Tom?"

That was Dink, and Dink, thinking fast, had wheeled back, leading one of the saddled PX horses. Tom mounted again while Dink spoke fast.

"Got both them blasted PX riders! The other men have gone on! This ain't no time to stop! Basco'll lead 'em right! Them Peyton skunks'll walk out o' the lava now if . . . !"

The rest was lost as Tom put the new horse into a gallop. They sighted the last of their own riders ahead in the moonlight, lost them again, and suddenly the narrow break in the high lava dyke was in front of them.

Tom galloped past a dead man sprawled on the ground. A Hyde man standing night guard up on the lava must have spotted trouble and shot one of the advancing PX riders. The fast-running horse bolted into the split rock where stirrups all but scraped the sides.

The funneling racket of gunfire came into Tom's face. He raced out into the bright moonlight again and the gunfire was a crashing, echoing discordance laced by the high, shrill scream of flying lead. Gun flashes stabbed the night like monstrous fireflies. The Peyton men had come through and scattered to the low growth along the dykes where shadows still lay black. They were working toward the old chuck wagon and the handful of trees. Their guns covered all the moon-drenched open. They had the camp party trapped in that narrowing space at the north end and were raking the chuck wagon and the trees with lead as they worked closer.

But they had not yet reached the camp. In that first sweeping look Tom marked the red lash of gunfire behind the chuck wagon and among the first trees. It was camp lead that ricocheted off the sheer lava near him and screamed viciously through the high moonlight. If Jeanie were alive, her gun might have fired that ricocheting bullet. Jeanie would be as cool and dangerous as any of the men, not afraid for herself, no matter what fear she felt for her brother. Tom had a flash of understanding. It wasn't fear for herself that had made Jeanie want to quit. She had not talked about herself or her safety. She had been afraid for Jack, as Tom now was afraid for her. His fear became a hard, savage anger at Buck Peyton.

The seven riders who had not waited for him and Dink had wheeled sharply to the right inside the lava slit, dismounted, and tied their horses to the nearest brush in the black shadows next to the lava wall. They were about a hundred yards ahead now, all but invisible as they crept forward, holding their fire. All that registered and flashed through Tom's mind. Dink reined up beside him.

"What do we do now, Tom?"

"Gun those Peyton men out into the moonlight where the camp can get a look at them!" Tom said savagely.

He spurred into a gallop along the narrow belt of shadow, Dink following, and, when Tom yelled, Dink yelled. Dink's gun opened up a second behind Tom's gun, firing at the red flashes ahead. Between shots Tom caught startled shouts of warning from Peyton men. He saw gun flashes lick toward him and Dink. They reached their own men and Tom made a flying drop from the saddle.

"Let's go! Run 'em out away from the lava!"

Tennessee Red whooped. But it was big Basco Sweet who led

them into a run after Tom. And it was Dink, still on his horse, who led them all. Bent low in the saddle, yelling, gun spurting red, Dink rode ahead through the narrow belt of shadow like a night fiend bringing death. No Peyton man was more than half a dozen steps from Dink as he passed. The racket of gunfire rose to a crescendo as the startled Peyton tough hands opened up on the howling, blasting rider sweeping by them.

Dink was drawing attention and gunfire. It was like Dink, unselfish, daring, and dangerous. Tom cursed the little cowpuncher huskily. He should have ordered Dink to the ground and made the ride himself. Then the running men behind closed up. The first flashes of the Peyton guns were just ahead. The blast of their own gunfire echoed off the lava and crashed out through the moonlight as they ran forward.

Tom glimpsed Dink's horse bolting out of the lava shadow into the moonlight, staggering, faltering. He thought he saw Dink leaping from the saddle, but he was not sure. He had no time to look further. What he had planned was happening.

Peyton men had strung out along the sheer lava dyke where they could shoot freely at the camp, dodge, hold to cover. Eight roaring guns advancing together were routing them. Not a man waited to fight it out face to face. Tom counted four men shot down as they scrambled up in running retreat. They had not expected this. Gunfire from two sides was raking them and they had no stomach for it—not to please Buck Peyton and old Samshu Peyton. Retreat would bring them closer to the camp. The lava dyke was too sheer to climb. A man made his choice and bolted out into the moonlight, crouching, dodging as he ran across the wide sweep of grass toward whatever safety he could find in flight. Two more followed, then others.

"Don't let 'em get back to our horses! Keep 'em afoot and running!" Tom shouted.

He had passed four men shot down. None had been Buck

Peyton. He guessed that Buck had been at the front, leading the men. They would have been watching him closely for sign of fear. Tom reloaded his handgun and scanned the running figures out in the moonlight. Beside him, Basco Sweet drove rifle lead at the retreat.

"It's turnin' into a rabbit hunt!" Basco said loudly, joyously.

"That looks like Buck Peyton," Tom said suddenly, and he left Basco standing there and ran from the lava shadow into the moonlight, angling out to cut off the tall, running figure that had broken into the open ahead.

He cut the distance down to half. The man shot at him, veered away. That way led toward the camp and men were running out to help finish the fight. The man swerved back, running harder. But he had lost ground. Tom had him cut off now, and, as distance shortened between them, Tom saw that it was Buck Peyton, hatless, rifle in one hand, short gun in the other. Tom stopped.

"You looking for me, Peyton? I'm Gannett!"

Buck Peyton stopped, too, and then frenzy seemed to seize him.

His handgun erupted in a burst of shots as Tom ran at him.

One bullet hit Tom hard in the leg. He stumbled. The shock brought him out of the hot, savage fury that had sent him at Buck Peyton. He was panting, but calm, steady as he stopped, set his legs, and snapped up the rifle. The last shots were pouring wildly from Buck Peyton's gun; he looked big and close to the rifle sights when Tom squeezed the trigger. The one shot was enough. Tom had known it would be. He was lowering the rifle before Buck Peyton dropped. The hot fury had drained out of him as he limped forward.

Buck Peyton was squirming, tearing at the grass, choking on blood that filled his throat. He got his throat clear, his still-swollen face was contorted, and an agony of fear was in his hoarse cry. "You killed me!"

Tom looked down at him soberly, as close to regret as he could go. "Tell Soapy that when you meet him," he said. "And watch Soapy laugh."

Buck Peyton was dead when Tom limped toward the camp. Shorty Case was the first man he met.

"You hurt?" Shorty demanded, panting.

"Bad leg. Can't run any more. Get out there and spread the word that Buck Peyton's dead. Any of your bunch hurt?"

"Think they got Pop Skivvy. He was watchin' again tonight. Shootin' woke us up. Your brother got hit in the arm. He and Jack Hyde run out ahead of the rest of us. Then they had to come back when they seen how many had jumped us. Can you make it?"

"Easy," Tom said, and limped on.

Behind him he could hear the shooting, scattered out now, less frequent. The slim figure that came running from the chuck wagon wore riding pants and carried a rifle, but Tom knew her, and he called: "Get back there out of sight until this is over! Think you're a man?"

"I'm as good as a man," Jeanie answered him. "Here, let me help you walk."

"I can get along," Tom grumbled, and then let her place his arm around her slim, strong shoulders and bear part of his limping weight. "I got some help and tried to head them off. Didn't quite make it. I'm sorry."

"Be still," said Jeanie crossly. "Who asked you to be sorry?"

"I said I'd keep this away from you."

"They're killers," Jeanie said, and her voice shook. "They tried to kill us while we were asleep. Now they'll never drive us out while we can fight them."

"You'll lose those fifty years of peace."

"Don't laugh at me," said Jeanie fiercely. "I'll spend the next

171

fifty years trying to stop those . . . those killers."

"I wouldn't know you now," Tom marveled. "But you can grow old peacefully. I saw Garcia. He won't trouble you. Buck Peyton's back there dead. And even if old Samshu didn't get caught in this, he won't be much of a problem now. I've hired enough men to make us strong, and I'll hire more. You can use those fifty years to suit yourself. I might even let you come back on the ranch I leased from your brother. . . ." He broke off and looked at her sternly. "But if you're laughing about it, maybe I won't."

"I'm not laughing," Jeanie quavered. "I'm crying."

"But it's going to be all right. I'll be around here to make sure you don't have any more trouble."

"That's why I'm crying. I'm happy."

Tom chuckled, not feeling the hurt in his leg now as he drew Jeanie closer.

"It doesn't make sense to me, Jeanie Hyde. But I mean to spend the next fifty years finding out about it."

★ ★ ★ ★ ★

A BULLET FOR THE UTAH KID

★ ★ ★ ★ ★

The author's title for this short novel was "Showdown in Blood" when he completed it on January 19, 1948. His agent sent it to Mike Tilden at Popular Publications who bought it, but changed the title to "A Bullet for the Utah Kid" when it appeared in *Fifteen Western Tales* (8/48). T.T. Flynn netted $454.00. For its first appearance in book form the magazine's title has been retained.

I

The first thing Johnny Rance noticed about Tule City was an election sign. The second, a pretty girl. The third was a man due to be killed. And none of it seemed half as important as the business Johnny Rance was riding on.

The four-day ride from the far harsh Phantom Mountains on a sag-backed red pack mule had been a hard one. And hungry. Johnny had eaten yesterday by knocking off a jack rabbits's head with his last rifle cartridge, and had hated the waste. You learned to shoot right when you lived and prospected with old Hook Adams. There was never enough money to buy extra cartridges.

Johnny cut into a dusty road miles out from town, so no one could back-trail him. He grinned as he remembered Hook's anxious orders.

"No whiskey or gamblin', Johnny. No girls, either. Git you in trouble. Tend to your business quick. Keep your mouth shut. Don't leave tracks when you ride out of town. Watch your back trail like a lead-holed grizzly. We've got the world by the tail if we don't make a slip till snow comes."

A bright red sunset blazed and waned fast into purple-black dusk as the mule shuffled dust to the edge of town. A black-lettered cloth banner, stretched overhead across the road by lines tied in opposite trees, said: *RE-ELECT WALT POWERS— SHERIFF.* Johnny pulled up the mule and stared at the sign. Memories, bitter and sorrowful, still able to hurt, galled hard for a moment before he rode on.

He was twenty-one and had never voted. Never wanted to vote or think about it. It was ten years since he'd been near an election. Big Bill Rance, his father, had won that election, back in Wyoming. Three months after pinning the nickel-plated sheriff's badge on his gray flannel shirt, Big Bill had been shot to death by nester rustlers, the same ones who had helped vote him into office. Nothing had ever been done about it. Johnny had run away before neighbors could ship him back East to be raised by strange relatives.

The next spring he'd fallen in with old Hook Adams and stayed with Hook, prospecting sun-blasted deserts and high far-back mountains. They'd been in a gold stampede or two and had seen other men get rich. Old Hook had stubbornly insisted: "We'll git our luck. Bound to come."

When he got old enough, Johnny had worked every now and then for ranch wages to get the next grubstake together. By then he knew old Hook Adams would die prospecting. But Hook had filled a hungry kid's skinny belly and taken him along. Johnny had promised himself old Hook would never die alone back in the mountains or out on the dry desert. He'd stay with Hook. It was a good thing he had.

The town crowded around. Dogs ran out and barked. Kids playing in the open whooped at the young stranger on the gaunted red mule with the cracked leather saddlebags. The mule flattened his ears nervously. Johnny had the same crowded-in feeling, even as he grinned at the kids. He was half-wild, he guessed, and looked it. Scraggly yellow hair fell down over his ears and over the open collar of the patched, sun-bleached shirt. Faded denim riding pants were patched in knees and seat. He hadn't shaved on the trip. Pack rats had chewed holes in his stained old black hat.

Two girl riders overtook him at an easy gallop. They looked

at the red mule and rider as they passed. One girl said something to the other, and laughed. Johnny knew he was something for the town girls to laugh at. But one girl's laugh didn't set right.

The girls stopped not far ahead at a house set back behind a white picket fence. They watched the approaching mule. He reined over and spoke across the mule's big ears.

"Mind telling me how to find the office of lawyer Spencer Wales?"

The girl on the right, sitting side-saddle, was the one who had laughed. Johnny could barely make out her long thin nose and small mouth. She answered him with wangy nasal assurance.

"Do you mean old Acey Wales?"

"Could be, ma'am."

She laughed again, and glanced at her friend, riding man-style in overall pants and soft leather boots, with fringed gauntlet gloves, and a wide-brimmed hat hanging back on small square shoulders.

"Judith, won't Acey Wales be keeping office hours in the Acey-Deuce Saloon this time of day?"

Judith was smiling, too, but it made her oval face look friendly in the deep dusk.

"He probably is," Judith agreed.

"Sounds like he might own the place," Johnny said, trying to see more of her friendly oval face, framed by the back-slanted hat.

"He may have bought it," the other girl said. Her laugh sounded malicious.

"Thanks," Johnny said evenly, and rode on, thinking about the one girl, slim and straight in her stock saddle.

He came in toward the plaza, night shrouding thicker, and passed a blacksmith shop, closed for the night, then a wagon yard fenced with rough poles and marked by a dim smoked-up oil lantern hanging at one side of the gate.

A street lamp on a high post ahead marked the northwest corner of the plaza. A rider turned through the feeble yellow glow and came at a shuffling trot, looking long and lean in the saddle, with a dark mustache and canted gray Stetson. The man stared hard at mule and rider, as if trying to place them, and lifted a hand silently as he went by.

A moment later Johnny heard a voice, guarded, sharp enough to carry over the *clip-clop* of hoofs in the street dust.

"Hank Willis!"

The rider answered: "Yes?"

His horse broke rhythm, halting. In the same instant a gun blast shattered the night. Johnny made a cat-quick instinctive turn in the saddle as the startled mule buck-jumped and bolted.

The faintest beam from the puddling yellow glow at the plaza corner reached along this side street, touching a shadowy figure at the corner post of the wagon yard fence. The figure held a shotgun. Its second barrel crashed, spurting light across Johnny's fast backward glance.

His left foot had almost lost its stirrup. Johnny was busy the next moments fighting the mule's hard mouth, while men came running under the plaza light. A hard-spurred horse lifted dust spurts past the light. More men came on foot and horseback as Johnny fought to quiet the mule.

One of the riders wheeled back from the target spot. He caught up with the mule almost at the plaza corner. A bone-handled Colt was in hand as he reined up by the mule's head.

"You have anything to do with killing Hank Willis?"

"Hell, no!" Johnny denied, short-reining the jumpy mule. "Is he dead?"

"Blowed all over the street! You were fogging off fast when I seen you! Who'n hell are you, anyway?"

Black-hatted, wiry, with a tied-down gun holster, the man had a short crisp mustache and hard demand in his voice.

"Name's Rance," Johnny said. "Get your hand off my bridle rein!"

Other riders and men on foot were gathering around them. The black-hatted man shoved his gun back in the holster.

"Mouthy, ain't you? What happened?"

"Willis rode that way easy. Fellow with a dark hat stood back there by the corner post of the wagon yard and called his name. Then cut loose with the shotgun. This fool mule lit out."

"Dark hat, huh? You seen the man?"

"Sort of."

"Know him again?"

"I might," Johnny admitted. "Have to get a good look at him. Seemed to have on a haired-skin vest where his coat was open. Not too tall."

A flat silence fell.

"I've got on a vest like that!" one rider called. "What about the man's face?"

"I'd have to look at it."

"How about his voice?"

"Maybe I'd know that. Didn't sound like your voice."

"Makes me feel better," the rider said sarcastically. "I was afraid I'd kilt him."

Johnny still had the hemmed-in feeling.

"Where'd you come from?" the wiry black-hatted man demanded.

"I just rode in," Johnny said vaguely. "Never saw your town before."

"What's your business here?"

Johnny took his time about answering. "I rode in to see Lawyer Acey Wales."

The same flat, unfriendly silence dropped again. It was the

kind of silence that had meaning.

The black-hatted man said: "What' your business with Acey Wales?"

"He's a lawyer, ain't he?"

"What kind of law business?"

"I'll tell it to him."

Someone farther back called: "Here's the sheriff!"

Johnny watched a rider crowd a big bay horse slowly to them. A big man with a bulgy face under a fine white sombrero, the sheriff wore a flowered vest, a loose-knotted yellow silk tie, and had no gun belt showing under his open coat.

He peered at the mule and rider: "What's this?"

"Stranger who wants Acey Wales," the black-hatted man said across the mule's neck. His voice had a new, cold note. "Says his name's Rance. He saw Hank Willis stuffed with buckshot. Claims he might know the man. What do you make of it, Walt?"

"I'll see what he knows. Do you make anything of it, Rip?"

"I'm asking you."

"Willis was a deputy. He's been working hard in the election. Maybe too hard. I'll damn' well find out."

Rip said: "You've got your witness handy and everything. A stranger who just happened to drop in town. And already he wants Acey Wales for his lawyer. Ain't it a miracle?"

The sheriff's answer roughened with temper. "Hell, you've electioneered enough, Rip. I never saw this fellow before. If he can spot the killer, he's my man. I mean to get the one who killed Hank, and get him before election, if possible. Maybe it'll change a few minds around here. If he wants Acey Wales for a lawyer, that's his business."

"Going to lock him up?"

"That's my business." The sheriff's hostility turned on Johnny. "Think you can spot the man who did it?"

"Maybe, mister. But I'd rather mind my own business."

"Well, what the hell is your business?"

"I rode in to buy some grub."

Rip said, coldly jeering: "He wants Acey Wales for his lawyer so he can buy some grub. Walt, I don't believe he learned his story straight."

Temper mottled the sheriff's face. "I don't know a damn' thing about him . . . but I will." The sheriff turned in the saddle and called: "Hondo!"

"Here, Walt!"

"Ride along with this stranger."

Johnny set his jaw. "I want Lawyer Wales."

Rip said, jeering: "He learned Acey Wales's name anyway."

"He can have any damn' lawyer in town," Walt Powers said loudly. "Rip, I know what you're driving at. I'll get you answered and pretty damn' quick, too." Powers reined hard back toward the dead man. Rip eyed Johnny.

"Maybe I got around the corner just in time, young fellow. Take my advice. Be damned sure you're right in everything you say."

Johnny said tightly—"I usually am."—and cut it short by riding on.

Hondo was a tight-mouthed, raw-boned man, his flat-crowned hat pulled forward and vest open over a gun belt. A deputy's badge was pinned to his vest. Chewing tobacco bulged one cheek. As they skirted the tree-filled plaza, Hondo turned his head, scowling. "If you mess Walt up in this election, God help you."

Johnny said nothing. Talking seemed to make it worse.

Sheriff's office and jail were in a small, two-story brick courthouse, built squarely across the end of a short way running south from the plaza.

Johnny dismounted stiffly at the long tie rack. Afoot, he was tall and lean, fined to muscle and bone. Even with saddle stiffness he moved with loose ease, Indian-like, from footwork in the mountains. He wrapped the reins slowly on the tie rail, delaying, trying to think what to do. If he carried the heavy saddlebags into the office, Hondo might get curious. If he didn't, and was locked up tonight, the saddlebags would be investigated. All hell would break loose.

Johnny envied Hondo's fast-looking black horse. With a horse like that, he'd chance a break out of town. Things promised to get worse.

"Need all night to tie that mule?" Hondo growled. Then he looked back toward the plaza. "Here comes your Acey Wales."

Johnny let out a soft breath of relief. "I need to talk to him alone."

"Walt didn't seem against it," Hondo decided reluctantly. The hurrying lawyer reached them and Hondo said: "Here's your man, Acey. Talk in Walt's office. I'll wait out here."

"Heard you wanted me," the lawyer panted, as they started in. "Retainer'll have to be ten dollars." When he got no reply, he cleared his throat nervously. "Five dollars then."

Johnny waited until they were in the office, where an overhead lamp with a tin reflector cast revealing light. He took time to close a front window and turned, expressionless. "You're a hell of a looking lawyer," Johnny said coldly. "Who sent you around to say you were Acey Wales?"

"Young man, I resent. . . ."

The protest faded out. He was a small thin man with a tobacco-stained gray mustache. He needed a shave and haircut. A frayed, stained, black frock coat was buttoned loosely over a soiled, collarless shirt, open at the neck. The frock coat looked as though it had been slept in.

Johnny's look traveled down to a split shoe. The old man seemed to wilt. He sat slackly in the swing chair at the sheriff's roll-top desk.

"Thought I had a client," he said dully. "Might have known better." He nodded dismally. "You called the turn, young man. I'm a whiskey-head barroom bum. I don't resent anything, any more. This was a trick on me, wasn't it?"

"Ever hear of Hook Adams?" Johnny demanded.

The ghost of a smile came under the stained gray mustache. "That was a long time ago. Adams came as near a hanging sentence from old Judge Abbot as any man I ever heard of. It was close . . . but I got him off."

"You must be lawyer Spencer Wales," Johnny muttered, dismayed. "Hook was broke. He didn't have a chance. You were the best lawyer in these parts, and you took Hook's case for nothing. Saved his neck and gave him fifty dollars for a grub-stake."

"I had fifty to give then," Acey Wales said with a wan smile. He stood up, drawing on some forgotten dignity. "Nice to think about it, young man. I bid you good evening."

Hondo opened the door. "You two get your business settled?"

"Not yet," Johnny said. He waited until Hondo closed the door, muttering displeasure. "Got an office safe?" Johnny asked under his breath.

"Good God, no. I haven't an office, unless it's the Acey-Deuce Saloon."

"Hook Adams never forgot what you did for him," Johnny said under his breath, watching the door. "Hook remembered you as a square-shooter. I've got to trust you. Looks like I stepped into a gopher hole by being near that killing."

"You sure did," Acey Wales agreed. He studied Johnny with bloodshot eyes. "Rip Madigan and his friends mean to have Walt Powers out of the sheriff's job Saturday, when the voting is over. Hank Willis was brother to Whitey Willis, who owns the Acey-Deuce. Walt Powers is Whitey's man for sheriff. Hank Willis has been using pressure, in Whitey's name, to get votes for

Walt. Pretty raw pressure. Looks like someone on the other side had enough of it and gunned Hank down."

"So that's it," Johnny murmured.

"It's enough," Acey Wales said with exasperation. "I hear you're the only witness. The side that killed Hank will lose the election. Each side thinks the other planted you there. A stranger like you would make a fine witness to throw the blame on the other side."

"I'll keep my mouth shut."

"Too late," Acey Wales muttered. He opened a desk drawer and found a half-empty pint. His veined hands shook as he pulled the cork and tipped the bottle.

Johnny frowned as the whiskey gurgled steadily. Acey Wales was emptying the bottle with a sort of fierce thirst. Johnny caught it away.

"That's enough. I need you sober."

Acey Wales drew a shuddery breath and wiped a hand across his mouth.

"Needed it," he said shakily. "Can't think without it." He closed bloodshot eyes for a moment, then squinted doubtfully. "Where you from? How can you prove you're a stranger, not mixed up in any of this?"

"Can't say where I'm from. Can't prove anything," Johnny admitted dismally.

"Why not?"

Horses were coming to the hitch rack.

"Must be the sheriff," Johnny guessed. He spoke rapidly. "Get my mule. Put him up if you can. But burr to my saddlebags. Hide 'em."

"Young man, I'm usually dead drunk by bedtime."

"You're Hook Adams's lawyer now," Johnny urged harshly. "You're that square-shooter Hook counted on. Whiskey don't rob a man of that. Hook told me to trust you."

"God bless him . . . the deluded fool," Acey Wales said huskily. He pulled out a soiled red bandanna and blew his nose. "Been a long time since anyone trusted me."

Johnny took a breath and gambled everything.

"There's about seven pounds of placer gold dust and nuggets in the bottom of those saddlebags. One fourth is yours. There's a wagonload more in the creek where it came from. You share in that, too. Hook Adams said so. He never forgot what you did for him."

Acey Wales said, his voice unsteady: "You'd trust me like that?"

"Got to. The creek ain't big. A stampede would clean it out fast. We're out of grub and money. Tule City wasn't the nearest town. But I traveled here because Hook said you were the one to help. If I try to sell that dust, God Almighty can't stop men from trying to find where I got it."

"They'd put guns in your back."

"Hook Adams was too poorly to make the trip. He figured a fine lawyer like you could handle the dust on the quiet. I could load up with supplies and disappear. Give us till winter and we'll have all we need out of that creek."

Acey Wales was trembling, husky-voiced. "All I live for is rot-gut whiskey. I'm not worth putting on the Injun list at the bars. If I was caught with placer gold like that, I wouldn't have a chance."

Boots scuffed the courthouse steps. Muffled voices were audible.

"Hide it until I see what happens," Johnny said fiercely as the door was shoved open. "You've got to."

Half an hour later the bulgy-faced sheriff stabbed a blunt finger at Johnny's face. He stared at him.

"You're lyin'. There's only two bits in your pocket. You

185

couldn't have rode in to buy grub."

The closed office was hot from the big lamp overhead. Walt Powers had stripped off his coat, unbuttoned his flowered vest. He was perspiring. Johnny sat on a hard chair against the wall, stubborn now, tight-lipped. "I had a mule and a rifle to sell, Sheriff," he reminded.

"To Acey Wales, I reckon."

"A fellow who knew him a long time ago said he was a big lawyer in Tule City."

Hondo had gone out. Another deputy named Red leaned against the desk, smoking. Red had bowed legs and eyes the color of gun metal. His narrow face was hard to read, but now he spoke mildly. "Don't lose your temper, Walt. He might forget who really killed Hank Willis. Rip Madigan and his friends would like that."

"You got any ideas, Red?"

"Maybe he is busted. Maybe he did think old Acey was good for a touch. Put a big steak in this stranger's belly. Get him washed and shaved like you'd do for any other young fellow down on his luck. Get him a room at the Western House, so he can have a good sleep."

"Cigars and liquor too?" Walt Powers suggested with a dangerous edge.

"Might do him good. He'll feel more like spotting the fellow who shot Hank. I'll stick with him, so that gun-toting Rip Madigan and his hardcase friends can't threaten him."

Walt Powers thought that over. His anger smoothed out. "Sure," he said finally, temper gone. "Losing Hank made me jumpy. Go out and grab something to eat. Get cleaned up. Then start lookin' for the killer. Red'll go along with you."

Johnny considered it. "Nice of you, Sheriff. Want to lend me a hundred dollars? I'll pay you back before I leave town. Won't need Red for a nursemaid, either."

Walt Powers exploded softly: "A hundred. . . ." He caught himself and looked at Red.

"Learns fast, don't he?" Red said, grinning. "I'd take a chance, Walt."

The gold double eagles felt good in Johnny's pocket. He got a haircut, a shave, and a bath at the barbershop. In the General Store he bought a canvas jacket, new pants and shirt, and changed in a storeroom at the back.

He came back out to the gun case and bargained for an old cedar-handled .44, and the soft-worn belt and holster the gun had been in. Cartridges were still in the belt loops, which had been in a back corner of the case, neglected.

The sharp-eyed clerk grinned when he had his money. "You got it cheap because it's Dave Scrutchfield's gun that Dave was using when Walt Powers killed him on a rustling case last year. It's a dead man's gun with a Jonah on it. Dave took it off a dead man, too."

"You might get it back off me," Johnny said, notching the belt in an easy slant across his hips.

"I was wondering," the clerk said, losing his smile. "Ain't you the stranger who saw Hank Willis killed?"

"I don't know what I saw. I was riding by and heard it."

"Better get hard of hearing then," the clerk advised brusquely. He turned away, as if he'd said too much.

The town seethed uneasily over the shotgun killing. Even women had come to the dim-lit plaza, some in buggies, where they could sit and watch, others nervously with their menfolk. Even a stranger could guess deep passions behind this election. The killing of Hank Willis was a bloody sign. Johnny idled around two sides of the plaza, his own memories bitter about the long-gone election that had sent Big Bill Rance to his death.

Here was another election. Here was death again, trouble building. Election signs and banners were everywhere around the plaza. Johnny resented them. He hated to think about elections. They stirred memories of Big Bill Rance, hearty and laughing and kind. That freckled button of a kid years back had worshipped his big father, who'd come in a rough wagon bed from a lonely coulée, blood-covered, stiff and cold. Not even a last good bye.

The Acey-Deuce, windows bright-lighted, half doors swinging busily in and out, seemed the biggest bar. Johnny turned into the place, searching for Acey Wales. The red mule had been taken from the courthouse, and the little lawyer had vanished.

Faces had turned to watch Johnny's idling progress around the plaza. But here in the noisy barroom, layered with blue tobacco smoke, rank with beer and whiskey, hot from big overhead lamps, he was ignored at first. Johnny saw himself in the barroom mirror. He halted, studying the smooth-shaven, lean, saddle-brown face and wide, grave mouth. Barbering and new clothes helped. He wondered if the two town girls would laugh at this one in the mirror. He grinned a little at the thought.

Acey Wales was not in sight. Johnny glanced at the two stud games in the back, and stood thinking. The little whiskey-hungry lawyer might have started a big drunk, might already be showing placer gold in public. Men would quickly know where he'd gotten it. Tule City would be like a kicked hornet's nest. Johnny had seen what a gold strike could do to men. Hundreds would try to trail him when he left town. He might be rustled quietly away by men who'd try to make him talk. Or he'd be delayed until even the porcupines gave out for old Hook Adams.

A man came in fast through the batwing doors and paused with a group at the bar. He glanced back toward Johnny, nodded, and came on back. The fine tailored broadcloth and white linen shirt belonged to Whitey Willis, gambler brother of the dead man.

Johnny stood waiting, marking the long, dead-white face and

silky brown mustaches, the spotless white silk vest crossed with a massive gold chain, the costly hand-worked gun belt and silver-mounted gun showing under the open coat. The man was bareheaded. Carefully trimmed and parted hair set off his high forehead and pale eyes that halted level with Johnny's. Talk had died away. The man's voice carried through the long smoke-filled room.

"I'm Whitey Willis. They say you're the one who saw my brother killed."

"I'd ridden past the spot," Johnny said carefully.

"You claimed you saw the man who did it!"

"Just a look. It was dark where he stood."

"Changing your story?" The gambler's dead-white face had no emotion.

"Just telling you how it was."

Whitey Willis turned, looking the long length of the barroom. "Anyone in here look like the man?"

"I'd go more by his voice."

The gambler wheeled back, his voice holding its flat unmoved resonance. "I'll pay a thousand gold money to have the right man pointed out."

"Not to me. I'm not after blood money."

"What do you want?"

"Nothing."

"Everybody wants something," Whitey Willis stated his flat belief. "Maybe this will interest you. I mean to get the man who shot Hank. I'll kill any man who covers up for him by lying about who did it."

Johnny thought it over and nodded. "Don't know as I blame you. That's your business."

Johnny stepped past the gambler, and walked a staring, suspicious gauntlet to the swing doors. Men from both sides of the election were here in the Acey-Deuce—and all distrusted him.

He added it up with wry resentment. The law and Whitey Willis were hunting the killer. Johnny Rance's knowledge of the shooting was death to any man he indicated. Johnny Rance was death itself, walking around town, waiting for a victim. Neither side in the election trusted him. Each side thought he was mixed up with the other side. It made him a liar and sneak to everyone.

Every man his eyes dwelt on would wonder if Johnny Rance meant to point him out as the killer. And the killer himself would be wary, waiting, watching him. Johnny stopped outside, under the wooden canopy, wondering dismally who would take the first shot at him. Or use a knife. He remembered Acey Wales and moved on, looking. The little whiskey-head lawyer was the one man in town who might be a friend.

Then, abruptly, Johnny noticed the girl he wanted to see again, sitting alone in a buggy close by the dusty plank walk. She'd been in his mind when he borrowed money from Walt Powers to clean up quick and get some decent duds. He could almost hear Hook Adams warning him: *No girls. . . . Git you in trouble.*

Johnny stepped off the plank walk to the buggy. "I found my lawyer, ma'am," he said gravely.

II

She was silent a moment. "You look different," she said, and then: "I hear you were the only witness to the killing."

"The sheriff thinks one thing. This Rip Madigan thinks another. They're both down on me," Johnny told her. He smiled. "Everyone else seems to line up with them."

She was leaning forward a little, studying him. "Which side are you on?" she inquired gravely.

"My side. I'm a stranger. Your election doesn't mean anything to me."

She said: "It does to me. I'm Judith Madigan."

She was about his age, Johnny guessed, and wearing a white dress now, with ruffles, and bits of ribbon at the bodice. Her black hair was caught back loosely behind her ears, under a small hat with a saucy tilt.

Feet scuffed by on the plank walk. Eyes would be noting this talk with Rip Madigan's daughter. It would travel fast. Johnny didn't care just now. Judith Madigan was speaking evenly.

"You're not the only stranger who has drifted in, and your lawyer has been fed and kept drunk by the one man who doesn't want decent law in this section. What else can my father and his friends think?"

"I didn't know how it was, ma'am."

"You could get another lawyer."

"No," Johnny said. He looked at her and shook his head. "No . . . he'll have to do."

She studied him. "Why?" she asked quietly.

"Well, I can't change lawyers now."

She watched him, tall by the dusty wheel. In the shadow under the tasseled buggy top she gradually became remote, withdrawn. Johnny tried to recapture something close and breathless that her nearness had brought.

"It's not what you think," he tried.

She gathered the slack reins, bringing the drooping sorrel horse alert and turning out.

"It's not what I think," her light cool voice said indifferently. "It's what my father thinks. What his friends think. Try to convince them. And you'd better do so."

She left him standing there, watching the buggy turning the plaza corner out of sight.

Johnny stepped back on the plank walk, knowing morosely the Tule City election had become his business. He had the deciding vote. A bloody vote. And Johnny guessed when he cast his vote all hell would break loose in Tule City. That was the

191

way it added up from what he knew, what he'd seen and heard. None of it ought to matter to him. But what she thought mattered. *No girls. . . . Git you in trouble.*

Johnny grinned ruefully and looked for the little lawyer. Acey Wales wasn't around the plaza, up any of the side streets. The red mule wasn't at either of the two feed stables.

A one-eyed hostler at the second stable showed yellowed teeth stumps in a sly grin. "So you give old Acey your mule to watch? Likely he's swapped it into whiskey by now. Or he's tryin' to."

"Does he do things like that?"

"A whiskey-guzzler like Acey'll do anything when he's dry. Hell, he was a big man oncet. He swapped that for whiskey. What's an old mule to him?"

Johnny was too hungry to wait longer. It had been a long time since the tough unsalted jack rabbit yesterday. In the Angel Café, on the west side of the plaza, he told the thick-armed, smiling waitress: "Biggest steak you've got. Lots of potatoes and anything else you can pile on. Coffee and pie right now."

He was cutting into the last of the thick steak when Red, the spraddle-legged deputy, came in. Johnny put down knife and fork and waited impassively as Red walked back and sat down beside him.

The deputy's face was no easier to read than it had been in Walt Powers's office. His gun-metal stare could mean anything. Red spoke quietly, any threat as light as blood taint on a wandering breeze.

"Been friends with her long?" Red asked. He started a brown-paper cigarette with nimble fingers, his look searching Johnny's face.

Red could only mean Rip Madigan's daughter.

"Not long," Johnny said carefully. "On my way in town I asked her where to find Lawyer Wales." He forked a bite of steak with pensive deliberation. "On the plaza a little while ago she told me she was Madigan's daughter. She said Acey Wales is Whitey Willis's man. That true?"

Red let the question stay unanswered.

"You were mighty friendly with her," Red said evenly. He pulled a match head to spluttering flame under the counter edge and drew the cigarette alight, his stare unblinking.

"She was waiting in a buggy. Why shouldn't I speak?" Johnny picked up the fork. "You nurse-watching me after all?"

Red glanced down at the blue smoke lazing up from the cigarette in his stubby fingers. He had a baffled look, as if his fixed ideas had struck uncertainty. He shrugged finally and reminded: "Walt Powers is trying to be your friend."

"He said so and made a loan," Johnny agreed. "When I start asking who Powers has been talking to, come around and ask me the same. Seen Acey Wales?"

Anger stirred in Red's gaze and was masked. He glanced around. His voice dropped. "Walt knows who shot Hank Willis. We'll ride out tomorrow and get him. All you've got to do is take a look at the skunk and say he's the one you saw. That'll be enough."

"Who is he?"

Red's look was flinty. "You'll know when he's stood up in front of you."

"Sounds like you're sure of it. If the sheriff knows, why does he need me to say so?"

"Makes it more convincing."

Johnny thought it over, studying Red. "Suppose the man doesn't look right to me?"

"He will." Red pulled on the cigarette and let the blue smoke come between them. "He damn' well better look right to you," Red said thinly through lips almost locked. "You ain't packing enough gold dust to buy your way out of jail . . . an' there's always a chance of a prisoner getting killed when Walt tries to make an arrest."

Red slid off the stool quickly as Johnny put the fork down. Red's thumb rested on his gun belt, above the holster. "Grab holt of that fork," Red ordered in the same thin, stiff-lipped tone. "You ain't in no danger while we're friendly. This is advice about who your friends are. And, fellow, you need friends if a stranger ever did. Rip Madigan's mealy-mouthed, sin-shouting friends would put guns at your back and run you to Walt's jail door fast."

"Why?" Johnny asked slowly.

Red grinned unpleasantly. "Crawl in the bed Walt's rented for you at the Western House and sleep on it tonight. If you get ideas about shaking your hocks outta town before you point out the man who shot Hank Willis, swallow 'em. We'll be watchin' you till then. After that you get your pockets full of money and a good horse. Suit you?"

Johnny said: "Maybe. Where's Acey Wales?"

Red stood a moment short and spraddle-legged, his thoughts not readable. "Acey's dead drunk by now. He'll be around tomorrow for another bottle. But you don't need Acey now, kid. You got Walt Powers as long as you keep friendly. He's worth a hundred busted-down whiskey soaks to you. Don't forget it."

Red swung on his heel and walked out. Johnny sat there, stirring a piece of steak with the fork, while his anger went against the double-crossing little whiskey-hungry lawyer.

III

The Western House was a sprawling clapboarded hotel between the plaza and the railroad station. Johnny slept like a drunken man in a back upstairs room.

He came off the creaking green-painted iron bed with sunshine stabbing bright blades through holes in the drawn window shade. He ran up the shade, marked the sun's height, pulled on the new denim pants, and jerked the door open suddenly.

The door opposite was standing ajar. It opened a little more. The raw-boned, tight-mouthed deputy named Hondo peered out.

"Sleep good last night?" Johnny asked with irony, and shut his door on Hondo's muffled curse.

That opposite door had been ajar when the fat hotel clerk brought him up to this room last night. Johnny had guessed then that a man would watch him all night. He looked out the back window. A blue-painted buckboard and a black buggy with shafts stood under trees.

A man lolled in the buggy seat, idly whittling a stick. Johnny marked the amount of whittling he'd done, and then leaned out the window. The whittling stopped. The man turned his head a little, watching.

He'd been out back all night watching this back window. A few feet below the window was the slant cedar-shingled roof of a porch or addition across the back of the hotel. A man could move quietly over the shingles, drop to the ground, and be gone—but they weren't taking chances on that.

Johnny whistled softly as he poured water from the big white pitcher into the wash bowl and washed and dressed. The thick steak and the long sleep had made a new man of him. But when he thought of old Hook Adams, alone far back in the Phantoms, hungry and trusting a crooked town lawyer, Johnny fell silent, his anger building again.

He buckled on the gun belt, glad he'd borrowed enough money from Walt Powers to buy the gun. He tried the slip of the old cedar-handled .44 in the oiled holster. He made a practice draw, and another, and tried the hammer, examining the gun with pleasure. Then Johnny swore softly. The hammer was resting on a live cartridge, so that the dead safety cartridge would turn under the firing pin when the first shot was tried. It made a man worse than unarmed. Lacking a gun, a man might back off from trouble. But a gun that wouldn't fire on the first shot was a dead man's gun.

Dead man's gun! The store clerk had warned him. Johnny wondered if Dave Scrutchfield, who'd owned this gun before him, had met the same trouble when Walt Powers killed him. The gun had been loaded right at the store last night. He'd made certain. Since then it hadn't been pulled from the holster.

Johnny sat on the edge of the bed, took the gun apart, and checked carefully, then he put it back together, slipped in the sixth cartridge, and walked out.

Last night the fat desk clerk had said Johnny Rance's door key was lost. It was a lie. Hondo had been ready to slip in and turn the gun cylinder. That meant they expected Johnny Rance to pull his gun. They meant him to be a dead man when it happened. Dead man with a dead man's gun. . . .

A sign over the lobby desk said *RE-ELECT WALT POWERS*. The dining room on the left was open for breakfast, dishes clattering, voices audible.

Johnny walked out and went back to the Angel Café. The same thick-armed, cheerful waitress brought him coffee, ham, and eggs.

Johnny grinned at her. "Who'll win the election?"

Her good nature went away. She said—"I don't vote."—and walked back to the kitchen.

Other men at the counter had heard him ask it. They looked his way and stayed quiet, busy with their food. A stranger couldn't tell who any man favored.

Hondo wasn't in sight when Johnny paced around the plaza. Tule City was a solid prosperous town on the railroad, serving ranch country far back toward the Phantoms, far in other directions. It was not a dead town at any time. But this morning an unusual number of people seemed to be stirring around. Cardboard signs and election banners were everywhere. This was the day Walt Powers meant to make sure he was re-elected. Johnny turned off the plaza to the wagon yard where Hank Willis had been killed.

The smoky lantern was gone from the gatepost. The yard was half full of wagons and rigs, teams unhitched and tied under an open-front shed at the back. A group of men loitered at the post where the dim figure had stood last night with a shotgun. Marks of the trampling crowd were still visible. Suppressed and bitter antagonisms around that killing still seemed to linger in the clear sunlight. One man nudged another, and heads turned as Johnny came to the spot.

A stranger couldn't tell here, either, who favored Walt Powers or Judith Madigan's father. A broad-faced cowman with worn, serge pants tucked into hard-used boots asked brusquely: "You seen anyone yet who looks like the killer?"

"I've just had breakfast."

It was no answer at all. The ranchman knew it by the way his mouth corners tightened.

A small trash-bordered wagon way ran between the wagon yard fence and the rear of buildings that fronted on the plaza. One of the men said: "Red Kinzie, the deputy, found the shotgun last night. It had been throwed over the fence there into an empty wagon bed."

"I hadn't heard," Johnny said. "Whose gun?"

"They're trying to find out."

"Any tracks where the man stood?"

"Tromped out. . . . Looks like it's up to you."

They studied him. None was friendly. They had the edgy look of men who waited, not knowing what would happen, or what to do about it.

Johnny nodded and started back to the plaza. Halfway there he halted, hardening, as a magnificent rig and matched bays swung smartly off the plaza toward him.

Brass-studded harness glinted in the sunlight. The sleek bay horses, pride of any livery barn, had been curried to a silken sheen. The high single seat rig, washed and polished, was elegant with tasseled pearl-gray sun top and curving dash.

The driver sat stiffly erect, fingering reins and long red-handled carriage whip. In shiny new silk hat, starched collar, black string tie, fine broadcloth frock coat, expensive yellow gloves, old Acey was elegant and carefree as he flicked the whip.

Johnny came out of the stunned surprise and lunged into the street. The bays shied. He grabbed a rein and stopped them, knowing every man at the wagon yard was watching.

"A salubrious good morning to you, my young friend!" Acey Wales called cordially. "You rested well last night, I trust?"

"Hold this damned team. Get over on that seat," Johnny raged under his breath.

"Join me, sir," the little lawyer urged. He moved over as Johnny went up fast beside him.

A barber had worked hard, trimming shaggy hair and stained gray mustache. The face that had been haggard, not too clean, glowed pinkly from massage. Acey Wales stank of powder and cologne water, and the rich odor of cloves and whiskey.

"I ought to gut-shoot you right here," Johnny raged. "Drive on, you pocket-picking, low-down, lying old thief. Drive out of town while I make up my mind."

"Indeed, yes, my young friend."

The long whip sent the spirited bays smartly on past the wagon yard. Every man there gaped.

Acey Wales was beaming. Farther on he bowed to a lady sweeping her porch, and swept on past, leaving the lady in frozen, open-mouthed astonishment.

"Missus Tilly Hobson," Acey confided to Johnny. "The dear lady stopped speaking to me some years ago."

"She showed sense," Johnny snapped. "More sense than I did. Drive on and keep your mouth shut. That butter voice of yours riles me more each time I hear it."

Acey Wales drove on grandly, bowing to right and left as they passed startled townspeople on walks and porches.

Johnny set his mouth hard when he saw what was going to happen when the splendid rig and pair passed the white picket fence where Judith Madigan had waited on her horse yesterday evening. Judith was at the front gate, talking with her father. Rip Madigan recognized them first, and said something to his daughter. Both were looking as Acey Wales saluted them with a bow and lift of the red whip handle.

Rip Madigan in the bright light of day lacked the look of a town man. A long-barreled roan horse stood ground-tied at the walk. He was in plain black broadcloth pants and coat, and pinch-top black hat. His short crisp mustache was graying. His tied-down gun showed under his coat. A saddle gun was on the horse, and Madigan stood, unsmiling and level-eyed, as they rolled by. His daughter seemed to grow taller and more remote as her own look ignored the lift of Johnny's hat and Acey's bow.

Johnny jammed the hat back on his head. His face was red, and he was inwardly raging. Anger at the dressed-up old faker beside him was getting dangerous as they passed under the cloth election sign at the edge of town.

Acey Wales thrust reins and whip at Johnny and slumped in the cushioned seat.

"Been wantin' to do that for a long time," Acey confessed unsteadily. "Sundays I used to drive out like this, sober like I am now, proud as any man in town."

Johnny pulled the bays to a walk.

"I trusted you like Hook Adams said to. And got double-crossed fast as your thieving hands could get in my saddlebags. Went straight to the sheriff with everything, didn't you? That deputy, Red, knew about the dust last night."

Acey Wales put the silk hat on the seat. He wiped perspiration from his forehead with a new linen handkerchief.

"I need a drink," he groaned. "It was Whitey Willis I went to. Used my judgment as your lawyer."

"And cashed in my gold, and started on a big drunk."

"Whitey would question me anyway about your business in town, and Walt Powers would, too. I took the poke of dust you said was mine, and one poke of yours. I told Whitey how you were in trouble and had to get rid of it quietly. Whitey and Walt Powers understand things like that."

"I wasn't in real trouble until you got greedy for whiskey money."

"You were broke, son, and so was I. Had to have money. If I'd said you panned that gold yourself, all hell would have started. I had to make everything reasonable to Whitey Willis."

"That was your crooked whiskey throat talking. I could have told him I had gold dust."

"Not like I could, boy. Not like old Acey, your lawyer. I told Whitey how you were on the run from a shooting scrape in Utah when your horse gave out. I told him how the old prospector whose mule you took raised a fuss about giving up his gold dust and you had to kill him."

"I never killed anyone, you lying old whiskey gut."

"Whitey understands how a young fellow on the dodge and needing money quick would hunt up a lawyer he'd heard of, and have to keep close-mouthed to others. Whitey paid good for the gold, figuring to use you in this election."

"You bleary-eyed old liar. Making a thief and a killer out of me."

"A big lie is better'n a little one," Acey Wales said huskily. He held trembling hands out and tried to steady them. "Only had one drink for breakfast. Not enough to hold off the shakes for very long." He reached in his coat. "Here's your half of what Whitey paid. I had to take paper money, so 'twouldn't weight me down. Your mule is in a Mexican's shed at the edge of town. Friend of mine. I dug a little hole in the corner of the shed and buried the other two pokes of dust. They're safe. You're the Utah Kid now . . . a hardcase young killer from up north, drifting toward the border. Whitey and Walt Powers won't give you away."

Johnny took the money and said: "The Utah Kid." It stirred him to wry humor. "You lie big when you start trying."

Acey Wales looked out across the yellow-cured short grass and dusty-gray sage clumps. He spoke low. "Been some time since anyone has needed me. It did something. I dressed up and hired this rig and started for a drive to keep my mind off the bottles on the Acey-Deuce backbar."

Johnny put the roll of bills in his pocket. "Hook Adams was right about you, mister. We'll ride back to Hook Adams's creek together. Ain't a drink of whiskey in a week's walk there. You'll be cold sober for life, and rich, when you come out."

Acey Wales sat rigid. "Sounds like a whiskey dream," he said huskily.

Johnny leaned out and looked back. Two riders were jogging out of town after them.

"You played hell with your Utah Kid," Johnny decided. "Walt Powers thinks he can crowd me now. Red Kinzie laid it out last night. I wasn't sure what he meant. I see now. If I don't take their brand in this election, I'll be arrested as an outlaw killer. They'll probably shoot me down if they try an arrest. Red Kinzie made a strong hint it'd happen that way."

The little lawyer was disturbed. He muttered: "I sure didn't expect that."

"If Walt Powers arrests me, the gold Willis bought can be used for proof that I am a killer," Johnny said. "The only way out of that would be to prove where I got it. I can't, without killing Hook Adams's luck. Hook's waited all his life for it."

"Messed everything up, didn't I?" Acey all but groaned. "The election didn't seem very important last night."

"It is now," Johnny said soberly. He drove for some moments in silence. "Would Rip Madigan make a good sheriff?"

"The best," Acey Wales said without hesitation. "Rip was a fighting deputy in Texas as a young man. He trailed two outlaws over into this country and had to kill one. Rip met a girl here, and came back and married her. They lived in Texas, then moved here and bought a small ranch out toward Big Elk Cañon. Got a fine little ranch out there now."

"He's a damned fool to want the sheriff's job," said Johnny almost resentfully. He leaned out and looked back again. The two riders were keeping their distance, pacing the buggy.

Acey Wales drew an unopened pint from inside the new frock coat. Johnny looked in silence. Acey hesitated, sighed, threw the bottle out into ragged gray sage beside the dusty road. He clenched shaky hands on his knees and spoke without emotion. "Whitey Willis is the biggest man for a hundred miles. Owns the most land, cattle, and horses. He started broke, dealing a faro bank. Now he's got his hand in everything, including who's elected to any office. He looks out for his friends. It makes some folks speak well of him."

"He could be worse."

"A rattler," said Acey, "is bad, and lets the world know it. I've heard the Mexicans talk about a little gray-backed snake that can hardly be noticed in the sand. A man is dying before he knows that snake bit him."

"Like Whitey does?" Johnny asked thoughtfully.

The little lawyer watched the walking gray horses. His new

finery and dignity just missed being pathetic.

"Whiskey didn't stop my eyes or ears," he said nervously. "Made me hear more if anything. I wasn't worth bothering about. Folks who cross Whitey Willis get run over. They get rustled and hit with hard luck. Sometimes they get shot. Walt Powers is the man who makes the law work for Whitey. The right kind of sheriff would clean up a lot of gun-toting men Whitey can count on for anything. It would jam a big spade bit in Whitey's hungry mouth."

"And Rip Madigan wants to be that sheriff?"

"Seems so. He might as well move on if he loses. Whitey and Walt Powers won't forget him after this election. Rip's talked plain, trying to make folks see what's happened on this range."

"Madigan hasn't got a chance," Johnny said flatly. "Walt Powers has already picked the man he'll charge with killing Hank Willis."

Acey Wales was startled. "Who is it?"

"I don't know. Bound to be one of Madigan's friends. I'm to swear he's the one I saw with the shotgun. Red Kinzie warned me last night. If I don't point right, I'll be killed when they arrest me as the Utah Kid."

"They'll do it, too. I thought I had a few brains left when I tried to explain everything by making you an outlaw."

"It made Red Kinzie tip their hand last night. Election's tomorrow. Not much time . . . but I've got a cold ace. I know who killed Hank Willis."

The little lawyer started. "Who did it?"

"It'd scare you straight to a whiskey bottle. Let me worry about it."

Acey Wales wiped the white linen handkerchief over his tired face again. "As your lawyer, I can't advise you to get killed. Drive on to a ranch. Buy a horse. Keep going. You can get grub for your partner at some other town."

"Look behind us."

Acey Wales looked. He mopped his face again as he faced front.

"One of them is Hondo Matthews."

Johnny's grin spread thinly. He took the bays to the roadside, and sharply around, turning back. "You're the Utah Kid's lawyer, mister. Might say you're his daddy. Get your backbone stiff. I'll need you."

Acey put the shiny new silk hat back on his head. His thin shoulders straightened in the new frock coat.

"There was a time I wasn't afraid of any man if the cause was right." Acey leaned forward, studying the two riders ahead. "That's big Charley Nash with Hondo," he said with concern. "Nash is Walt's deputy at Wildhorse. He's killed a man or two and whipped other good men. Walt must be bringing in his men for trouble."

Johnny slashed lightly with the red-handled whip, and the bay horses jumped into a hard run.

"I'll stop off at Rip Madigan's house," said Johnny, tight-lipped now at what lay ahead. "You drive on and get my saddle and rifle. Have that rope-held stirrup fixed quick as a shop can get leather on. Then buy me a fast saddle horse. I'll give you money and meet you on the plaza."

"You'll need a fast horse when Walt Powers and Whitey hear you've stopped to see Madigan," Acey Wales said nervously.

"They won't get dangerous until they bring Madigan's friend to town for me to look at," Johnny guessed. "The minute they don't need me, I'm a dead man walking."

"I hated to tell you." Acey held the silk hat hard down on his head as the running pair whipped wind around them. He sounded fatalistic. "You know too much. Might talk. Whitey's too smart to take a chance."

"Hook Adams used to say there never was a wolf so smart he

couldn't be caught."

"He never knew Whitey."

They whirled gray dust by the waiting deputies. Johnny marked the Wildhorse man, big and flat-faced and surly—a man for trouble.

The roan saddle horse was gone from Madigan's house. Johnny gave the reins to Acey Wales, peeled off bills to buy a saddle horse, and got down.

"Missus Madigan's mother lives here, but it'll mean the same to Whitey," Acey said. He tried to smile. It was a haggard effort. His hands were shaking again. "I could use a bucket of whiskey," he said huskily as he drove on.

Johnny walked to the neat white-painted cottage and knocked.

Judith opened the door and stood unsmiling. Her silent antagonism held him off, a stranger, challenging his presence at this door.

"I stopped to see your father," Johnny told her, too abruptly, he realized. Her level, gray-blue gaze pushed at him.

"Rip isn't here, and he doesn't want to see you. He's seen enough already."

The strike of shod hoofs came abreast of the house, and Judith looked out at the deputies. One horse audibly pulled to a slow walk; the other went into a faster lope after Acey's rig. Johnny did not look around.

She said with slow contempt: "Your friend is waiting."

It was the way she said it. The way she looked. Nothing Johnny Rance said was going to be believed. Anger was a thing he hadn't counted on. But it came, flaring at her. He knew it was too late to stop.

"None of this is my business. I'm a fool to try and help Rip Madigan. I don' know why I'm here."

Judith colored. Her own anger was quieter, but as blunt.

"How much were you paid to try this? Acey Wales wore rags yesterday. You were as bad. Now you both have money to throw around." She hardly paused for an angry breath. "Tell Whitey Willis that Rip isn't interested, whatever the scheme is."

She was closing the door when Johnny blocked it with a quick foot and spoke to the small opening. "My father won his sheriff's election in Wyoming when I was a kid, and in three month he was shot by rustlers. I had him on my mind when I stopped here. If you've got sense at all, tell your father, if he wants to win this election, he'll have to fight."

Her breathlessly angry voice came back through the blocked opening.

"Rip wants to be sheriff because it's his duty to friends and neighbors!"

"Then they'd better help him. One of his friends will be arrested today for killing Hank Willis."

"Which friend?"

"I don't know."

"I don't believe you."

Johnny took back his foot and the door shut with hard finality. He swung off the porch, anger still building to an unreasonable pitch.

Hondo had pulled up a little beyond the property, lounging in the saddle, looking back at the cottage porch. He waited now, and, when Johnny came abreast and hauled up balefully, Hondo gave him a surly comment, shot with malicious pleasure: "Looked like she shut you out."

"Where's the sheriff and Red Kinzie?" Johnny asked.

"None of your business if I knowed, which I don't. They rode out." Hondo spat. "A gutter bum like Acey an' a burr-tailed range tramp like you sure flew high today. Whitey must've greased your hands plenty . . . and it wasn't fer nosin' around a fancy-stepper like Madigan's gal."

There was a silent second in which Hondo sensed his danger. His hand swayed near his gun butt. His surly readiness was confident. Johnny wheeled toward the plaza.

Rip Madigan was not there. Johnny made the circuit, noticing again that the town had the look of filling for the day—and not for business. There was a kind of loitering, tense anticipation under the drench of high-climbing sun. It was a feeling that might have run out from the crowded plaza last night, and across the range, the way important news could race.

Johnny stopped in front of the bank on the east side of the plaza. He was there, facing the hitch rack, saddle horses and buckboards before him, when Judith Madigan rode her blue roan gelding into the plaza at a fast lope.

She pulled to a slow trot, riding side-saddle today, and scanning faces along the walk and in the center of the plaza. It took a moment to realize how quickly she must have changed into the darker riding skirt, the soft buckskin jacket, and same wide-brimmed hat dropped back over her shoulders.

Johnny stood, not moving, as Judith pulled up before the barbershop on the north side of the plaza. A tall black-bearded man standing there stepped out to her.

They talked for brief moments. Then Judith reined around and shook the horse out. She left the plaza, riding west at a gallop.

The black-bearded man in turn went back fast to the barbershop door and evidently summoned another man out. Johnny could see the second man, a ranchman also, nodding and instinctively hitching his gun belt, as if the six-gun entered his mind from their talk.

The two men parted there, the second man starting across the plaza with long strides. The black-bearded man walked to a dry-goods store and turned in with a look of haste and purpose.

Hondo's surly suspicion spoke at Johnny's left shoulder. "She came quick to find Bob Abbot. He's Madigan's best friend. What'n hell did you say to her that riled 'em fast like this?"

Johnny started to leave, not answering.

Hondo's grab at his elbow stopped him. "Stand still, you damned saddle tramp! What you up to?"

Johnny turned, jerked by his elbow. He was hard, lean from mountain work and placer digging. All of it—muscle, bone, and thought of the dead man's gun fixed for him last night— smashed behind his balled fist.

Hondo hadn't expected it. A gun, maybe. Hondo's squinty scowl was on the holster when hard knuckles tore his mouth against his teeth.

Hondo rocked back a step, spraying red droplets as he spat a tooth chip. He gobbled fury and pain and snatched for his gun.

"I'll kill you fer that! I'll gun-whip your face flat! Git back . . . !"

Johnny followed him, furious and fast, not talking as red spittle and fury spewed from the mashed mouth. Hondo was banking on the dead man's gun not firing—he was dizzy and slow anyway. Johnny, out of Hook Adams's hungry prospector camps, used to making each cartridge count, had the edge. Hondo was a dead man and didn't know it.

Johnny had a choice in the flash it took to crowd in and yank his dead-man's gun. He let death go by and clubbed the steel gun barrel in under the black hat with his own cold fury. A skull-sledged steer at Eastern packers never dropped quicker than the Tule City deputy. Hondo hit the dusty walk boards hard, hat falling off, gun sliding from his lax grip, blood dribbling from his mashed mouth.

Breathing hard, Johnny holstered the gun.

Then it hit him like a low punch. He'd done publicly what Acey Wales had done on the quiet. He'd stepped into outlaw boots. He'd gun-slugged a law badge, like the Utah Kid might have done. He was outside the law now. They could handle him like an outlaw. And they would when Hondo mouthed his raging suspicions. And that would be soon enough. There hadn't been time for Acey Wales to buy a horse. The Wildhorse deputy wasn't in sight when Johnny looked around. Nearby men were running toward the bank. Two men stepped out of the bank and blankly eyed the blood-dribbling deputy.

Johnny said: "When he gits up, tell him to keep away from me."

He walked with fast strides toward the Acey-Deuce bar. And old Hook Adam's warning mocked him. *No girls. . . . Git you in trouble.* He could hear that voice repeating it over and over again.

IV

The barkeep in the Acey-Deuce said Whitey Willis was back in the office. Word of the trouble hadn't reached here. But attention left the faro game against the wall, heads turned from the bar, following Johnny back to an open passage and a door on the right marked *OFFICE*.

Johnny walked in on low-voiced talk between the gambler and the flat-faced Wildhorse deputy. Their blank regard suggested they'd been talking about him.

"Your badge partner is stretched in front of the bank," Johnny brusquely told the deputy.

Whitey Willis sat at a roll-top desk in shirt sleeves. A window let light against his ash-pale stare and unmoved comment. "I didn't hear a shot."

"I buffaloed him."

The Wildhorse deputy spilled a surprised oath. Whitey touched the silky brown mustache with absent habit and shrugged.

"That Hondo tries to stir up trouble. Ed, tell the fool he's lucky he isn't dead."

It was an order and a dismissal. It said Whitey Willis thought Rance, the stranger, was dangerous. Ed stood in new caution, and then walked out.

Money had evidently changed hands in here. A lacquered money box stood open on the desk, gold coins beside it. Willis picked up a double eagle and tapped the edge slowly against the desk wood.

"Slugging Hondo helps, Kid. They won't think you're friendly to us now. I bought your gold dust. Madigan wouldn't have touched it. Why did you go to Madigan this morning?"

He might have been impassively cutting cards in a high-stake game, quiet, sure of himself. But Willis owned the Acey-Deuce and no telling how many of the men and guns along the bar. He owned Walt Powers and the law. He was a smart gambler, not worried by a young drifting outlaw.

"I didn't see Madigan," said Johnny shortly.

Hook Adams claimed any wolf could be trapped. Johnny wondered about this wolf while he watched sensitive fingers turn the gold coin so swiftly it seemed to disappear in the turn, Willis not even glancing at it.

"Set your sights high, didn't you, Kid? I hear she slammed the door in your face."

"You paid for hearing it."

"I get what I pay for. And I bought your gold dust. . . ."

"From my lawyer. Got what you paid for, too. Gold dust."

"Want more?"

"I want plain talk. Red Kinzie says I'm to swear a certain man killed your brother."

Willis nodded. "Walt and Red are bringing him to town now . . . a loud-mouthed, two-bit rancher named Cultis Day, who's been going broke on the sage flats over toward Salt Creek. Hank loaned Day money . . . my money, but Hank held the notes. When Day started riding the fence lines, electioneering for Madigan, Hank talked to him and got cussed out. Hank attached Day's cattle. They had words about it yesterday in George Howard's Drugstore."

The door was shoved open. The barkeep thrust his head in. "Whitey, they just carried Hondo Matthews over to Doc Sweetwater's office. You hear about it?"

"Yes. Don't bother me."

Johnny relaxed as the door closed. "You think this Cultis Day shotgunned your brother?"

The coin flipped again in the fast fingers. Whitey Willis shrugged indifferently. "He could have. Day was drinking yesterday and hating Hank. Day is a widower. He thought he was courting a certain lady last night. When he claims he was with her, she'll swear he wasn't. No one else can say they were with him at the time."

Johnny grinned thinly, studying the gambler. "So you've got him cold-decked and me to swear I saw him shoot. You'll hang him for it, knowing he was with the lady at the time. Last night you wanted the man who shot your brother. Now any sorry trap bait will do."

Willis said with sudden viciousness: "We've been talking election."

It was the first break in his cold calm. He slammed the gold piece in the money box, scooped up the other pieces, and slammed them, too, and carried the box to a green-painted iron safe. His chalky face was drawn as he yanked the fancy-tooled gun belt and silver-mounted gun off a wall peg.

"Cultis Day is business. Walt Powers thought of using him, and planted Day's shotgun in the wagon yard. Walt's got a head on him when he doesn't get too greedy. I need Walt re-elected. This two-bit Cultis Day will swing the election. I didn't get where I am by overlooking sure bets like Day, who's against me anyway."

Whitey Willis gave a vicious yank buckling the gun belt on. His long soft hand drew the silver-bright gun like it had flipped the gold coin. Too fast to follow.

"Hank was my kid brother. The only one I trusted. I'll bury Hank this afternoon. Then I'll find who really killed him. How do you stand on this Cultis Day?"

"Take that damned gun off me. I didn't kill your brother." Johnny took the roll of money from his pocket. "Madigan's side knows your fat-faced sheriff is crooked. They don't trust me. When I say this Cultis Day is the one, I'll be a gun target. I borrowed a hundred from your sheriff last night. Pay him."

Willis took the money. A thin grin quirked one side of his mouth. "Your liver crawling, Kid?"

"Make your own guess."

Whitey Willis brushed the silky brown mustaches, in the way of a man who thought well of his looks. The half smile lingered. "You're safe, Kid. This two-bit Cultis Day is only bait. A man Madigan thinks is boosting him will start the trouble. Then they'll bury Rip Madigan tomorrow instead of voting for him. Step out to the bar and size up the men who'll be close when you run the iron on Cultis Day."

Johnny stood at the back end of the long bar, drinking beer, eyeing the men Willis spoke to. Hardcases, gun-hung, expectant, when Willis came along the bar. Men like that had killed Big Bill Rance years ago in Wyoming. The memories still vivid, Johnny held the wet beer glass hard, wondering if Rip Madigan's girl would have the same strangled silence after guns blasted her father down. Rip Madigan didn't have a chance. He was cold-decked, with the dead-man's card ready for the cut. Johnny Rance had stirred it up. Johnny Rance had baited Judith into thinking this election was important. She'd know different when

Rip Madigan lay bloody at her feet.

Johnny took a hard bitter swig of beer against tightness in his throat. *No girls. . . . Git you in trouble.* He was thinking of it when the bat doors slapped open. The fast entrance of Red Kinzie made Johnny set the beer glass down hard.

Red's urgent harshness rang through the long barroom. "We just brought in the skunk who kilt Hank Willis! We're gettin' argument about it from a hunch led by Bob Abbot! Walt Powers needs deputies!"

Johnny turned away abruptly while every eye was on Red. He was half running as he went back past the saloon office. He heard the gritty resonance of Whitey Willis demanding: "Who was it killed Hank?"

Then Johnny was out the back door and they hadn't seen him go, and he ran through the trash-cluttered alley to the corner and wheeled toward the plaza. Silence seemed to crouch over the plaza in the bright midday sunshine. That was the first impression. Taut silence was building in fine dust drift raised by many feet. But threading the silence was a stirring undertone of movement and talk, and the brisk thud of booted feet on boardwalks leading to the plaza.

It was as if Tule City had been waiting. Saddle horses, buckboards, and buggies had brought men and women in off the range all through the long sunny morning. The hurried moves of Judith Madigan and Bob Abbot, the quick savage fracas with Hondo, had helped crowd the plaza quickly with men primed for trouble. The movement was toward an uneasy focus on the north side of the plaza. Johnny was brought up short by a tall bearded man on the corner, watching.

"Rip Madigan over there?"

"Nope. But he'll be here quick, I hear."

The splendid livery rig Acey Wales had hired could be picked out as far as a man could see. It was there on the south side of the plaza, in front of a saloon. Any other time the run of a man across the open plaza, under the tall cottonwoods, would have caught every eye. Now with the focus of attention on the north side, and other men moving fast toward it, the run Johnny made caught scant attention. Mounted men were at the center of the gathering crowd. The bulgy angry face of Walt Powers on a horse showed there. Powers was talking vehemently.

Acey Wales stepped out of the saloon as Johnny sprinted to the buggy. "Where's my horse?" Johnny snapped.

"Saddle won't be ready for an hour."

Johnny swore softly. "This rig will have to do. Get in. Are you sober?"

"Too sober," Acey Wales groaned as the rig lurched around. "I stepped in the Eaglehead for one short bracer. Then I asked for water. Drank it, too."

Johnny swung the fast matched bays west out of the plaza and cut with the red-handled whip and they bolted. Acey Wales snatched off the new plug hat with trembling hands.

"I heard you'd gun-whipped Hondo Matthews and guessed you were ready for a break out of town. It's the best thing to do. A lawyer can't do much for you on dropping a deputy. Not here in Tule City. I was trying to find you to tell you the saddle wasn't ready."

Johnny steadied the wild-running bays. He had to lift his voice above the trip-hammer beat of racing hoofs. "We're after Rip Madigan. His daughter rode this way. I'm taking a chance she went after him."

Acey Wales looked sick. "You aren't leaving while your skin is safe?"

"Don't know what I'm doing."

"Acting like a lovesick young fool, it sounds like."

"That's whiskey talk."

Johnny peered at two riders heading toward them, one riding

side-saddle. They were coming fast.

Rip Madigan's leather-hued face held hard suspicion as he pulled the sweat-streaked roan up beside the tassel-topped rig. Acey Wales held the reins now and Johnny was standing by the near front wheel.

"Got news for you," said Johnny soberly. "Better light and talk it over."

Madigan stepped down, holding the bridle reins, a wiry short man, level-eyed and searching.

Johnny met the look. "Walt Powers has brought in your friend, Cultis Day, for shooting Hank Willis. It's a frame-up."

Madigan's face darkened. "How do you and Acey Wales know so much about it?"

"Whitey Willis told me. The idea is to suck you into gun play over Cultis Day. He's the bait. Then they'll get you and settle the election today."

The weathered face with squint wrinkles at the eye corners went to the expensive livery rig and Acey Wales in all his new splendor. Madigan's gaze dropped back to Johnny with hard clarity. "You think I'd better stay out of town?"

A false mildness in the question brought brusqueness to Johnny's retort. "It's a cold-stacked deck. I didn't know how bad it was when I was at your house."

Madigan's slow smile laid on contempt. "Tell Willis I'm obliged for sending you. When I get to town, he'll see it didn't work."

Rip Madigan was turning back to his horse when Johnny said softly: "Mister Madigan. . . ."

Judith cried a warning as her father turned back. Rip Madigan caught at his low-tied gun. Johnny's whipping gun barrel was already in under the black hat, and Rip Madigan went down. The sweaty saddle roan snorted, sidled uneasily as Johnny caught the limp figure out of the road dust with a heave and a grunt, and loaded it into the rig at Acey Wales's feet.

"Drive him as far from town as you can get, Acey."

He heard the quick-urged move of Judith's horse. Johnny turned and heard a carbine levered hastily. Judith's order was almost a gasp of anger. "Both of you stay where you are!"

Acey's thin, shaky certainty came at Johnny's back from the rig seat. "You ain't lovesick, Johnny, you're crazy! I can't law you out of things like this."

Judith had Rip Madigan's carbine. Above the swirl of her skirts on the side-saddle, her white anger sighted along the barrel.

"Take him on, Acey," Johnny repeated, not looking around.

Judith squeezed the trigger, and her horse jumped as the shot slammed. Johnny's upper left arm got the sledging bullet. It rocked him with a numbness and a moment's fog of purpose while the frightened livery bays were bolting.

They raced away from Tule City with Acey Wales's helpless protest. Judith's horse was halfway across the road before she levered in a fresh shell and got control.

She gasped: "Stop him!"

Johnny stood in silence as she gave the impossible order in thin huskiness. Judith looked after the buggy, then tried to sight along the wavering gun barrel. She suddenly let the carbine drop to the road dust and said: "You're bleeding." She bit her lip, swallowed hard, and sat looking at him in white misery.

Johnny glanced down at his sleeve, holed front and back on the upper arm and already staining dark with new blood. Judith came off the side-saddle unsteadily against him and he steadied her as if used to it.

"When your father sits up, he'll do better rawhiding Acey Wales than busting into town and getting voted out with hired guns. They're waiting for him," said Johnny soberly. "I was eleven when they brought my father home in a wagon. Don't want it to happen to you?"

He released her arm then, not sure she'd paid attention, for she ordered: "Take off your jacket."

The wound was a raw tear through muscle. Johnny surrendered his knife on request and turned his back while cloth ripped under Judith's skirts with hurried urgency. She was pale when she finished the bandaging and helped him back into the new canvas jacket.

Johnny dusted off her father's carbine, thrust it back in the saddle scabbard, and said: "I'll borrow his horse."

There was no remoteness now in Judith's look or her quiet demand. "What will you do?"

"Ride back to town and see what's happening," said Johnny vaguely. Her knit brow warned that he'd not told enough. Johnny added reasonably: "I think I know who killed Hank Willis. Can't let this Cultis Day take the blame."

She said then abruptly: "Would your father have gone out that day if he'd known what was going to happen?"

Johnny nodded, not having to wonder about it. Always, forever, he'd have that prideful knowledge about Big Bill Rance. "He had the badge," Johnny said, not suspecting his look as he said it. He only felt sure and proud about Big Bill. It helped his grin as he gave Judith a hand up to her side-saddle and made his own climb to Rip Madigan's horse.

Judith said, and tightness made it an effort: "Be careful until Rip can get there."

"Tell him to stay out of town today."

Her smile had a look like his own feeling about Big Bill Rance. "Rip asked for the badge," said Judith evenly.

There should have been an answer to that, but Johnny couldn't think what it should be as Judith lashed the long rein ends and rode fast from him, west again, where Acey Wales's gleaming livery rig had vanished in the growing swell and break of the tumbled range.

Johnny reined Rip Madigan's horse toward town, sobering, thinking again of old Hook Adams. . . . *Git you in trouble.*

It hadn't taken long to drive swiftly out of town and ride back fast. But in that time the plaza had filled, and tempers were frayed. Johnny sensed it when he reached men clotted at the plaza corner and heard a challenging call: "That's Rip Madigan's horse! Where's Rip?"

"Coming!" Johnny called back. "Where's the sheriff?"

He was answered from the crowd in grim sharpness. "Right where he was, until Rip gits here!"

Johnny felt tightness, too, as he walked the sweating, dust-caked roan toward the point where Walt Powers was still at bay. He made a guess why the prisoner hadn't been taken on to jail. The courthouse would block off the crowd, cut off what was said, make a gun trap for Rip Madigan almost impossible. A stranger, not caring what happened, could have appreciated this trap held open with gambler's patience.

Walt Powers had put his prisoner on an empty freight wagon. The weathered wagon sheet was rolled to the back bow, and Walt Powers and the handcuffed prisoner sat on the board seat, facing rear. Red Kinzie stood, spraddle-legged and alert, in the wagon bed, smoking a cigarette. He had a peaceful look.

Recognition ran ahead as the dust-caked roan horse picked a slow way past men in the street. Johnny saw Red Kinzie say something that brought Walt Powers hastily off the seat.

He noted Whitey Willis on the boardwalk in the crowd, standing passively. Scattered in the crowd around the wagon were faces Willis had spoken to in the Acey-Deuce. Everything was under control, waiting for Rip Madigan.

Walt Powers's loud demand held temper as Johnny rode up beside the wagon. "What you doing on Madigan's horse?"

"Riding it," said Johnny amiably.

Powers's temper was rising, but when Hondo Matthews climbed fast over the off front wheel, doctor's white stickum tape closing a gash over his ear and his bruised his lips snarling, Walt Powers snapped: "Keep out of this, Hondo!" And then to Johnny: "How'd you get that horse? Where's Madigan?"

Now silence around the freight wagon had a deadly weight. Johnny eased himself in the saddle and grinned. "Madigan had an accident. He's coming. That the man you say did the shooting last night?"

"Never mind that! We're waiting for Madigan!"

"What's Madigan got to do with it? Did he see the shooting?"

This wasn't the way it had been planned. Powers let his temper go. "Madigan's friends are butting in! This fellow's guilty as hell an' he's going in jail quick when Madigan gets here!"

Back in the crowd a man yelled: "Stranger, you seen the shootin'. Take a look at the man Powers brought in!"

Johnny turned in the saddle. "What's the evidence?"

The same voice answered: "They found Cultis Day's shotgun in the wagon yard last night. Day says he left his shotgun an' spotted hair vest in his lady friend's kitchen while he took a nap on her sofa after supper. When he woke up, his gun an' his vest were gone an' Hank Willis was dead. He rode home to think it over an' the sheriff got him this morning."

"A man who sleeps when calling on a lady ought to sneak home and think it over." Johnny grinned, and heard scattered laughter as he turned to the wagon. "Sheriff, what does the lady say?"

Walt Powers scowled at him. "She says it's a lie! Didn't feed no one last night! A committee asked her while we sat here! You saw the shootin'. Here he is, short, with a dark hat like you seen. Stand up, Day!"

Johnny eyed the sallow, uneasy prisoner, short and thin, with a flat-crowned black hat and handcuffed wrists. Cultis Day had a dazed look, as if not sure what was happening to him, and beginning to be frightened by it.

"A short man with a spotted haired-skin vest and a dark hat shot Hank Willis," Johnny said loud enough to carry. "If the lady told the truth, this fellow wasn't at her house. So no one stole his gun and vest. You found his gun. Where's his vest?"

They were listening on all sides of the wagon, not moving, sensing from the reasonable questions and Powers's growing anger that something important was happening, waiting to set their minds and perhaps to act.

Walt Powers stirred angrily. His voice carried in a heated blare. "He threw the damn' vest away! It wasn't at his place! He's the one, ain't he?"

"A man fool enough to throw his shotgun away and use a lady he hadn't talked to for a lying alibi would be fool enough to shuck off his haired vest, too." Johnny grinned. "Sure the vest wasn't in the wagon yard, too?"

An incisive demand rang out. It was Whitey Willis, edging forward among the men on the plank walk. "What are you driving at, Kid?"

Johnny thought of the streaking gun draw Willis could make. He set feet with slow firmness in the stirrups and cut the deadman's card before all the crowd. "If the lady told the truth, this Cultis Day is a blind fool. If Day told the truth, some man who knew he was at the lady's house killed your brother and planted the gun after the killing. Use your head, Willis. The killer wore the haired vest. I said so last night. Saw it plain when he stood spraddle-legged and called to your brother."

"Spraddle-legged?"

The tight-wound crowd caught the ferocity in Willis's cry and moved uneasily.

Red caught it. Walt Powers swung, startled, toward the tone, shouting: "He's a damned liar, Whitey! He's throwed in with Madigan, like Hondo said!"

Whitey Willis sounded strangled, all his gambler's calm gone. "I didn't think of that haired vest, you fat bushwhacking snake."

"Red!" Walt Powers bawled, ducking, clawing the Texas holster inside his coat.

Red was whirling in a crouch toward Willis when the gun blast on the plank walk shattered the last peace. Johnny didn't see the draw. He doubted if anyone else did, either, even Walt Powers. But the sheriff's bawl to Red had held a snapping fear, and the fear was on the mottled sag of his bulgy face. A .45 slug caught that blotchy fear on a cheek bone, mushrooming, tearing out the front part of Walt Powers's heavy face.

Walt Powers went limply around, his arm flying out and his greenish eyes bulging. His horrified knowledge of death looked out over the crowd as a second shot sledged through his thick chest. Powers fell hard against the wagon side, all of it in an exploding moment. The crowd's sound was like a fast sigh, then a frightened shout, and then the tumult of a stampeding herd.

Johnny saw little of it. He was watching Hondo's bruised mouth turn hard at the corners with purpose. He lost sight of the deputy for an instant as Walt Powers staggered around and fell, and the prisoner lunged in fright flat onto the wagon bed. Hondo was pulling his gun when Johnny saw him again. Johnny wondered, as stirrup-firmed feet braced his draw, if Hondo still banked on the dead-man's gun not firing. He drew and fired as you had to do when living with Hook Adams—not missing because cartridges were always few.

Muzzle flame and black powder smoke topped Hondo's shot, driving it awry, doubling the raw-boned man half over as the slug tore through his middle. He'd die slowly, but he'd probably die. He was paralyzed by shock now.

Madigan's roan horse jumped as Hondo went back against

the board wagon seat, both hands pressing his belly. Guns were still crashing. Red's fast-drawn gun, Whitey Willis's gun, and abortive firing came from the stampeding crowd through which the roan horse was trying to bolt.

Johnny brought the roan to its haunches after two men had been knocked aside, one falling and scrambling up and plunging away from the gun battle. Then, almost violently, quiet struck through the gray dust haze.

As Johnny brought the snorting roan around, a few men, six-guns in hand, stood in the open near the freight wagon. He recognized several of the men who had been in the Acey-Deuce. Willis's men were waiting, wondering. They stood scattered now in the armed frame of the trap set for Rip Madigan. They'd had their orders and none of this had fitted the pattern of the trap. They stood in a kind of loose uncertainty, Walt Powers dead and Red Kinzie down out of sight in the wagon bed.

The roan sidled unwillingly to the wagon back, snorting at the blood and powder reek. Johnny looked past the wagon at a thin sensitive hand hanging over the edge of the plank walk. The silver-bright gun lay in the dirt below. Men were peering cautiously that way from store entrances.

Red Kinzie sprawled in the wagon bed. Hondo had slid down, sitting, still holding his belly, face like loose putty, a faint slobber of red seeping from his bruised mouth. The flat-stretched prisoner lifted a chalky face. Gun still cocked, he faced west, where men cautiously ventured out into the plaza again. Beyond them, beyond the plaza, dust lifted behind a tasseled rig top racing into town. A side-saddle rider was keeping pace.

Johnny wheeled the roan away from the wagon and spoke flat truth to the uncertain men scattered out, not sure what to do now that Willis was dead.

"Be a new sheriff tomorrow who won't like what Willis had in mind."

He left them with that disturbing thought and spurred the roan toward the oncoming rig.

Rip Madigan was driving. The set of Madigan's leather-weathered face had disturbing purpose. He brought the sweating bay team up blowing when Johnny reached them beyond the plaza. "Johnny, he's riled," said Acey Wales shakily.

Rip Madigan's clipped promise struck harder than a threat. "We'll talk it over later, Rance."

"Might as well now," said Johnny mildly. "The sheriff, Red Kinzie, and Whitey Willis are dead."

Judith, on the other side of the foam-flecked bays, sat with her pale, determined manner softening in relief.

It was Acey Wales who groaned. "I could go into court on one shooting, Johnny. But not three. Not those three. You better ride."

"They killed each other, Acey."

Rip Madigan's glance, questing ahead to the plaza, snapped back in clouded caution. "Tell me what happened?" he demanded.

Johnny told it briefly. At the end Madigan's clouded squint was puzzled. "The haired vest started Willis shooting?"

"Whitey Willis, Red Kinzie, and Walt Powers were the only ones who understood," Johnny explained. "Last night in the sheriff's office I was sure Red Kinzie did the shooting. Those spraddle-legs were plain. But who'd believe me? Walt Powers wouldn't arrest himself or his deputy for getting greedy and trying to move in whole hog on Whitey Willis by killing the brother first. Maybe there was another reason. They got Cultis Day's shotgun and vest and made a point of finding the shotgun in the wagon yard, and let Whitey Willis know how slick they were framing your friend Day.

"Willis thought the frame-up happened after his brother was dead. Red Kinzie had worn Day's haired vest, in case anyone

223

saw him. He forgot that, if the vest was part of the frame-up to throw suspicion on Cultis Day, it also gave proof that the man who was framing Day was the same one who had murdered Hank Willis. No one knew it was a frame-up but those three. I helped Willis straighten it out in his mind before the whole town. He saw quickly that the man who framed Day had to have been wearing the haired vest when Hank Willis was killed. And Willis knew who had framed Day. No one else did. That was Willis's weak point . . . his brother. And there was Red, spraddle-legged in front of him, and Walt Powers looking guilty. Whitey forgot everything else and pulled his gun. They just naturally killed each other off, once it started." Johnny grinned. "I've got a friend who always said there never was a wolf that couldn't be trapped some way."

Acey Wales said almost reverently: "A lawyer ain't what you need, Johnny."

"What do I need?" Johnny asked lightly.

Acey Wales rubbed the dusty new plug hat on his coat sleeve as Rip Madigan shook the harness reins and stated: "I'll look into all this."

Acey Wales, in splendid, sober dignity as the rig moved forward, called out: "You need a wife, Johnny, who'll keep you in line with a gun!"

The startled turn of Rip Madigan's head weighed that idea and seemed to hesitate. Then Madigan dropped the long whip on the bays and they whirled the fine rig on, leaving Judith, uncertain, on her horse.

Johnny thought she was ignoring him until he saw red creeping up where her profile had been pale. This was something gold hunting back in the high mountains had never taught. Johnny had to sit thinking desperately before he seized on anything to say.

Then it seemed to be what he felt. "Acey's a fine lawyer,"

Johnny said diffidently.

"He used to be," Judith agreed. She sat quietly, not looking at him. Johnny held his breath until Judith said: "He must still be a fine lawyer." A faint smile touched her mouth corner. "Very sensible," Judith added.

Hook Adams would have warned against it: *Git you in trouble.* But Hook wasn't a fine lawyer like Acey Wales. Johnny didn't think of it anyway as he sent Rip Madigan's roan horse over beside Rip Madigan's daughter, knowing Acey's advice hadn't been needed anyway. This had been in mind since yesterday.

ABOUT THE AUTHOR

T. T. Flynn was born Thomas Theodore Flynn, Jr., in Indianapolis, Indiana. He was the author of over 100 Western stories for such leading pulp magazines as Street & Smith's *Western Story Magazine,* Popular Publications' *Dime Western,* and Dell's *Zane Grey's Western Magazine.* He lived much of his life in New Mexico and spent much of his time on the road, exploring the vast terrain of the American West. His descriptions of the land are always detailed, but he used them not only for local color but also to reflect the heightening of emotional distress among the characters within a story. Following the Second World War, Flynn turned his attention to the book-length Western novel and in this form also produced work that has proven imperishable. Five of these novels first appeared as original paperbacks, most notably *The Man from Laramie* (1954) which was also featured as a serial in *The Saturday Evening Post* and subsequently made into a memorable motion picture directed by Anthony Mann and starring James Stewart, and *Two Faces West* (1954) which deals with the problems of identity and reality and served as the basis for a television series. He was highly innovative and inventive and in later novels, such as *Night of the Comanche Moon* (Five Star Westerns, 1995), concentrated on deeper psychological issues as the source for conflict, rather than more elemental motives like greed. Flynn is at his best in stories that combine mystery—not surprisingly, he also wrote detective fiction—with suspense and action in an artful balance.

The psychological dimensions of Flynn's Western fiction came increasingly to encompass a confrontation with ethical principles about how one must live, the values that one must hold dear above all else, and his belief that there must be a balance in all things. The cosmic meaning of the mortality of all living creatures had become for him a unifying metaphor for the fragility and dignity of life itself. *Travis* will be his next Five Star Western.